KT-179-553

8/09

501 471 482

THE
SHADOW
SPEAKER

THE
SHADOW
SPEAKER

NNEDI OKORAFOR-MBACHU

JUMP AT THE SUN

HYPERION · NEW YORK

TEEN- OKOR

501 471 482

Copyright © 2007 by Nnedi Okorafor-Mbachu

All rights reserved. Published by Jump at the Sun/Hyperion Books for Children, an imprint of Disney Book Group. No part of this book may be reproduced or transmitted in any form or by any means, electronic or mechanical, including photocopying, recording, or by any information storage and retrieval system, without written permission from the publisher. For information address Hyperion Books for Children, 114 Fifth Avenue, New York, New York 10011-5690.

First Edition

1 3 5 7 9 10 8 6 4 2

Printed in the United States of America

Library of Congress Cataloging-in-Publication Data on file.

ISBN-13: 978-1-4231-0033-1

ISBN-10: 1-4231-0033-6

Reinforced binding

Visit www.jumpatthesun.com

Dedicated to my father, Dr. Godwin Okorafor,
a healer of the heart and a man of peace

PROLOGUE

❖

Ejii was lying on her bed typing into her e-legba when the ground began to shake. From the kitchen, she heard the clank-bang of a pot falling and then her mother's shout of surprise.

"Mama!" Ejii shouted, dropping her e-legba and rolling off the bed to a crouching position on the floor. She listened, sweat forming on her forehead, her eyes darting around her room. Two books on her desk were shaken to the floor. The model globe on her dresser bounced onto its side and bumped against the wall. The clothes in her closet danced on their hangers. Outside her bedroom window, the red-flowered tree softly quivered to the beat of the earth.

"Come on!" her mother shouted, now standing at the door. "Out . . . outside! I don't know what this is!"

Ejii was too afraid to move. The ground joggled her about, even as she crouched. She heard the crash of things falling and, outside, people screaming and crying.

"Oh, Allah, save us!"

"Please, not again!"

"Take us into your arms, *o* !"

1

"Come on," her mother said again, this time more softly.

Ejii fought against her surety that this time the world really *was* ending; that the Sahara Desert was finally finishing what it had started, swallowing up the rest of what was there.

Then the room darkened. She felt *them* press against her. They were almost pushing her up. The shadows.

Ejii stood up, grabbed her e-legba, and ran with her mother to the front of the house. She tripped over a fallen chair, her mother stumbled over a framed family painting; they both leaped over a toppled houseplant and a large beaded ebony mask, the groans and shakes of the earth slamming them against the walls.

When her mother threw the door open, Ejii saw that outside was chaos, too. Everyone had run out, sure that this was finally the end of days. A young child ran and tumbled about crying, his father chasing after him. People dropped to and hugged the ground, praying to whichever gods they worshipped. A woman tried to stop her roaring camel from running off. Other camels ran about in large circles, confused and horrified. A brown goat stood defecating and several chickens huddled against a child's legs.

Two men, even as the earth shook, tried to salvage the round stacks of flat bread that had fallen from their cart. Another man laughed wildly as he stared at the sky where many birds and bats circled. Ejii also spotted a windseeker woman flying with them. She could see that the woman's face was wet with tears. The windseeker wailed and flew even higher, several bats and birds following her like babies trailing after their mother.

Other people just stood, as Ejii and her mother now did, looking south, past the houses and buildings, and palm and monkey-bread trees, into the Sahara Desert. Something was coming. Ejii could see it far better than everyone around her.

Something green.

Like a green egg on the horizon.

As it grew, the earthquake subsided. Soon everyone was looking. Green air spread over the sky, quickly approaching them. Ejii grasped her mother's hand and touched the amulet that hung from her neck with her other hand. *"Inshallah,"* God willing, her mother whispered. Then the green wave came with a *WHOOOOSH!* Its wind pushed everyone a few steps north, the toddlers and the very old fell to the ground. Palm trees bent northward and monkey-bread trees lost all their fruits.

The strength of the wave forced Ejii to inhale deeply as it passed. It smelled of a thousand roses blooming at the same time in the same place for the same reason. She sneezed and looked at her mother, and they both pressed closer to each other. It wasn't the end. It was another beginning. But of what?

✛

CHAPTER ONE

STATIC

KWÀMFÀ, Ejii's home, was a town of slim palm trees and sturdy gnarled monkey-bread trees, old but upgraded satellite dishes, and sand brick houses with colorful Zulu designs. It was noisy, too; its unpaved but flat roads always busy with motorbikes, camels, old cars and, during certain parts of the year, even the occasional truck. Kwàmfà was also known for its amazing carpets and after the Great Change, in the shadier parts of the market, its *flying* carpets.

After the recent earthquake, Kwàmfà was abuzz with rumors. But as the small town had moved forward after the Great Change, it moved forward again after the earthquake. Two days later, following a massive cleanup, the market, shops, and schools had reopened and people stopped preparing for the end of the world. Now, another twelve days later, people no longer talked about the earthquake with as much urgency as before. Kwàmfà was a resilient town, even with its troubled past. This had always made Ejii proud. Of course, that didn't mean that the town's ghosts didn't haunt her. Especially in the dark.

"Ejii, please turn on the lights," her history teacher, Mrs. Nwabara, said.

Ejii didn't sit that close to the light switch, but her teacher always asked her to turn them on after the class had watched a digital in class. It was a cloudy day and with the shades drawn and the flat screen off, the room was pitch dark. It was logical for Ejii to be the one to turn the lights on. Mrs. Nwabara had entrusted Arif and Sammy, who were also shadow speakers, with the same job when they were in this class last year.

Ejii flipped the lights on. Everyone in the class blinked except her. As she returned to her seat, she was aware of their usual stares.

"Any questions about the French Fifth Republic?" her teacher asked. The class was silent. She smiled. "When did Niger achieve independence?"

More silence. Ejii and two boys raised their hands. The teacher picked one of the boys. "Raji?"

"August third," he said. He paused, frowning. "Ninteen-ninety?"

"Close," Mrs. Nwabara said. "August third, nineteen-*sixty*. It may have been over a century ago but it was a turning point." She leaned on her desk's edge. She wore light-blue pants and a matching silk top; an ensemble that Ejii both liked and was bothered by. Mrs. Nwabara was the only female teacher in the school who had the nerve to wear pants.

"It's good that all the hype about the earthquake has died down." She paused again, pinching her chin. "But after it happened, I got to rethinking your next assignment. I have

5

something better for you to do. Forget the oral presentation but . . ." Mrs. Nwabara paused dramatically.

An anticipatory silence fell over the class; Ejii wasn't the only one who couldn't help grinning. She picked up her e-legba, highlighted the "oral presentation" link, and happily deleted it.

"I want this new assignment to be long enough for you to efficiently explore the topic," Mrs. Nwabara said. "At least seven pages."

A groan swept through the class and Mrs. Nwabara laughed. "Would you rather do the oral presentation?"

Everyone quickly responded "No!"

"Okay, then. Write an essay answering this question: What is history? We've just watched a digital about the French, the people who colonized our country long ago. That is history, but do you feel like you are a part of it?" She waited. "Well, do you?"

Ejii shook her head and said, "No." When she realized she was the only one who'd spoken, she felt embarrassed. The teacher smiled at her.

"Most of our history books are about foreigners or royalty or the wealthy or the murderous, they rarely focus on people like the farmer who lived and died on his farm or the mother who raised her ten children, the majority of people. Yet, we can't move forward unless we understand the past. Where do *you* fit in? Who *are* you?

"I want you to write yourself into history because no matter what history books say, even *you* are a part of it. Tell me about some historical event and how you figure into it." She paused as several students raised their hands. "No questions asking me what exactly I want from you." All the hands went down. "This is an open assignment. It's up to you to write it however you want. Dazzle me. You have a week."

As Ejii typed notes into her e-legba, she could still hear the shadows; their sound was like the soft static of an e-legba with a broken receiver. She frowned. The shadows had been trying to speak with her since the day of the earthquake. But no matter how hard she tried, she just couldn't understand what they were saying. Still, there was one thing she was sure of. Something bad was going to happen soon.

She blinked, suddenly knowing exactly what she would write for her assignment . . . if she could ignore all the noise of foreboding.

✝   ✝   ✝

That night, she quickly did her other homework and moved right on to her history assignment. She worked feverishly, finishing around four a.m. She put her e-legba down and went to the bathroom. She ran some hot water over a washcloth and pressed it to her face, which was swollen from crying. Her eyes burned, her head ached, and her stomach felt sour. She looked at herself in the mirror and wanted to punch her fist through it. It was always this way when she thought too deeply about her father. In her ears she could hear the shadows; their voices were still nothing but aggravating static.

"I don't understand you!" she said to the shadows, looking

at herself in the mirror. She felt like sobbing. Instead she sighed and tiptoed back to her room. She reread her essay, putting a few finishing touches on it. Then she turned her e-legba off, put it on the floor, climbed into her bed, and didn't sleep a wink.

✝   ✝   ✝

"Are you sure you want to give . . . all this detail?" her friend Arif asked, still staring at the essay on Ejii's e-legba. He looked very disturbed. "I mean . . . this is . . ."

Ejii snatched her e-legba from him. "It's history," she snapped. "It . . . it's the truth."

"I didn't say it wasn't," Arif said, taking the e-legba from her again and looking at it. He paused. "It doesn't exactly follow the assignment, and it's kind of long."

"It's what happened and where I fit into it," Ejii said. "It's what happened, Arif."

"Ejii, I *know*. We were all there," Arif said. "I'm just saying that this is so . . . personal. Mrs. Nwabara won't understand all the . . ."

"I want to get a high mark in the class," Ejii said defensively. "Plus . . . I don't *care* if she's shocked or doesn't understand. The truth hurts and doesn't always make sense."

Arif looked Ejii in the eye. She looked away. "Make a second file, then," he said. "Keep this one for yourself. Write a lighter version for class. This is . . . the violence . . ."

The bell rang. "I'll do what I want," she grumbled, taking her e-legba.

Arif caught her free hand before she could leave. "We'll meet you after class?"

"Sure. Fine. By the dead palm tree," Ejii said crossly.

All day Arif's reaction bothered her. What happened had been bad. Her father and his twisted ways. All that he'd done. That day. That historic day. The day that haunted every move she made, always lurking behind her efforts to be happy and normal.

After school, she waited for her friends at the dead palm tree that the school would soon cut down. She had her e-legba in hand. She could hear the shadows whispering their staticky whispers.

"Leave me alone," she said out loud. But of course, they didn't.

She shielded her e-legba's screen from the sun, began to reread what she'd written. Arif's right, she thought. She had to change it. Even five years later the incident was disturbing.

CHAPTER TWO

✛

THE ESSAY

Ejii Ugabe
History Class
"What is History?"
Thursday, The Seventh Eke Market Day

History is change. The great change, the change of my father, the change in Kwàmfà, the change of my mother, the change of me. The reason anyone writes history is to record big changes. If history is change, then I'm definitely a part of it.

The greatest change in my history was when I was nine years old, when Sarauniya Jaa, the Red Queen of Niger, returned to cut off my father's head. It is Kwàmfà's most famous and infamous day. I hope this essay will become a sort of historical document in itself.

Kwàmfà is a great place because of Jaa. There is only one book written about her. There should be a million. She came decades ago with her nomads, when Kwàmfà was just a tiny village. With her leadership, people were able to organize, build, and develop. Kwàmfà became a town. Years later, right after Jaa decided she'd done all she could for Kwàmfà and hopped onto her camel and rode back into the Sahara, things changed again . . . because of my father.

I'll tell you a bit about him because there should be history books about him, too. He was of the Wodaabe tribe and very tall. My mother told me that when he was a child his mother and sisters used to pull his limbs to increase his height. They wanted him to gain great status when he grew up.

Unlike my father, my mother is dark-skinned and short and believes in peace. And she is of the New Tuareg people. The New Tuareg are a group of ex-Tuareg slaves and those who wish to join them. Jaa is of the Hausa tribe, but her nomads were New Tuaregs.

Anyway, my father was wealthy and respected. When he spoke, people listened. My mother said he was born with a "sugared tongue." And because he was beautiful, he was popular among the women. When he was in his twenties, he was the winner three years in a row of Gerewol, a celebration of and contest between the most handsome men in Niger. To win more than once is unheard of.

"It was those eyes," my mother told me. "He could make them each go in a different direction at once. The judges loved that."

My parents were friends as children and they fell in

love when they got older. Even when he was winning the contests, he refused to take a second wife. My father sold and bought houses for a living, but he was most interested in politics. He never missed town meetings, and he was most attentive when Jaa was speaking.

My mother didn't think anything of it. She also liked politics and attended the meetings with him. She had no idea that my father and his circle of friends took serious issue with Jaa and how she ran things. Sometimes I wonder just how well my mother knew my father. Or maybe there were things that my mother chose to ignore.

Anyway, the day Jaa left Kwàmfà, my father left too. All he told my mother was not to worry. He returned a month later a changed man. He rode into town on a bejeweled camel, wearing a golden caftan and turban and an equally golden smile. My father was light in skin tone, the color of tea and cream. But that day, my mother told me, he was much darker from traveling in the sun, and it made him even more beautiful. More freshly brushed camels marched behind him, ridden by his close friends. They threw naira notes to the gathering crowd and the crowd gathered faster.

"Jaa is gone, but don't worry!" he shouted in his booming voice as he smiled and winked at the women in the crowd. "I will make sure Kwàmfà remains the great town Jaa built! Make me your chief and you won't have to worry about greedy, shady men destroying her council!"

My father was playing off people's fears of change, that without Jaa things would crumble back into corruption. In a matter of days, Jaa's Kwàmfà had its first chief, my father. Months later, after throwing a lot more money around, flashing his smile, making sure he had the right people on his side, after he'd made even more promises and silenced Jaa's most devoted devotees with money or threats, my father was able to make a lot of . . . changes.

This was all before I was born.

When Kwàmfà was Jaa's town, everyone learned how to shoot a gun, ride a camel, take apart and rebuild a computer. Girls and women with meta-abilities were allowed to hone their skills and learn from elders. My father put an end to all this.

"Women and girls are too beautiful to dirty their hands with such things," he told the people with a soft chuckle. The men would agree and the women and girls would feel flattered and demurely smile. My father also thought women and girls too beautiful to be seen, so he brought back and enforced the requirement of wearing a burka or veil at all times. And he cut off several food and housing programs, which left many people very poor.

"Once I have put my great design into motion, we won't need such programs," he told everyone with a wink.

I was months from being born at this time. My mother said that most people backed my father in his fight against crime. Kwàmfà was safe, but no place is ever totally crime free. My father wanted perfection. Soon there were public canings, hands and ears being cut off, and in the rare cases of murder, public beheadings. All in the name of

Jaa, he constantly said. But Jaa would never have approved of these things.

I was a month from being born when my mother decided to leave my father. She tried to sneak out but he caught her. It was the only time she ever spoke directly to him about what he was doing.

"You really want your daughter to grow up like this?" she asked him, clutching her bags.

"Nkolika, it's all falling apart," my father said. "My way, the old way, is the best way for our children and women to be protected, for me to protect you and our child. The old way isn't perfect but it's best, most durable. You have to give up some things."

My mother looked at him, chuckled, and shook her head. Then she moved past him and that made him angry.

"Get out then!" he shouted for all the neighbors to hear. "I don't want you if you can't support me!" My mother said he had tears in his eyes; that it was the only time she'd ever seen him cry. So maybe he did have a heart. But then again, this was my mother's version of the story. I hate thinking about this . . . he grabbed her bags and threw them out the door. Then he pushed her out.

"But not hard enough so that I would fall," she told me. As if that made it any better. What if she'd fallen anyway? She finally told me all this . . . history . . . last year. All I knew up to then was that over the years, my father didn't visit me. I'd thought that it was because I was a shadow speaker. But it had nothing to do with me.

My father didn't fear Jaa. He was sure that she would

14

never return. My mother watched him become a different man. It must have been so painful for her when, to top it all off, he started marrying more wives. The better to look the part of the "big man." He was like one of those crazy magicians in the storyteller's stories. Talented, arrogant, and always wanting to eat power. The magic and spells that my father used were woven from politics. He had the perfect plan, his "Great Design." As with all magicians who go wrong, it was bound to come back on him.

It happened during the New Yam Festival, nine years after I was born. Ten years since Jaa had left and my father took over.

My father liked to have an opening ceremony where he gave a speech and ate the first piece of yam. This day, a high golden canopy covered the stage, and its floor was covered with a thick, red cloth, Jaa's color, and decorated with soft red and gold pillows.

As usual, there was a specific spot next to the stage for plenty of journalists. Part of my father's Great Design was to "put Kwàmfà on the map." They brought their digital cameras, and the footage and photos would be streamed to the popular Nigeria Net News, broadcast from down south in Nigeria, and talked about on the Net radio stations. The air already smelled of palm oil, pepper soup, sweat, and cologne. It was supposed to be a fun day.

I sat on some of the gold pillows with my half brothers and sisters. I wore my yellow veil over my long, blue dress. The veil was of the type that I knew my father would have approved of if he ever turned my way. It may sound strange but I wanted to be there.

"Look at this goat girl who thinks she should be here," Baturiya my half sister said to my half brother Azumi. They were two and three years younger than I was. She screwed up her nose. "I hate smelling her."

Azumi looked at me and frowned. I wanted to slap the frown off his face. I hated them both.

"I don't know why she comes," Baturiya said sucking her crooked teeth. "She should be ashamed."

"She'll accept scraps," my half brother Fadio said, his eight-year-old face twisted like a bitter old man's. It was Fadio whom I hated most. He was the meanest.

My mother sat in the audience. Even if she hadn't divorced my father, she still would have refused to sit with the other wives who were all closer to my age than hers. Only during public appearances did he acknowledge me as his daughter by sending a messenger to tell me my "presence was demanded." During these events, he'd either ignore me or look at me with disgust. A year earlier, during the Yam Festival celebrations, he'd pulled me aside.

"How old are you now?" he asked.

"Eight," I said. He'd never really asked me anything before. I remember staring into his eyes, and for a moment, just for a moment, him staring into mine. He stepped back, maybe not liking what he saw in my eyes.

"My cook's son has agreed to marry you. Be glad someone will."

I was horrified. I knew my father's cook's son. Aside from the fact that he was more than three times my age, he was known for harassing women and refusing to learn recipes from his father. I had been betrothed to a cook's laziest son. That is the kind of man my father, the chief, was. I never told my mother that this was what my father planned, and I never will. I didn't and still don't want to hurt her.

Though I looked more like my mother, the whole town knew I was his daughter and he'd have looked stupid pretending that I wasn't. "Is it a wonder that she has those strange shadow speaker eyes?" people would say. "Look at what her father could do with his! Moving them about like that."

So his solution was to marry me off as soon as possible, make me someone else's responsibility. My father knew the power and the rules of marriage. That's why, right after he'd banished my mother from his house, he went on to marry five very young wives. I think he married so many to spite my mother, too.

As I sat there onstage, waiting for my father to finish his speech and trying to ignore my half siblings, a blue scarab beetle climbed up my sandal. I brought out my magnifying glass to look more closely at it. I liked studying this kind of insect, so I always carried the magnifying glass in my pocket. As I looked, I knew to tilt the magnifying glass with great care. If I moved it in the wrong direction, the insect would fry.

Sometimes these kinds of scarabs spontaneously

multiply. My mother says that these ones aren't native to Earth; that they come from that other place. Anyway, scarabs are a sign for rebirth, especially this one . . . because I was about to be reborn. I dropped my magnifying glass when I felt a rhythm vibrate through the stage, like a heartbeat. Maybe even a little like a tiny version of the earthquake two weeks ago, now that I think of it.

"In the new year . . ." my father was droning. He was draped in the red cape that he always wore for speeches. He'd just broken the four-lobed kola nut and given the pieces to the elders present. ". . . I will make sure elections run smoothly, and that every man running has his say. In the name of our nurturing queen, Sarauniya Jaa, I will . . ."

"You dare speak my name?!" said a voice, high-pitched like the sound of a bamboo flute. "You dare say your words are in the name of Jaa?"

A whisper flew through the audience. The soft thump of camel feet on sand grew closer coming from behind a building. With my peripheral vision, I saw my half siblings all running in different directions. I looked at my father. His eyes were wide and his upper lip quivered as he stared at his fleeing audience.

"Kwàmfà is mine now," he shouted. "You won't take it . . . you witch!"

There were shouts of surprise, as people jumped and threw themselves out of the way. Journalists continued recording and snapping pictures. My mother remained where she was, her hand pressed to her chest. My half brother Fadio stood behind her. Only my father and I were onstage. Then I saw them.

I have seen many camels. People ride them and use them to carry burdens. They smell like desert wind and have long eyelashes, rough fur, soft lips, and knobby knees. They roar with protest when mounted and many of them can speak human languages. But I have never seen camels of this size. I wondered how such a small woman (at the age of nine, I was as tall as she was) could climb onto that kind of beast, let alone ride it. Her two husbands weren't much taller, their camels equally as huge.

The camels wore no jewels and had no saddles or reins. And their eyes were wild. Yet they traipsed through the fleeing crowd swiftly and with care. Not one person was trampled. I could see Jaa's face clearly through her sheer red burka as she approached. She was very, very dark, her skin almost blue, like mine. She had a smile on her round face, just like in the stories.

Once everyone was out of the way, she picked up speed and unsheathed her sword as she barked something to her husbands. I speak Hausa, French, Igbo, Yoruba, English, and Arabic. But I couldn't understand the language she spoke. Her husbands stopped their camels, but she continued with her sword held high.

I gasped.

My father's mouth was in the shape of an O, a guttural grunt coming from his throat that was probably meant to be a scream, or perhaps words. He swayed slightly, paralyzed with indecision, awe, and fear.

Jaa's camel leaped onstage.

The scarab beetle landed on my shoulder. It made a soft popping sound as it multiplied, the second beetle appearing on my other shoulder. I didn't brush them off. I was barely even aware of them because of what happened next.

Shhhhooooomp! With a swipe, she took my father's head right off.

Everything around me looked as if it were made of metal—shiny silver, gold, copper. I felt sick and there was a pain in my chest. All the blood rushed to my head, but no scream came from my throat. And there was something else, something . . .

I'm still disgusted with myself to this day. I . . .

I was *glad*.

I was relieved, so happy with what she did.

I could have screeched with joy.

Finally, I thought. He deserved it! I was appalled, but I felt this way.

Something is wrong with me, o!

The camera flashes made the scene even more gruesome, lighting up the shade and highlighting the horror. So many witnesses. I felt as if I would die. I could not look at my father. Jaa's camel had leaped off the other side of the stage. Now it had climbed back up and was approaching me! I still didn't move, though at this time I was shaking. I heard a crunch. Her camel had stepped on my magnifying glass. Jaa reached down and pulled off my yellow veil. I felt naked in my blue dress.

"Are you his daughter?" she asked me in Igbo.

A red flower fell from the sky, bounced on my head, and fell to my feet. Even in my horror and terror and happiness, I couldn't deny who my father was.

"Y . . . yes," I said, tears in my eyes. I sniffed and tasted blood. My nose was bleeding.

"What is your name?"

"Ejii Ugabe," I said. Warm blood crept from my nose toward my lips.

She laughed and brought forth her sword. I took in a sharp breath, still trembling as she flicked the scarab beetles off my shoulders. They caught themselves in midair and flew up and away.

"Chief Ugabe, indeed," she said. "I hope you are nothing like him." She squinted at me, her head cocked, as if assessing me. I just stood there looking at the strange blue eyes of her camel and the smear of my father's blood on her sword.

Her sword is legendary. It's made of a green clear metal that people say has no earthly name because it doesn't come from Earth. Rumor has it that the sword's blade comes from the body of another place called Ginen. People say her sword smells like rain-soaked, dark, true soil. It is thin as paper, but strong enough to cut diamonds without a scratch. I believe all of this.

"Ejii," she said. "You'll hate me for this, but one day you'll understand why I had to do it. He was a weed in my garden; a weed's nature never changes."

I only stared at her.

"Where is your mother?" she asked, after a moment.

I looked around. My half brother Fadio was on the ground, passed out. Jaa's husbands, Gambo and Buji, their shoulder-length dreadlocks swinging as they maneuvered their camels, were telling people to go home. My mother was still standing there, her hands on the stage. I ran and jumped off the edge of the stage and stood in front of her.

"Leave her alone!" I shouted.

Jaa trotted up to me on her camel. I waited, trembling, sure she would raise her sword and behead me and then my mother. Jaa leaned to the side to see past me and said, "Greetings."

"It's a good time for you, Gambo, and Buji to return, Sarauniya Jaa," my mother said, pushing me aside.

"Mama, no," I whined.

She caught my hand and held it. Her face was sad. She wiped tears from her cheek, but they kept coming as she stood there. Jaa laughed as if my mother were an old friend; no longer did Jaa look like a crazed warrior. I tried to figure out her age, not wanting to look at my father's body. Jaa seemed both ancient and the age of my mother.

"You will handle this town when I'm next gone," Jaa told my mother.

My mother nodded. Then her shoulders curled and she sobbed. And that is how my mother became Kwàmfà's councilwoman who answers only to Sarauniya Jaa. My mother is like Merlin to King Arthur, except I'm not sure if

my mother is older or younger than Jaa, and Jaa probably has more mystical abilities than my mother.

Everyone knows that my father's head was never
found. The bush it rolled under was one of the new type,
the carnivorous type. I was the first to start looking for it,
minutes later. I was in shock but I had to find it. But I was
too late. Those few minutes were enough time for one of
these bushes to devour flesh and bone. So my father was
buried without his lovely head. The burial ceremony was
so big that Kwàmfà had to be shut down for the day.

I still have the flower that fell when Jaa spoke to me. I
planted it and over the years it has grown into a tree next to
my bedroom window. I also still have horrible nightmares
about that moment. Sometimes I hear the sound of her
camel's hooves, or I see my father's head roll. Other times
I see my father and he's winking at me. He never winked at
me when he was alive. But I don't cry as much anymore.

It's been five years since all this and so much has
changed in Kwamfa. Everything changed. And now there
is the earthquake from two weeks ago. There have been
tremors since the Great Change but nothing that violent,
so similar to that huge earthquake that happened on the
day of the Great Change thirty-something years ago.
People are saying things about what they think the latest
earthquake did, and all of them are scary. And there is a
static in my ears as the shadows try to tell me something
that's probably earth-shattering, as if the earth could
endure more shattering.

I think about the mark I want to make on the world,

my place in history, and I know that I don't want to be a councilwoman like my mother. I want peace but deep down I wonder if I am peaceful. I wonder if I am more like Jaa. I think I want to be more like her. Is that wrong of me since she killed my father?

But who knows, maybe I'll never have the chance to make history because of the way things are going around here. Mrs. Nwabara, you said that we can't move forward unless we understand the past. Well, I don't think there is anything from history that can prepare us for what's coming.

CHAPTER THREE

✛

FADIO'S NEWS

Ejii looked up from her essay. Her hands shook as she suddenly wanted to smash her e-legba against the dead palm tree. I wish Arif and Sammy would get here. I need to focus on something else, she thought. What's taking them so long? She clicked the essay closed. When she looked up, her half brother Fadio was standing before her. He was the last person she wanted to see. She sucked her teeth loudly and rolled her eyes.

Fadio was born normal. To Fadio, the shadows were places sunlight couldn't reach. His eyes were dark brown with round pupils and white whites. He couldn't see farther than any other normal person. And at night, when he walked into a room, he'd need to turn on the lights. Ejii, on the other hand, was a product of the fallout from the Great Change.

She'd been born with the ability to see in the dark and she could see as far as fifteen miles. And for as long as she could remember, day or night, the shadows were alive and drawn to her, often pressing close and trying to speak to her. Ejii's eyes

25

were golden with black pupils that were horizontal slits in the light and large and black in the dark, like those of a cat's. She was only one of four shadow speakers in Kwàmfà.

"Look at you!" Ejii's half brother, Fadio, said, looking Ejii up and down, his face twisted with exaggerated disgust. It was a look he often gave Ejii, a look that marked Ejii as abnormal.

"Look at *you*!" she spat back. Immediately she felt she should lower her voice and act more like a lady. Fadio smiled knowingly and Ejii felt more irritated with herself.

Both of them knew that when it came to looks, Fadio had the easy advantage. His dark brown skin was flawless, his lips were like two lemon segments, and his black hair was thick. On top of all this, Fadio had the magnetic personality of their father and for this reason, he had many friends. Many even said that Fadio was their father reincarnate. Fadio used this to make Ejii's life miserable.

"Not only are your kind ugly, you attract evil. You and the others are the source of all of Kwàmfà's diseases and bad luck." He turned his head and spat.

Compose yourself, Ejii thought. She hated all the stupid superstitious rumors that people had for metahumans, especially windseekers and shadow speakers.

"You all should be afraid," he said.

"Of you?" Ejii retorted, looking him up and down. "No such thing."

He stepped closer, his arms around his not-so-narrow chest. "Haven't you heard?"

She waited for him to say what he seemed to be itching to say. Her hands prickled and her face felt warm.

"Six days," he said, making eye contact, something few people ever did. "In six days, the Red Queen will be leaving."

And right in that moment, the shadows that had been whispering to her stopped. Silence. The news hit her hard enough to make her temples ache.

"What?!" she gasped, standing up.

"You remember what happened last time that witch left?" Ignoring her shock, he stepped closer. "It'll happen again. No one will protect your pathetic mother. Kwàmfà will become the town Father wanted."

Ejii's composure was cracking. Jaa was leaving, she thought frantically. How *could* she? When Ejii refused to look at him, Fadio stepped closer. She could smell him, soap, scented oil, and power.

"My mother was talking about you yesterday," he said.

"So?" she said, finally finding her voice, looking angrily into his eyes. Fadio immediately stepped back. She frowned to keep the tears in her eyes from falling. "Why should I care what your mother says about me? She could easily be my older sister!"

Taken aback, Fadio's eyes grew wide. "You're a curse!" he shouted. "That's why you look like that, with those damn eyes. That earthquake was probably an attempt to swallow you back to hell. Everyone knows evil spirits hang around you. Like moths to light at night. Once Jaa gets out of here, all of you unnaturals will be properly dealt with."

"Your mother is ignorant and illiterate," Ejii shouted back.

"Your mother is a whore!" Fadio shouted back. "You aren't *really* the first child! I am! *You* were a mistake! Look at your mother! She couldn't even stay in her husband's house. Maybe you look like that because she hit the ground too hard when he threw her out and . . ."

And that was when she sprung forward and threw herself at Fadio. She plowed into his chest, wrapping her arms around his waist and they both fell to the ground. Releasing her rage into him felt wonderfully sweet. They were an even match. At fourteen, Ejii was gangly and full of spit and fire. And at thirteen, Fadio was tall and strongly built but taken by surprise. They had both inherited their quick reflexes from their father, but Ejii got her powerful arms from her mother.

Dust flew up as they punched, scratched, bit, and grabbed at each other. It was not a children's fight. This was a fight poisoned with hate and resentment that was older than both Ejii and Fadio combined. They threw each other off and jumped back onto each other. Fadio tore at Ejii's now dirty green dress and Ejii tore at Fadio's dirty white caftan and pants. Ejii punched Fadio in the face and Fadio punched her in the belly. A crowd gathered, some cheering Ejii on and others cheering for Fadio.

Ejii had no idea how long the fight lasted. She didn't recall what her classmates were yelling. She wasn't sure if her friends Sammy and Arif finally came. All she remembered was wanting to tear Fadio apart. She wanted to shut him up once and for all. She wanted to pummel his beautiful face.

It took several teachers, the school headmaster, and a bucket of cold water to finally break them apart. And by this time they were battered and bruised.

"I hate you!" Ejii screamed, her voice cracking. "I *hate you*!"

But even as she screamed this, again she could feel it— satisfaction at the release of it, the violence of it. Fadio had had it coming. Like her father.

That evening Ejii knew that everyone was talking about two things. The earthquake was still a favorite. Some said it was a warning from Allah of what was to come in seven years, in the seventh month, on the seventh day at seven o'clock from a seven-year-old daughter of seven children. Others said that the earthquake opened up portals to hell and that people needed to somehow open up portals to heaven.

Others believed these portals led to heaven and people needed to make sure the ones to hell never opened. Several people said that only a sorcerer in Kenya named the Wizard of the Crow could predict what would happen. Some speculated that now monsters roamed the earth.

Nevertheless, the news of Jaa's impending departure topped even the earthquake. The news of the fight between Ejii, Chief's Ugabe's first child, and Fadio, Chief's Ugabe's first son, only added to the fear of Kwàmfà becoming unstable again upon Jaa's departure. People said that this fight was ferocious, and there was a rumor that Ejii had knocked out one of Fadio's front teeth. Ejii rubbed at her bruised hand. There were people who were born with the ability to disappear at will. She wished she was one of them.

"What started it?" her mother asked after their evening prayers. It was the first question her mother had asked about the fight.

Ejii only shrugged, ashamed. "Mama, it started a long time ago." Her mother nodded, pulling her blue wool robe more tightly around herself.

That night was the second night that Ejii lay in bed awake with a swollen face. Last night the swelling was from crying; this night it was from Fadio's fists.

CHAPTER FOUR

✤

WALKABOUT

EJII'S mother allowed her to stay home from school, as long as she did her homework and some extra reading. Tomorrow was Saturday and schools would be closed the days before, of, and after Jaa left. Ejii would have plenty of time to get herself together to face her schoolmates.

She ached from her bruises but she ached more from guilt and shame. Over and over she asked herself how she could have lost her mind the way she had.

"People are talking, right?" she asked Sammy and Arif when they came to see her after school. Sammy laughed as he slapped the back of his hand to hers three times, the handshake of friendship.

"Yep," Arif said.

"You sure you want to know?" Sammy asked.

Both shadow speakers, Sammy and Arif were also her best friends. Arif was a wiry boy with a knack for noticing details. It was his description of the earthquake and subsequent green wave that everyone at school liked to hear most. If he'd witnessed Ejii's fight with Fadio, he'd have recalled everything, including the reactions of others.

Sammy was a strongly built boy who even Fadio knew not to mess with. Nonetheless, Sammy had a gentle soul. He'd spent the hours after the recent earthquake helping the men rescue people from fallen buildings. Being a shadow speaker, he was especially useful when night fell. If he'd been there when Fadio had harassed Ejii, she wouldn't have gotten in the fight in the first place.

Sammy and Arif had been trained from the day they were born. Five years ago, after Jaa returned and righted the wrongs of Ejii's father, Ejii began attending the special lessons with them. This marked the start of her friendship with them. The lessons were given by an older shadow speaker named Godwin. Ejii, Arif, and Sammy called him Mazi Godwin; "Mazi," a title of respect for adults.

"Of course people are talking about the fight," Arif said, grinning. "That's what people do. Don't worry about it so."

They sat in the darkness on the steps behind the house facing her mother's small garden. She watched a fat, black beetle walk up a long, yellow stem. The beetle was too heavy for the stem and the stem slowly bent as the beetle tried to move higher. Neither Arif nor Sammy liked Fadio. Aside from the fact that he was Ejii's nemesis, Fadio was known to talk garbage about all metahumans who had pointedly odd abilities, like shape-shifters, windseekers, firemolders, faders, and rainmakers.

"Where *were* you guys?" she asked.

"Talking to a teacher," Sammy said. "The shadows didn't warn us with even an unintelligible whisper. I guess they didn't think you needed our help."

Ejii almost laughed at this. "So . . . was Fadio . . . ?" She stopped when she saw them exchange a look. She cocked her head. "He wasn't at school?"

Arif and Sammy burst out laughing. But Ejii felt more horror. "It's true then?"

"Yeah," Sammy said. He pointed to one of his front teeth and said, "This one."

"Now people will really think I'm dangerous," she said.

"I wish I was there to see you do it," Arif said, looking at Ejii with admiration.

Ejii felt warm under his gaze. "I don't know what came over me," Ejii mumbled.

"If he'd said that about *my* mother, I'd have beaten him to mash, too," Arif said.

"I didn't exactly win the fight," Ejii said.

"Yes you did," Arif said. He and Sammy laughed some more.

"And even if you didn't," Sammy said. "You got in some good hits."

"Stop being so hard on yourself," Arif said. "He had it coming."

"No!" she said. "It's not right to think like that." Ejii looked away, frowning. "I've just . . . had a lot on my mind lately."

"Have you tried to consult the shadows?" Sammy said,

33

growing serious. It was always Sammy's first reaction when things went wrong—to consult the shadows.

Ejii shook her head, feeling slightly embarrassed.

"Why not?" Sammy said.

"I can't understand them really," she said. "I'm not like you guys."

"No, you just don't try hard enough," Sammy said.

"Or maybe you don't really want to hear what they have to say," Arif added.

✝   ✝   ✝

For the third night in a row, Ejii lay in her bed unable to sleep. She glanced out the window, remembering that tonight was a full moon. It was about eleven o'clock. Quickly, she dressed and went to her mother's room.

"Mama," she said, peeking in.

Her mother was leaning back in her chair facing the open window, her e-legba in one hand and a cup of tea in the other. She didn't look up. "Mm-hm?"

"Is it all right if I go listen to the storyteller?"

Her mother turned and looked as if she were about to say something but then decided not to. She nodded. "Some fresh air should help. Try to enjoy yourself."

Clear, full-moon nights were the safest nights in Kwàmfà. On these nights, almost everyone would shut off the lights in their homes and open their windows and doors. It was traditionally believed that good but self-righteous spirits walked the streets on these nights. For these reasons, no one dared commit an act of lawlessness under a full moon.

This was also the night the storyteller sat under the old monkey-bread tree next to the marketplace. Children were allowed to walk alone to the tree and listen to his stories. Even during Ejii's father's reign, this was one of the few freedoms that remained. The last time Ejii had gone to listen to the storyteller was when she was nine years old, days before Jaa had returned and changed her life. Her decision to stop going hadn't been conscious; she'd stopped doing a lot of things after her father's death.

Ejii arrived just as the storyteller was saying, "All of you shut up! My goodness, you give me an awful headache. I can't stand it!"

Ejii laughed. The storyteller still liked to drink his beer as he told his stories. And he still wore his old black caftan and black turban, too. With his equally dark skin, he looked like a shadow. There were about forty children sitting in the dirt around him. Ejii didn't see anyone who looked older than ten. For the first time she realized that she was now a little too old to be coming to the storyteller. A few feet from the group, she leaned against one of the wooden market space dividers with her arms around her chest.

The children quieted as the storyteller cupped his ear against the tree. He was waiting for the tree to tell him the next story, or so Ejii's mother said. Up until she was nine, Ejii'd believed that the storyteller was some sort of metahuman who could hear trees talk. But he was just a man with the gift of stories.

He told of the tortoise and his cracked shell, the chaos magician and his chemistry set, the palm tree bandit and her thievery, and the albino girl who could walk through walls. Sometimes he spoke in Arabic, other times in Yoruba, Hausa, or Igbo. He didn't seem too concerned about who understood or who didn't, and neither did the children. It was getting late when he finally came to the story Ejii was waiting for. This story was short and always told last. For some reason Ejii felt comforted by the fact that he still told this story at all. She'd thought that he'd stopped after Jaa cut off her father's head.

"The Legend of Sarauniya Jaa, the Red Queen, Princess of the Sahara," the storyteller said. "Yes, she is queen *and* princess. All queens come from somewhere."

He drank the last of his beer and belched loudly. Several of the children snickered. The storyteller glared at them and they instantly quieted. When he spoke, his coarseness was smoothed away and his true softer nature came forward. He told this story in the Hausa language, Jaa's native tongue.

"No, she isn't the daughter of the prophet as her name suggests. No, no. 'Fatima' is a name for a tamer woman. Merely the name her parents gave her. Her true name is Sarauniya Jaa, Queen of the Red. She is the dreamer. Simply call her Jaa. She is always accompanied by her two wild and sword-swinging husbands, Buji and Gambo; ask me for their stories and I will give them to you on another day.

"Jaa is a tiny woman, small like a worldly child. But size is deceptive. You do not want to be the enemy of her sword. Her voice is high-pitched and melodious. And sometimes when she speaks, red flowers fall from the sky. Legend has it that when she was a young woman, she was stolen by a group of New Tuareg nomads called the Lwa. They claimed that the reason for the kidnapping was because she was their queen. They were right.

"Soon, the queen in her awakened, and before they knew it she was laughing loudly and telling men to straighten up their clothes and women to learn to ride camels; and, to whomever would listen, she told the stories of her past life as a daydreaming medical student. This was just after the Sahara was no longer the Sahara and the world had changed. In next to no time, Jaa was ruling the new land with her army of devoted nomads. She feared none of the talking sandstorms, flocks of carnivorous hummingbirds, or the nuclear fallout that drifted from countries away. The subsequent return of magic to the world didn't bother her.

"I tell you, if it were not for this woman, death and blood would have soaked the sands. No empire would have thrived. The same goes with now. But it is not Jaa's wish to rule. Whenever things grow calm, she and her husbands ride off to Ginen. This time is different; there is business she must attend to. But Jaa always knows when to return, so it's best to behave well in her absence."

The storyteller looked up, past the children, right into Ejii's eyes. After several moments, all the children turned and looked at her, too, wondering what the storyteller was staring at. Ejii wrapped her arms more tightly around her chest, and went home.

As she walked in the cool night, all she could think of was the last part of the storyteller's story, Jaa was leaving. And I'm already fighting, she thought. She was annoyed with the storyteller for calling her out the way he did. As if Fadio's stupidity was my fault, she thought. None of this badness is my fault. She rubbed the sides of her head.

There were troubles brewing in Kwàmfà, all right. Her father's wives were young and ambitious and cruel like her father. And since becoming young widows, they had become even more so. Not long after her father's death, they had gotten themselves educated, studying careers in architecture, real estate, and Kwàmfà law, and other advanced studies online. They claimed that they did it only to better preserve their husband's legacy, but Ejii knew ambition when she saw it. Would her mother be safe with all those women brewing and stewing?

When Ejii got home, she lay on her bed and stared at the ceiling. Then she sat up and punched her pillow. It's all his fault, she thought, thinking bitterly of her father. Why did it seem as if men caused most of the world's problems? Even the Great Change. Sometimes, Ejii thought that if it weren't for men, magic would never have retreated from the Earth in the first place. But, as her mother always said, "Nothing is a coincidence." Maybe man was meant to do what man did. Was woman?

Before Jaa had returned—no matter what her mother said—Ejii had been sure that girls were to simply marry and give birth to and raise sons. When Jaa returned, and more aspects of school were opened to girls and women, suddenly

Ejii was expected to hone her shadow-speaking skills; she could be a wife and mother, but there were other options that seemed attractive, too. It was up to her to wear her burka or not. She had to learn to ride a camel, to speak up, all these things. Too many choices. Ejii sighed.

Two hours later, she still couldn't sleep. As she was busy tossing and turning, she heard voices from down the hall. It had to be well past three a.m. She stopped moving, listening with every part of her body. Her mother was talking to someone. A woman. With a high voice. She sat up and crept out of bed. Slowly, she cracked open her door and peeked down the hall. The kitchen light was on. Now she could hear the voices clearly. Holding her breath, Ejii tiptoed down the hall and peeked into the kitchen. Cups of tea in hand, her mother and Jaa sat close, speaking in hushed voices.

Ejii stared at Jaa, taking in Jaa's heavy red dress and pants. Jaa also wore a light but long veil that reached the floor. She looked at Jaa's fingernails, which were cut short and neat. Ejii's own fingernails were jagged and orange with chipped nail polish. Jaa wore green bangles on her wrists and a red bead necklace around her neck. And there was her sword, hanging sheathed at her hip, peeking from underneath her veil.

"I have sources," Jaa was saying in her singsong voice. "They're calling it the great merge. That last earthquake destroyed what was left of the boundaries between the worlds I've told you about."

Silence. Jaa took a sip of her tea as she looked intensely at Ejii's mother.

"But this is too big!" her mother said. "What could this Golden Dawn Meeting possibly accomplish?"

"Nothing, Nkolika," Jaa said, looking disgusted. "It's the Ginen chief's idea. His only goal is to silence my husbands and me, as we are his greatest challenge; most of the openings to Ginen are here in the Sahara, my territory. After what happened with that failed envoy, he hates all things having to do with Earth."

Ejii's mouth fell open. She was just learning that there *was* a place called Ginen, and now she was hearing that the people from that place might declare war?

Suddenly, Jaa slammed her fist on the table. "I'll cleave that man's head in half!"

Her mother looked Jaa keenly in the eye and leaned forward. "Gandhi once said, 'I object to violence because when it appears to do good, the good is only temporary; the evil it does is permanent.'"

"He also said, 'It is better to be violent, if there is violence in our hearts, than to put on the cloak of nonviolence to cover impotence,'" Jaa retorted.

"Only if need be," her mother flatly replied, after a moment.

"Nkolika, those people have weapons that no one on Earth would have a chance against," Jaa said. "My own sword is from there and you see what it can do."

"That has more to do with the fact that it's you wielding it," Ejii's mother said.

"Their hatred of Earth is very strong," Jaa said. "The best

plan is to pretend that we come in peace and as soon as the chance presents itself, lop off that chief's head."

"And how will that establish better relations with the people of Ginen?"

Jaa chuckled. "You think I am the only one who wants that tyrant chief dead? Almost every citizen there will rejoice."

Silence. Her mother sipped her tea and Jaa tugged at her red sari.

"I have something to ask of you," Jaa said after a moment. "Right now is ripe. A new world has just been born and we're on the brink of war." She paused. "It's likely that something may happen to me in the near future. I need to start grooming an apprentice, a successor." She sipped her tea, looking into Ejii's mother's eyes. The two women stared at each other for what felt like a full minute. Then her mother slowly shook her head.

"Yes, Nkolika," Jaa countered. "It's known that shadow speakers are born with leadership potential, and she's your daughter. She's strong. I want her to come with me."

Ejii covered her mouth, shocked. A swirl of conflicting emotions flew through her. Fear of Jaa, joy that Jaa had noticed her, anger at Jaa—she didn't want to go, but she did.

"She's the one," Jaa insisted. "I heard about how she took on her brother Fadio. Your daughter is a born warrior, like me. She's . . ."

"No," her mother flatly said. "I'm honored, but you have to understand . . . talk to Godwin, her instructor. He'll explain why I can't let you take her."

"I know why," Jaa said. "But like I said, Ejii is strong. It's worth the risk."

"No," her mother said again, this time more firmly.

Jaa looked hard at Ejii's mother. "Fine," she finally said. "For now."

Ejii frowned. With all that was going on, who knew if Jaa would ever return to Kwàmfà after she left? Does Mama think I'm so pathetic that I couldn't survive as Jaa's apprentice, she wondered. I know I could . . . maybe.

"Exactly," her mother said to Jaa. "Maybe when she's older."

When the two women got up, Ejii quickly tiptoed back to her room. She leaned against her door and let out a sigh. Whenever her mother met with Jaa for council meetings, Ejii wasn't allowed to go along. It was adult business. But for the last four years, her mother had brought Ejii to see Jaa once each year. Jaa herself had requested it.

During these meetings, Ejii always felt as if she would explode with nervousness. Thankfully they were always very short. Jaa would sit behind her desk, look Ejii over, and ask her a few insignificant questions. Whenever Ejii replied, she'd had the strong feeling that Jaa wasn't listening to her words as much as watching how she spoke them. Now Ejii understood why. Ejii wanted to run to her e-legba and record the moment. She wanted to call and tell Sammy and Arif everything. She decided against doing either one. Her mother had said no, so that was the end of it.

She picked up her e-legba and began to read through its expansive dictionary encyclopedia at random, hoping to get her mind off of how irritated she felt. She clicked on the radio, which was playing Arabic music, and turned it low. She could feel the shadows pressing in on her again. As she stared at her e-legba, reading definitions and entries, she stopped on a particular entry—*walkabout*. She read it over and over, her sense of foreboding increasing every time she read it. As daybreak neared, finally—maybe it was due to a clarity brought on by fatigue or maybe it was that Ejii finally pushed aside her subconscious reluctance—for whatever the reason, Ejii could suddenly understand the shadows for the first time ever. She listened to them. And what they told her dashed sleep from her body for the rest of the night.

CHAPTER FIVE

✛

RED STEW

Ejii chopped red peppers, onions, and tomatoes and dumped them into the large pot. She would have used the blender, but a powerful thunderstorm had recently passed by and the electricity was out again. Her mother turned over slabs of beef in a pan and added red and black pepper, salt, green curry, and thyme. Ejii looked up.

"So . . . why is she leaving?" Ejii asked, breaking the pleasant silence.

"It's complicated," her mother said without looking up.

"Are you worried?" Ejii asked, gently pressing the bruise above her left eye. There was juice from the peppers still on her fingers and it stung the sore spot. Even two days later, she still ached all over from the bruises, scratches, and sore muscles.

"About what?"

"About her leaving."

"No," her mother said flatly. "And you shouldn't be either."

Ejii grunted, looking at the sizzling meat.

"Why do you ask, Ejii?"

Ejii shrugged. "Well . . . remember what happened last time?"

"Won't happen again."

"Fadio said . . ."

"You put too much weight on Fadio's words."

But Ejii knew that her mother knew better, that her mother was aware of her father's young wives. And though Ejii's mother, who was short but strong, could throw each of them with one arm tied behind her back, what could she do if the women rallied the entire town against her?

"How do you know things will be . . . all right when Jaa leaves?" Ejii asked.

"There are few people like your father."

Ejii wanted to say, His wives may be some of those few. Instead, she unintentionally asked something more upsetting. "Do you . . . miss him?"

"Sometimes," her mother replied quietly. Her hands quivered slightly as she sprinkled some salt on the beef, but her face remained calm. "When we were your age, just after the Great Change, he was so sweet and kind and he made me laugh." Her face grew dark. "But when Jaa cut him down . . . he was rotten."

For a while they quietly prepared dinner.

"Did she have to cut him down?" Ejii finally asked.

"He was my soul mate, Ejii. No one could love him as much as I did. . . ." She paused. "And no one could know him as well as I knew him. That's why I know that he couldn't be changed. He would have grown meaner. And as for Jaa, well, Jaa is Jaa."

Ejii mulled over her mother's words. Mama still considers him her soul mate? she thought. She dug her nails into her hands. The man barely had a soul.

"So who is Jaa? I know her history and all, but who *is* she, Mama?"

"Ejii, ask what it is you truly want to ask," her mother said.

"Well . . . Has Mazi Godwin told you about the urge to travel shadow speakers eventually have when they're of age? The Drive?" Ejii paused digging her fingers into her thighs. "I might be feeling that. It's not so strong yet. . . . But I'm old enough to . . ."

"You overheard us last night, didn't you?" her mother asked.

Ejii looked at the floor. "Yes, but . . ."

"You want to go with her?" her mother asked.

Ejii hesitated, frozen. "Yes," Ejii said. But even as she said it, she wasn't sure. "Here, look. It's what the shadows wanted me to read, I think." She held her e-legba up to her mother and said, "Akwukwo, tell Mama what I stored in memory."

Her e-legba spoke in a low mysterious lady voice. "In Australia, the indigenous tribes have an old custom called *walkabout*. This is when a young man leaves his daily life and walks alone across desert and bush country on a spiritual quest. The distance covered on walkabout may exceed one thousand miles. It is done without aid of compass or computer."

Her mother watched Ejii with piercing eyes. This look always made Ejii uncomfortable. Her mother had always had a way of seeing into people. It was a talent that made her such a great root woman. Aside from treating the sick, her mother also gave all kinds of advice for a small fee.

Ejii often snuck into the living room and watched her do this; she noticed that her mother always got an intense look on her face just after her client told her about his or her problem. The look of gazing into the individual's soul, Ejii liked to think. The same look her mother had on her face now. From her father's famous eyes, to her mother's ability to see what others could not, Ejii often wondered if her being born a shadow speaker was such a coincidence.

"And this is what you want to do?" her mother asked.

"The shadows told me I should," Ejii said.

"Told you? I thought you couldn't understand them, Ejii."

"This time I did."

"Does it feel like you *have* to go or you'll go crazy?"

"Well, no," Ejii said. "Not that strongly."

"Then it's not The Drive."

"If I'll travel eventually, why can't I do it before the urge gets as strong as . . . as Kambili's?" Her mother flinched. Bringing up Kambili was a low blow.

Everyone in Kwàmfà knew of the shadow speaker named Kambili and all but a few feared her. At twenty-seven years old, Kambili was Kwàmfà's oldest female shadow speaker. She'd felt The Drive ten years ago, during the height of Ejii's father's reign. But because of his strict rules, being a young woman, Kambili wasn't allowed to leave her home unaccompanied, let alone leave Kwàmfà. Instead, Kambili was quickly married off to her betrothed, a young man who'd been her best friend since they were very young. If Kambili had not been a shadow speaker experiencing The Drive, she'd have been happy.

Once she moved in with him, things began to go wrong fast. The first month, she cried and cried and her husband didn't know what to do. Three months later, a perpetual twilight created by the shadows fell over their home. Apparently, Kambili had crawled into bed, pulled the sheets over her head, and refused to leave the bedroom. By the end of the first year, her distraught husband had to move out because even he had started to hear the voices of the shadows and they were driving him mad. For Ejii and young shadow speakers in general, to understand the shadows took great great effort. For a non-shadow speaker to understand them so effortlessly was truly bizarre.

To this day, Kambili remained shut into what Kwàmfà people now called her twilight house, her heartbroken husband bringing her food every week. Anyone who got too close would hear terrible things like how they would die or their loved ones' darkest secrets; one could imagine what a tortured soul Kambili's husband was, since he still went inside every week. To this day, Mazi Godwin would not talk about Kambili.

Because of Kambili, the people of Kwàmfà saw female shadow speakers as a greater threat than the males. Female shadow speakers were dangerous and unstable. The people of Kwàmfà didn't understand that what had happened to Kambili could happen to any shadow speaker if he or she wasn't allowed to follow The Drive.

"You're not afraid of what might be out there, in the world?" Ejii's mother asked.

Without speaking his name, Ejii knew her mother had retaliated by hinting at Dayo. Two years after Kambili had gone mad, Dayo, a sixteen-year-old shadow speaker, left Kwàmfà to see what he could see. His body was found three months later, forty miles away. Mazi Godwin had gone off into the desert for a month to mourn him.

"Fear shouldn't be the reason I don't go," Ejii said, pushing Dayo from her mind.

"What of school?" her mother asked.

Ejii cringed. School? What about school? "I'll learn things along the way that I'll never learn in school," Ejii said. "And the trip won't be forever."

"What of your friends?"

Ejii shrugged. "They especially will understand."

Her mother sighed and sat down at the kitchen table, looking at her hands. Ejii sat down across from her.

"Have you spoken to Mazi Godwin about this?" her mother asked.

"Not yet."

Her mother nodded as if this explained everything. "Ejii, you can't run away from your problems."

Ejii frowned. "What do you mean?"

"You're ashamed of your fight with Fadio," her mother said. "Your father has *always* been under your skin. I see you with Sammy and Arif. They're your friends yet you walk behind them, you ask them what you should do instead of deciding for yourself, you lower your voice." She paused, pressing her lips together.

49

"Mama, I . . ."

"And you're afraid of dealing with your half siblings once Jaa leaves. Running off isn't going to make it better."

"It's not about any of that," Ejii said.

"Are you sure?" her mother asked, looking her in the eyes. Her mother never hesitated to look Ejii in the eyes. Her mother wasn't afraid of what she'd see in them. Her mother never yelled at Ejii when she'd find her studying in the dark. Her mother was never afraid when she sometimes saw shadows hovering around her daughter like black bats. This made Ejii trust her mother above all others.

Still, maybe Ejii did want to get away from all of the shame and the taunting and ridicule and guilt. . . . But that wasn't all of it. This went far beyond her feud with Fadio. The shadows had told her to go for a specific reason.

"Mama, you're right, but that's all secondary. The shadows told me there . . ."

"It's not secondary, Ejii."

"I'm not saying . . ."

"No," her mother said, shaking her head and frowning.

"Huh?"

"No," her mother repeated. "You're too young, too ignorant. Look at your face. All scratched up from that childish fight with Fadio!" She sucked her teeth and shook her head. "You haven't even had the courage to speak to Mazi Godwin about this."

"Mama, you're not being fair."

"Don't talk to me about fair, Ejii."

"I'm sorry," Ejii said, quickly returning to the plantain she was slicing.

"Ejii," her mother said after several minutes. "I know you're a shadow speaker and the shadows tell you things, but I'm your mother. I can't let you leave your home, your family, to travel with Jaa. Not right now. Talk to Mazi Godwin. He'll explain to you the true danger. You'll risk travel when you truly feel The Drive, in three or four years."

There was a knock at the door, and her mother looked at her and left the kitchen.

"Oh! Mazi Godwin," Ejii said, as he walked into the kitchen. She almost cut her finger. She looked at his bushy beard, avoiding his eyes, afraid of what she might see in them. "I didn't know you were coming."

He chuckled. "You didn't?" he asked. "I must not be teaching you much. Of course, how can I teach you when you skip your lessons?"

Mazi Godwin was a tall, bent man in his late forties. He'd traveled around the world, after being born in what used to be the United States. Ejii had gone through a year of being obsessed with all things American when she was ten, and this fact about Mazi Godwin still intrigued her. Above everything, not only was Mazi Godwin Kwàmfà's only adult shadow speaker, but because of his travels, his skills were exemplary.

Ejii took his red jacket and went to hang it up, glad to get out of the kitchen for a moment. He was sipping a cup of tea when Ejii came back in.

"Why weren't you at your lessons yesterday?" he asked.

Her mother moved about silently, setting more food at the table. Ejii knew not to avoid Mazi Godwin by helping her, so she just sat down across from him. "You already know about it, Mazi," she said quietly.

"A fight is no reason to skip your lessons," he said. "Tomorrow, the three of you will meet with me at my house to make up for your . . . day off. Don't pout. You have days off from school, you need something to do. Now, tell me about it in your words."

She told him everything, especially detailing Fadio's nastiness: what he'd called her mother, how when Fadio came, she'd been working on an e-letter to herself about her father's death, and how Fadio told her about Jaa leaving. When she finished, he looked at her for a long time; Ejii continued to avoid his eyes. The room darkened some and Ejii knew that Mazi Godwin was consulting the shadows. She sighed.

"Ejii," he finally said. "I'm disappointed in the way you handled your brother."

"*Half* brother," she said, frowning deeply, crossing her arms around her chest.

"*Ta!*" he snapped. "He's your brother, there is no in-between. And you knocked his tooth out! The boy was in the worst pain. Are you an animal?"

Ejii was taken aback. "But he . . ."

"A shadow speaker doesn't behave senselessly," he said. "You're brighter than that. Think of how people in this town already view female shadow speakers, Ejii."

"That's not my fault," Ejii said.

"No, it's not, but you should still keep it in mind," he said. "And remember, Fadio *also* witnessed your father's execution. The boy has the weight of that family on his shoulders being the first son. You're a girl and free to choose many things. Fadio will never be able to choose his wife or what he wants to do with his life. How is pummeling his face going to help? Eh?! *Think*, Ejii! *Think!*"

Ejii was terribly ashamed. But she was angry too. Mazi doesn't understand what it's like to be me, she thought. If he did, he'd have tried to smash Fadio's face, too. She'd intended to tell Mazi Godwin everything, about the great merge, Jaa wanting her to be her apprentice, what the shadows told her and how it all made sense. But now she decided against it. Let the shadows tell *him* if he's meant to know, she thought.

"What would you like to drink?" her mother asked Mazi Godwin.

"Beer would be fine," he said. "And give my student here a glass of palm wine to calm her down."

That night, as Ejii sat in her room looking at her e-legba, she frowned, thinking about the shadows. Those things that knew more than any human being ever could. She was just learning to communicate with them, and already they were telling her shocking things, that she had to leave Kwàmfà and join Jaa, that she had a part to play in this Golden Dawn Meeting that Jaa was going to attend.

She shivered. Jaa had spoken of the great merge, but online news stories mentioned no such thing. On the news, scientists insisted that the recent earthquake (there'd been news about it on the Net coming from all over Africa and even personal reports from as far as Spain) was not another Peace Bomb, that it was just another aftershock. Authorities and scientists reminded people that the infamous Peace Bombs were now as obsolete as maps. "As we all know, there have been a few of these aftershocks over the decades," reporters said. "Experts say that this recent one, though strong, is nothing to worry about. If anything, each aftershock has simply made a few new pieces of land, maybe a lake here and there."

Nothing was said about worlds merging with Earth. Still, Ejii believed Jaa. If there was one person who understood change, it was Jaa. On top of this, Jaa was known to have connections to Ginen, that other place that word of mouth said existed, and was hinted at by the occasional otherworldly item that popped up in the markets.

Most likely, people would remain ignorant and in denial, and the only thing people would do in the near future in response to the earthquake was make new maps. It's ridiculous, Ejii thought. And pointless. Her country of Niger was certainly more than what it had been back when it was named Niger, and even *that* name was artificial. She didn't understand why people still called the Sahara a desert when it was known to have some lakes and fragrant fields of grass and trees. There was more land, more places. All over the world, there were new forests and fields, lakes, oceans, and mountains.

What people called the Great Change happened decades ago, a result of nuclear and Peace Bombs being dropped all over the earth. The Peace Bomb was the tool of an enviro-militant group called the Grand Bois, headed by a Haitian man named Dieuri. The Grand Bois systematically blew up oil refineries, disabled and destroyed equipment used to cut down trees in the rain forest, and set loose chickens, turkeys, ostriches, pigs, and cows at slaughterhouses. Dieuri, himself, was responsible for crossing science and magic and creating the Peace Bomb, a weapon consisting of airborne biological agents meant to counteract the effects of nuclear missiles.

For a whole year, Ejii had been fascinated by old documents containing Dieuri's fevered writings. She even knew that his name meant "God laughs" in Haitian Creole and that he'd originally gotten the idea for the Peace Bomb from a dream. Dieuri's idea was that the Peace Bombs would create where the nuclear bombs destroyed and cause so many "glorious" mutations amongst humans (he called these potential people, metahumans) that no one would want to fight each other. There would be too much variety. Fights meant that sides had to be taken first. With so many differences, there would be too many sides taken for any kind of fight.

Dieuri got his chance to put his plan into motion when American intelligence found and disabled a nuclear bomb left in an empty warehouse in New York City. The president immediately accused North Korea and prepared its nuclear weapons for launch. North Korea adamantly denied planting the bomb and quite a few American intelligence officials said that the bomb was indeed planted by independent terrorists. To this day, no one knows who did it, and many speculated that the Grand Bois was the culprit, hoping to instigate a nuclear war so that the Peace Bombs could be used.

Nevertheless, the American president had the majority of support from her administration, and the world went to nuclear war. Dieuri acted immediately after hearing that nuclear bombs had been launched. He called on his Grand Bois International Underground Army, and the Peace Bombs were launched to hit all of the earth's continents. The Earth was changed forever, of course. The Great Change.

That fateful day, when Ejii's mother was just a little girl, a vast green-tinted wave flew over the earth. People said it smelled like thousands of types of flowers and that the air made one's skin feel tight. There were earthquakes, tsunamis, and tornadoes. Things collapsed, died, moved, were born, were erected, expanded. Things changed. But not in the way that Dieuri expected. No science or magic is so easily controlled by a mere human being. No longer did many rules of the earth apply.

Magic was no longer something that loomed underneath things. It flooded everything. What people did understand was that it was not safe to travel the world alone. Bizarre bad things tended to befall the solitary more often than when people were in groups. Out in the wilderness there were many spirits, creatures, and beings that had a specific appetite for the lonely. Thus, at least in Niger, people huddled mainly in their towns and cities and if they traveled, they traveled in large groups.

Soon after the Great Change, Dieuri disappeared. There were all sorts of rumors. Some said that he, himself, became a metahuman, that he sprouted wings and flew away. Ejii didn't quite buy this theory because metahumans were usually born with their changes; only rarely were people instantly changed. Others said he threw himself in the Caribbean Sea. He'd always said that that was the way he wanted to die. No one really knew what happened to him. His Grand Bois organization quickly dissolved after that.

Now, after the most recent earthquake, all the worlds were one and there might be another war because of it. And the shadows were telling Ejii that she had a role to play in what happened next.

I need to talk to Arif and Sammy, she thought.

✢

CHAPTER SIX

THE GREAT DESIGN

THE next day, they met at Mazi Godwin's house. Led by their instructor, they prayed and then spent three hours meditating, trying to get the shadows to tell them small things like the weather, and weaving tiny, tiny baskets from dried grass to exercise their hands, minds, and eyes. Ejii enjoyed the lessons, glad to get her mind off her problems. Her bruises from her fight with Fadio were also finally starting to fade. Afterward, when they were a few blocks away from Mazi Godwin's house, Ejii decided to bring things up.

"Stop, you guys," she said, nervously chewing on her lower lip. A wind chime hanging from someone's house jingled its sweet jingle as a soft breeze blew.

"What?" Arif asked.

Nearby, a white cat passed through the shadows. It paused to look at the three of them, and Ejii saw that it had lovely eyes. One was blue and one was gold.

"I have . . . I have a problem," she said.

The cat sauntered closer, keeping to the shadows. Sammy

crouched down and coaxed it closer. Sammy was the best at communicating with animals; the shadows allowed him to hear even the smallest bird. Ejii had her moments, usually with cats and small rodents, never birds. Arif couldn't hear animals at all.

Arif frowned. "Fadio didn't do something to you? Did he?"

"No, no," she said shaking her head. "But . . ."

"The chief's wives?" Arif asked. "I know exactly which one is the most . . ."

"Let her speak," Sammy snapped. The cat rubbed itself against his leg and purred.

Ejii opened her mouth and found that she couldn't speak. Telling Arif and Sammy what the shadows had said made it that much more real. Sammy, in particular, took what the shadows said as fact, and to him, to ignore their words was a sin.

"I can't," she said.

"Just spit it out," Sammy said.

Suddenly the cat lunged at Ejii and tried to scratch her. She jumped back.

"Did you make it do that, Sammy?!" Arif asked, looking very impressed.

"The cat wants you to speak," Sammy said.

"They just . . . settled on me," Ejii said. "And I *understood*! You know me, not good like you two. I can't understand *anything* they say. Not usually. They said that I had to go. 'Leave, leave, leave,' they said, with Jaa, to Ginen for some meeting. I don't want to go with Jaa anywhere, not really. I don't know. She asked my mother for me to come with her as her apprentice! She *murdered* my father and I wouldn't be here if it weren't for him, but I wouldn't be here talking to you if it weren't for her. I'd be hiding under my veil, giggling, all shyness and no confidence. Is it good or bad? Is *she* good or bad? To be with her up close is the best way to find out.

"If I don't go, they said, I'll be responsible for some war because all the worlds have merged and something's going to happen that I have to stop; that's what that earthquake and green wave were—all the barriers between the worlds dropping! Do the shadows tell *you* of any threat of war anywhere right now?

"Oh yeah, and my mother won't let me *go*! She acts like me seeing the world will kill me! She has no faith in me. I can take care of myself. . . ." She trailed off when she noticed the looks on their faces.

Arif was grinning and Sammy looked plain and simply awed.

"What?" she whispered.

"You've experienced The Drive," Sammy whispered.

She shook her head. "Maybe. It's not that strong. It's more like some woman telling me the right thing to do and me agreeing. Agreeing isn't the same as action."

Arif gently took her hand. "You know you have to go, right?"

"But my mother," she said.

"What war?" Sammy said.

"What's this great merge thing?" Arif asked.

"Earth, Ginen, and whatever other worlds, all now one, no boundaries," Ejii said.

"Allah protect us," Sammy whispered.

They stood there for a moment, all thinking. Then Sammy said, "Let's go to the graveyard. I think it's a good evening for it."

✠   ✠   ✠

The three of them liked to go to the graveyard to practice their shadow speaking abilities. Arif and Sammy had been going to Kwàmfà's graveyard for years before Ejii joined them. Of course when she did, they had to change their meeting place to as far from her father's grave as possible. The graveyard was old and had graves from well before the Great Change, and it was always deserted as soon as the sun went down.

Palm trees, green tall cactuses with sweet smelling flowers, and other plants were cultivated to make the graveyard beautiful. One of the strange carnivorous plants had grown near the center of the graveyard next to a giant cactus. It bloomed lovely blue flowers once a year and fed only on small rodents, so those who maintained the grave site left it alone. Sammy led the way, the cat at his heels, as they moved past the palm tree that they usually sat beneath. Ejii frowned.

"Where are we going?" she asked.

"Your father's grave," Sammy said.

"No! Why?" Ejii asked. Suddenly her armpits felt prickly.

"For motivation," Sammy said.

It was one of the first things that Mazi Godwin had ever taught Ejii. She was nine years old and her father had been dead for two months. Ejii had sat behind Sammy and Arif; she was unveiled and feeling terribly vulnerable about it. Mazi Godwin had taken them a half mile out into the desert and sat them down on the sand. As Ejii crouched low, trying to be invisible, she listened.

"Ejii, you've lived all your life in your body, but you're new to what you are, so I speak to you today," he had said. "Your abilities stem from sight. We shadow speakers are born eyes open and able to see for miles. We can see in the dark, and the shadows are with us helping our minds to see. They're Earth's messengers. Your eyes and mind will be further affected by them as you grow." His words pulled Ejii in. She sat up straighter.

"In a few years, you'll feel The Drive, you'll want to go out into the world and see and affect. And this very act of traveling will push you to progress, to evolve. It will happen in bits and pieces and it will be different for each of you. For now, to push your abilities, to push for The Drive, you must go to places that move your blood. It doesn't matter if this is in a good or bad way."

He'd then taken them over a sand dune where a spontaneous forest of beautiful flowers had grown. Ejii had laughed with delight. That was the first day Ejii had ever been able to hear the shadows' crackly whisper. Sammy's current idea of going to her father's grave site was a good one.

Ejii hadn't visited her father's grave for the exact reason that she was going to it now. It made her terrifyingly alert. Two years ago, she'd gone during the day on a whim, and when she got there, with each step she took toward the gravestone, the shadows that were always with her grew louder and pressed closer. She'd barely been able to throw the flowers she'd brought at her father's gravestone before fleeing.

His grave was the most grand in the cemetery. Jaa had let the chief's wives build it. Ejii guessed that the fact of his missing head gave Jaa enough satisfaction. His gravestone was carved in the shape of a detailed house made of solid black marble. It came up to Ejii's waist. The front of the grave house, facing his grave, was inscribed:

IN MEMORY OF
THE GREAT CHIEF OF KWÀMFÀ
YOUR GREAT DESIGN WILL BE ERECTED

Ejii, Arif, and Sammy stood before it for a moment. Ejii shivered. She could feel the shadows pressing. But they were silent. Sammy brought out a stick of incense from his pocket. It smelled like a field of sunflowers. Ejii smiled. It was her favorite and would help her focus. Arif used his e-legba's side socket to light it.

Ejii watched Sammy and Arif walk away and then turned to the gravestone. She stepped forward, placed a hand on the cool smooth marble, and sat down on the dry grass with her back against the stone. Her father's remains were right beneath her. She focused on the sweet-smelling incense. She thought of Mazi Godwin's words, "Don't try to listen. Relax and hear. It's not something you can force, it's something that happens."

For a few minutes, all she could hear were their usual soft

whispers. Her mind kept wandering to her father's moldering headless remains, so close. She was on the verge of running off when the darkness around her deepened. She froze. It was similar to what Ejii imagined a fish would feel like when it was thrown back into the ocean after being caught. Immersion. She felt at home and welcome and a little scared.

The sound of the shadows was like static softly blowing on her ear, or that high-pitched sound one often hears when things get really quiet. Now, again, for the second time in her life, these everyday sounds took shape in her head. Blue and round. It was such a satisfying feeling that Ejii found herself smiling. She waited, flaring her nostrils to inhale the smell of the incense. She heard the shadows laugh at her. She took in a sharp breath of surprise.

"Wow," she whispered, fighting to maintain her concentration.

Then they went silent. Ejii felt her legs falling asleep but she didn't dare move. She was hearing the rumble of gas in her belly, trying to keep all thoughts of her father at bay, when the shadows spoke. *Go*, they said in unison. *War will come if you don't. Go with the warrior Jaa. Go to the Golden Meeting.* There was a pause. *The box that sits in the center of your mother's glass people, go with that to the meeting as well.* Then in a teeny, tiny, tinny voice that Ejii had to strain to hear, they said, *You are growing. But you won't advance here. You are like a cow who has eaten all the grass in her field. The butcher has come. He is at your doorstep. Go.*

Ejii let out a loud breath and opened her eyes, feeling as if she'd stepped into a new world. Everything around her seemed to pulse with life and possibility, colors underneath the shadows. Oh yes, she could feel something stronger now. She covered her mouth with her hand and looked around. Her father's grave felt solid against her back.

"Okay," she said loudly. But what box are they talking about? She heard their footsteps from not far away.

"Well?" Sammy said.

"I *heard* them, again. They . . . they said that I was a fat cow and now the butcher was coming to slaughter me at home!" she said. "That I need to go. They mentioned war again. And that I have to bring some box that's in my mother's room."

"Do you need any more reason to go now?" Sammy said.

"It's not realistic," she said, rubbing her forehead. "It'll be like running away from my mother." She thought about her father's wives.

"It'll be what it is," Arif said. "If you're not running away, then it's not running away." He paused. "You don't normally disobey your mother. If you're going to do it now, it would be for a good reason, not an evil one."

"Yes, but . . ."

"The shadows never lie," Sammy said.

"No," Ejii said. She hated the thought of disobeying her mother like this, let alone leaving her. But to stay meant risking war and possibly a fate like Kambili's.

"So?" Sammy asked.

Ejii bit her lip and looked at the ground.

"Ejii, if you don't learn how to lead, you'll only be led," Arif said.

"I'll go," she said, looking up at both of them.

"We'll help you," Sammy said. "You have only a day before Jaa leaves. There's a lot to do."

Arif held out a hand and pulled her up.

✜   ✜   ✜

When Ejii got home, she was relieved to find that her mother wasn't home. She's probably at the market, Ejii thought. Not much time. She ran to her mother's room. The table that carried her mother's collection of glass people was tiny, only about a foot in diameter. It was made of braided wicker and dyed a dark blue. Ejii's mother didn't care for material objects; however, this was the one indulgence she allowed herself.

The figurines were arranged in a spiral that circled to the table's center. Ejii hesitated as she stared at the object in the center. The object was sort of an inside joke between her mother and her. It was egglike and about the length of her pinky finger. Its hard outside was a shiny, dark brown that would have been smooth if it weren't for the grooves carved into it. It looked as if some artistic insect had gnawed squiggles all over it. The squiggles revealed a light-brown corklike material.

Was it a seed? A piece of fossilized wood around which a substance had grown hardened? The home or egg of some sort of creature long dead, gone, or still dormant? A stone? Who knew? Ejii and her mother had been guessing for seven years. Since they joked about it so often, they had to call it something; they'd settled for "egg stone."

Seven years ago, a cranky old Igbo man had come selling all sorts of objects like jagged shards of quartz, old worn-out rings that looked as if they'd been worn by fat-fingered Yoruba kings, various colored stones, chips of silver, worthless things children tended to be attracted to. Ejii had been one of those children crowding the man, but it was her mother who had picked up the strange object.

"What's this?" her mother asked the old man.

"No idea," he said. "Found it in the sand on my way here. Buy it or put it down."

Her mother bought it for less than what it would cost to buy half a boiled egg.

It's sort of like a box, Ejii now thought. An oval box. There was nothing else boxlike on the table. She plucked it from its spot and quickly left her mother's room.

CHAPTER SEVEN

✦

THE NERVE

THE next day, Ejii met with Sammy and Arif at the market. When she passed the old woman who sold palm nuts at the entrance of the market, Ejii hunched her shoulders.

"Demon," the old woman shouted in her quivery voice, throwing a palm kernel at Ejii. "Ride the green wave back to where you came from, *o*!"

The kernel bounced off Ejii's chest leaving a tiny, oily red mark on her blue garments. Ejii bristled with anger but she quickly moved on. No matter what, the woman was still an elder and thus entitled to Ejii's respect. Still, respect for her elders didn't stop Ejii from *imagining* wringing the woman's neck. She had been harassing Ejii for years.

As Ejii walked through the market, she looked around. Everyone was going about their business as if the Earth were still just Earth, as if the world wasn't on the brink of war. What else should I expect people to do? she thought. Still, there were a few visible changes. The number of women selling veils had increased; people were buying them for their daughters out of fear that a new chief would pop up when Jaa left. Almost every vendor carried copies of the classic Chinua Achebe novel *Things Fall Apart* and the books were selling like crazy. And more people had their e-legbas tuned to the news, the volume turned high.

Ejii met up with Arif and Sammy in the fruit section. Sammy had borrowed a donkey from his aunt to carry everything. He said using the donkey was no problem, but Ejii had a feeling that he hadn't asked for permission. Sammy had a way of making things happen by quietly working around people.

They took out their e-legbas and looked at their list. Though Ejii would be traveling with Jaa, all three of them felt it would make a better impression to come to Jaa as an adult fully prepared to travel, with her own supplies. They'd each typed up a list last night and sent them to each other. Then, through a series of e-messages, they'd compiled them into one list, crossing out and adding items.

"Let's see what you have," Sammy said.

"Come closer," Arif said. The three of them stepped close to each other and Arif brought out a large wad of naira notes. Ejii's eyes grew wide. Arif glanced at her and shook his head. "Don't worry about it," he said, putting the roll back in his pocket.

"But it's your savings," she said.

"Only half," Arif said.

She'd brought all of her savings, but it wasn't a third of Arif's half. And Sammy, coming from an even poorer family, didn't have any savings at all.

"His parents are rich," Sammy said. "There's plenty more where that came from."

"Hey, I *saved* all this," Arif said. "As you said, my *parents* are rich, not me. They give me only what I need, not what I want."

"Anyway, there are ways of getting things without money," Sammy said, smiling mischievously at Arif. Arif returned the smile, giving Sammy a friendship handshake. Ejii felt uncomfortable. When Sammy and Arif shook on things, it often meant trouble.

As they shopped, Ejii noticed herself walking a few steps behind Sammy and Arif. It was habit. But since her mother had mentioned it, she was now conscious of it. She wondered if Sammy and Arif were aware of it at all. She didn't ask.

By the time they bought everything on the list, Ejii was glad Sammy had "borrowed" the donkey. It was a lot of stuff. Thankfully, Sammy and Arif didn't have to break any laws to buy things. But Sammy did have ways to save them money. They'd bought a camel saddle for next to nothing from a man who owed Sammy some huge favor. Another of Sammy's aunts gave them two pairs of sandals for the price of one. And an old man gave Sammy one of his smaller, more beat-up paring knives for free.

"I like this boy," the old man had wheezed, slapping Sammy on the shoulder. "Helps me set up every Saturday *and* Sunday!"

It was Ejii's idea to seek out fellow metahumans to do business with. "I think they'll go cheaper with us," she said. She was right.

They bought a leather camel bag decorated with orange

leather fringes for a more than reasonable price from a woman with long dreadlocks. The area in her booth was cool with a breeze that didn't seem to exist anywhere else. She was a windseeker, a metahuman with the ability to fly. Ejii recognized her as the woman who'd been flying in the air crying and wailing during the earthquake. They also bought a large, thick goathair tent treated with weather gel, and a wool rug from a merchant who had the ability to disappear. Many of his carpets were flying carpets and made a dusty racket because he'd had to tie them down. The merchant was a timid young man who kept fading away every time the carpets thrashed too hard.

The used capture station was the most expensive item. This small appliance would be Ejii's source of clean fresh water and out in the desert, water was life. They bought it from a young man who was, ironically, a rainmaker. "This one is very noisy," he said. "But it brings good water, as good as a mere machine can bring, at least."

"You can bring better, right?" Ejii said, smiling.

"Of course. But you can't afford my services," he said.

There weren't many metahumans who sold food. People were reluctant to buy food from them. But, between the three of them, the food market was full of relatives. In this way, they were able to buy all of Ejii's foodstuff heavily discounted. They avoided most of Ejii's relatives. They didn't want word to get to her mother too quickly.

The sack of sweet, juicy dates was Arif's idea. "They're delicious fresh," he'd said. "And when they dry up, they're still good for you. The perfect travel food."

The last item on the list was a haircut for Ejii. Ejii's idea. Arif didn't like it and said so, but Ejii insisted. She wore her hair in tight cornrows but she thought it best to cut her hair low. "For travel," she said. "Hair carries a lot of energy, I want to start fresh." Plus, it would be cooler in the sun and she wouldn't have to worry about washing it for a while. She'd also considered traveling disguised as a boy, but her already slightly curvy figure wouldn't allow her to really fool anyone.

"Oh," Arif said, when she stepped out of the hairstylist's tent. "That looks different. It actually looks really nice."

Ejii smirked. "Thank you."

"I hope it won't make your mother suspicious," Sammy said.

Ejii didn't think it would but the thought still bothered her.

"There's one more thing on the list," Arif said.

"No there isn't," Ejii said. "We're done." She held her e-legba up to him. "See?"

Arif barely glanced at it. "This way."

He stopped at a booth selling jewelry, looked for a moment, then chose a pair of silver hoop earrings. He bought them from the seller and presented them to Ejii.

"A going-away gift," Arif said.

"I can't take these. I've spent so much of your money already," she said.

"Just take them," Sammy said, taking the earrings from Arif. He shoved them into her hands. "You just shaved all your hair off. You need to . . . accessorize or something."

When she put them on and looked in the jewelry seller's mirror, she grinned.

"You look like a queen," Arif said softly.

"Yeah, a queen who was beaten up by her king," Sammy said.

Ejii punched him in the shoulder as she looked closer at her face. She touched the scratches on her cheek from her fight with Fadio. They were scabbed over and would soon be completely gone.

That night Ejii sat on her bed feeling guilty. Sammy had taken all the supplies to his house and hidden them in his father's shed, and she'd hidden her new earrings in her pocket. Her mother liked her new low-cut Afro, saying that it gave her a regal look. The secrecy made Ejii feel dishonest and sneaky. She hated how her mother was so unaware of what she was planning to do. She felt especially bad about the camel she was going to take. Earlier that night, she'd gone to his small hut behind their house.

"Onion, good evening," she said.

Onion the camel raised his head. "Good evening," he said in his guttural voice.

Ejii set the bucketful of onions at his feet.

"You have questions for me," Onion said, slowly getting up from his bed of dried grass. First he straightened his back legs, then knelt on his forelegs and stood up tall.

"Yes," Ejii said. She looked around. She could see her mother in the kitchen. "And you can say no, if you like. I'll understand." She told the camel everything. As she spoke,

Onion lowered his head into the bucket, crunching on the juiciest onions first.

Onion was not like other camels. He was one of the few who could speak; one did not have to be a shadow speaker or any other type of metahuman to understand him. After the Great Change, Onion had realized that he had a bulge near the top of his long neck—a large, developed voice box. He'd been hearing human beings speak all his short life, for he was just a calf. It was not hard to do the same. "Onion" was the name he chose for himself because he loved onions.

He'd belonged to Ejii's grandparents and Ejii's grandmother had been the first person Onion spoke to. Ejii's mother had grown up with the camel and she and Onion were inseparable. Ejii was quite prepared for the camel to refuse to go with her. But Onion might also feel better guarding her mother's only child. It was also possible that Onion would trot past her to the kitchen window and tell her mother everything.

"I will go," Onion said as he ate. He glanced at Ejii with his light-blue eyes and Ejii smiled. She patted Onion's muzzle and sighed with relief.

It was yet another night where Ejii could not sleep; she was too excited. Her mother would wake up around five a.m., pray, and then leave for a last meeting with Jaa. After her mother left, Ejii would ride Onion to Sammy's house. Jaa and her husbands would be giving their farewell at six a.m. and her mother would be there, expecting Ejii to come on her own and join the crowd. Afterward, Jaa and her husbands would ride off using the main road and Ejii would meet them at the border of Kwàmfà.

Ejii already felt as if she'd left. She just had to bring her body along. She shivered underneath her covers and not because it was a cool night. She was just starting to settle down when suddenly she felt the shadows press in on her. And then there was a wind in her ear. It suddenly focused and she understood. *Get ready* they said. Nothing more. She heard footsteps. It was only about two a.m. Strange, she thought. Before she could move, the covers were yanked off her.

"Terrible girl, *kwo*!" her mother shouted. "The nerve!"

Ejii gasped, realizing what was happening.

Her mother flipped on the lights. "How could you!? Ah ah! My own daughter, so conniving and selfish," her mother shouted.

"Mama, I didn't mean . . ."

Her mother held up a finger and Ejii immediately shut her mouth.

"Where is the medicine?" she asked in a low voice.

Ejii was so confused that she didn't know what her mother was talking about.

"Shut up," her mother snapped. "You took some of my medicinal herbs. I keep track of what I have, like any good root woman."

Now Ejii understood how she'd been caught. "I didn't take much," she said. "I was trying to think like you. In case I got sick along the way."

"Where is it?" her mother asked.

Ejii reached under her bed and brought it out. Her mother snatched the bag of herbs and threw it at Ejii. "Did you take my egg stone as well?"

Ejii felt her stomach flip again. So she *had* noticed. "I . . . for good luck?"

"Lies," her mother said, throwing her hands up. "And so secretive. *You* are not going anywhere! You're my only child. You're too *young*! You have no idea what it's . . ."

"Just let me go!" Ejii shouted. The combination of being caught so close to the time she was to leave, the lack of sleep, and all that she'd put into her plan made Ejii crazy with desperation. "It . . . it's the right thing to do. You have to sense it!"

"My eyes are on you, Ejimafor," her mother said. "They may not be as sharp as yours but they *see* you. If you leave here, don't *ever* return. You will not be welcome. I didn't save you from your father so you could die in the desert."

She sucked her teeth in disgust and left. Ejii sat there shaking. She could still hear the shadows whispering, urging her to go. I'm not going anywhere, she thought. She wiped the tears from her face and lay back down. There was the patter of rain outside and then the boom of thunder. Minutes later the rainstorm had passed. Come morning, there would be no sign that a drop of rain had fallen. Ejii turned over and was soon asleep.

The next day, Ejii stood with slumped shoulders in the crowd during Jaa's speech. In her left hand she clasped the egg stone. Doing so felt oddly comforting. There were several messages from Sammy and Arif on her e-legba. She'd ignored all of them. She wore her light-blue dress and yellow burka that covered her dress and the rest of her. Neither Sammy nor Arif would recognize her and that was how she wanted it. Ever since Jaa's return, she hadn't had to wear it in public and that was a relief. At first it felt strange, like being naked. But she slowly got used to it. And she actually came to like it.

However, Ejii was growing and boys and men were beginning to look at her differently, despite her being a female shadow speaker. They wouldn't say anything; there were no lewd comments. But there were eyes. Eyes that her sharper eyes saw and understood.

Thus lately, whenever she went to public events, Ejii preferred to wear her burka. Today, she wore her burka for different reasons. She wanted to be invisible. There were several Muslim women wearing burkas, so Ejii felt invisible on multiple levels.

She'd woken up at five a.m. crying. It was the most bizarre thing. She couldn't remember what she'd been dreaming about but she felt distressed. Then she remembered her mother's words, "If you leave here, don't you *ever* return. You will not be welcome." From outside she could hear the morning prayer being broadcast through the streets. After praying, Ejii had left her room and found that her mother had already gone.

Jaa's soft girly voice carried strong words over the large audience. "Buji, Gambo, and I are leaving you all now. We have reason. It is time that Kwàmfà stood on its own two feet. I have great confidence in you all," she said. "Kwàmfà will continue to prosper. A repeat of the 'chief' will mean a repeat of the 'chief's' fate."

The audience roared with applause. Ejii frowned as she looked around. These people had no understanding of Jaa's doublespeak. And how many of them had supported her father's Draconian nine years of rule? After Jaa, her husbands spoke and the audience cheered some more. Ejii enjoyed hearing Gambo speak; the energy he projected was so contagious. At the end, the three had lifted their swords in the air to salute their town and then ridden off into the desert. Many of Kwàmfà's children ran after the camels shouting good-bye. Ejii just stood there.

She was still standing there, her hand grasping her egg stone, as people left, walking around her. She was standing there long enough for Jaa's counsel to walk by, her mother among them. They were on their way to the town hall for a long meeting, Ejii knew. Her mother caressed the top of Ejii's head as she passed. Even through the cloth of her burka, Ejii could feel her mother's warm hand.

"Go home," her mother said softly to her. But Ejii refused to look at or speak to her mother. She just stood there as her mother went on her way.

"It's only a matter of time," a voice to her left said.

Ejii's entire body tensed. She could understand how her mother could recognize her with her burka, but Fadio? There he stood with his sister Wata. Both of them dressed immaculately. Fadio flashed a big smile, a smile with no gaps in it. The dentist had done a good job. Ejii put the egg stone in her dress pocket.

"Leave me alone, Fadio," Ejii said.

He ambled up to Ejii and looked her over. "It's good to see you dressed more appropriately," he said. "Wata, you should take an example from your half sister."

Wata looked scared. She practically worshipped the ground her older brother walked on. "I won't have to wear that thing, right?" she asked in a small voice.

Fadio only laughed.

Ejii suddenly felt a flash of rage so strong that she knew it was best to leave as soon as possible; otherwise she'd embarrass herself again. She began to walk away.

"Don't you walk away from me!" Fadio said, following her. He grabbed her burka and Ejii whirled around.

"Don't touch me," she hissed, snatching it from his hand.

"Brother, just leave her alone," Wata whined. "Ple-e-e-ease. Oh, this is bad."

Ejii was shaking with pent-up rage.

"You're too low to have so much pride," Fadio growled. "You should . . ."

Ejii threw up her burka with such force that it flew into the air. Then she stared long and hard into Fadio's eyes. Fadio practically jumped back, his eyes locked on hers.

"Leave me *alone*," she said.

Fadio grabbed his little sister's hand. "Mark my word," he said over his shoulder, "things will soon change around here."

"Let them change, then!" Ejii retorted.

"They will!" Fadio said.

"Let them!"

"They will!"

"Let them!" She watched them walk down the road. About a mile down, she could see her father's wives gathered. She laughed bitterly to herself.

CHAPTER EIGHT

✛

MY CYBORG MANIFESTO

"**Y**OUR mother said that?" Arif said, looking shocked. He had to shout above all the noise. "Why were you avoiding us like that? We didn't know what happened."

Ejii turned down the volume of her e-legba. In her e-legba's small screen, she could see that Arif was eating from a plate of rice and stew and Sammy was drinking a cup of palm wine, behind them the celebration of Jaa's departure was just kicking into high gear.

"I didn't want to talk about it," she said.

"We thought you'd left," Sammy said, trying to see into Arif's e-legba. "Or that you'd been caught."

"Yet there you are in the middle of the party," she said.

Sammy smiled. "What'd you expect us to do?"

"You feel okay, though?" Arif asked. "No . . . weird feelings?"

Ejii shook her head. "I feel depressed. Maybe my mother was right."

"Why don't you meet us?" Arif asked. "We're just out-side the town hall." Behind Arif, Sammy was laughing at a

80

street performer doing flips and complex dance moves.

"I don't feel like celebrating." She paused. "Would *you* have still gone after your mother said something like that?"

Arif looked at the street performer. Ejii frowned. "You have to think about it?" she asked, leaning back on the couch, holding her e-legba to her face.

Arif turned back to her. "This isn't some choice you pulled out of your ass," he said. "You should have gone once your mother left. I . . . I think you should still go."

"Jaa's gone," Ejii said, her throat feeling tight. She'd been thinking the same thing. "It's almost nighttime." She saw something sparkly fly past Arif's head. He yelped, and the picture went funny. He must have dropped his e-legba.

"Keep your e-legba next to you, Ejii. It's getting crazy around here," Arif said. She could hear Sammy laughing really hard. Then he was gone.

Ejii angrily stared at her e-legba. She cursed and threw it on the couch. By the time night arrived, Ejii was still lying on the couch in the dark staring off into space and her mother was still not home. There was knock at the door. She didn't bother turning on the porch light as she peeked out the window to see who it was. She went to the front door and opened it. Arif carried a plate of wrapped food from the celebrations.

"I know where Jaa will be for the next day or so," he said.

"Really?"

"You're not the only shadow speaker here," he said.

"The shadows actually *told* you that? Only Mazi Godwin could have . . ."

He smiled more broadly.

"You went to Mazi Godwin?!"

"Nah, Sammy and I overheard two of the chief's evil wives talking about it. Jaa's going to Agadez. It'll take her about a half day. She'll be there for two days, maybe less."

"And you still think I should go?" Ejii said.

"Yep."

"I couldn't make it there in time. Alone? You know how it is out there!"

"Ejii, there's more at stake than your welfare. You said it yourself."

"The war."

"Yes. And your *self*."

"My mother thinks I'm too young," she said, feeling angry.

"But the shadows don't lie," Arif said. "If they say there's going to be war if you don't go, then there will." He shivered. "Can't you just feel it?"

Ejii nodded.

"I heard that not far from here there's a huge hole that goes somewhere," he said. "If those Ginen people hate Earth so much . . ."

"Yeah," Ejii whispered. The thought of anything happening to Kwàmfà, all that she knew and loved, made her want to grab whatever was closest to her and use it as a weapon. She frowned. Then she looked up and said, "I *have* to go."

Arif nodded. "I didn't want you to go. I was so happy when you called and said you were still at home. I wasn't going to come here tonight." He sighed. "But when I heard the chief's wives . . .

you should definitely go. Something is going to happen."

"Are you talking about where Jaa is going or here?" she asked, frantic.

"Both. We'll keep an eye on your mother. Sammy says leave Fadio to him."

Ejii frowned. "What of the things my mother said? She'll never . . ."

"Ejii, make your choice. There are consequences in all directions," he said.

She chewed on her lips and wrung her hands. "Okay," she said. She nodded.

"Are you sure?" Arif asked. "Your mother won't be happy about it. The journey might cost you your life." He hesitated. "I can tell you still aren't sure that it's The Drive you feel. You might not make it to Agadez in time. You know how danger-ous it is for lone travelers. And you don't know what will happen here. I know for a fact that your father's wives have planned something. Fadio, he'll drag your name in the dirt as much as he can. And Sammy and I will miss you. I'll miss you."

A minute ago, he was telling me to leave, she thought.

They held each other's eyes for a long moment and Ejii felt a flutter in her chest.

"Yes, I'm sure," she finally said, taking his hand.

✝   ✝   ✝

As they walked to Sammy's house in the night, they passed many happily drunken revelers. The party in town square was still very alive. They went over things as they walked, Onion slowly plodding along behind them.

"Water pills, sun lotion, vitamins, hyena/monkey spray?" Arif asked.

"All in my camel bag."

"Did you get whatever box the shadows said you had to get?"

"Yeah," she said, patting her thigh pocket.

"You packed your copy of *My Cyborg Manifesto*."

"Of course," she said. It was her favorite book, as it was for thousands of other people. When she was down, all she needed was to read a few pages of it to lift her spirits. Sammy was waiting outside with her supplies when they arrived. They quickly packed her things on Onion. Arif handed her three pouches filled with money.

"Don't argue with me," he said. "One in your dress pocket, one in your saddle bag, and one in the pocket underneath your saddle."

"Fine," Ejii said. She understood why she had to break up the money. The possibility of being robbed along the way was one of her many fears.

"Catch up with them as quickly as you can," Sammy said, patting Onion's hide.

"Can you hear anything from the shadows?" Ejii asked.

"Some," Sammy said. "They tell me things that have more to do with Kwàmfà."

"Me too," Arif said.

"Like what?" Ejii asked, frowning.

"That's not your worry," Sammy said.

She gave Sammy the friendship handshake and a tight hug. "Hurry. Remember to listen and learn," he said, giving her a kiss on the cheek.

She turned to Arif who was frowning deeply. He didn't hug her, but he gave her a kiss on the lips that made Ejii feel both warm and afraid, afraid for what was to come.

"We'll tell Mazi Godwin tomorrow," he said, looking away.

Ejii knelt on the ground, pressed her head to the sand, and said a prayer to all the gods and goddesses she could think of. Then she climbed onto Onion and just sat there.

"Go on," Sammy said.

Onion started walking without Ejii's command and soon he'd worked himself into a trot. She looked back and waved. Arif was looking at his feet and Sammy was waving back. Onion walked a few blocks down the main road and then turned toward the narrow street, the road that would lead her out of Kwàmfà.

They passed Kambili's house. Darkened by thick brooding shadows, the small adobe house was practically invisible, but Ejii could hear the shadows whisper to her as she passed. Chilling words, and clear as a bell. *You will die out there and all that they will find of you are your damned eyes! All that you love will die here and people from Ginen will kill the rest, Ejii!* Ejii frowned wondering why these shadows weren't glad to see her leaving as they'd wished Kambili would have. Onion must have heard something awful, too, because he upped his pace to a gallop until the house was a half mile away.

In Kwàmfà's town square, the celebrating would go on well into the night. As Ejii rode in the opposite direction, the sounds of laughter and music grew more and more distant and she passed fewer and fewer people, all of whom were going to the celebration.

"Don't look back," Onion said when they reached the top of the first sand dune.

The words of the angry shadows hovering around Kambili's house were still with her. Ejii had to take one last look. She could see the top of her house. Her mother usually sat next to the open window to read. But tonight, that bedroom light was off and the curtains were drawn. Ejii looked back until she could no longer see her home.

✛

CHAPTER NINE

CACTUS CANDY

T WAS deep into nighttime, hours from daybreak, so it was cold. Ejii was glad for her long, blue dress, black wool coat, and thick veil that exposed only her face. She touched the silver amulet that hung from her neck on a delicate silver chain. Her mother had given it to her seven months ago for her birthday. It was a Cross of Agadez made of pure Tuareg silver and it was specially engraved with Nsibidi symbols of her mother's choosing. The symbols told the story of Ejii's family all the way back to her great-great-great-grandparents.

"Yes, including your father's," her mother had said when she saw Ejii hesitate as she put it on. "This amulet represents you, Ejii. *All* of you."

When Ejii got to the very edge of town and the land opened up before her, she looked ahead, scanning the night. "We'll be going south," she said. She squinted. "Okay, I see a speck . . . might be a monkey-bread tree . . . about twenty-five miles away," she said. "If we can make it there, we'll camp. That will be a start."

Onion took a step. "Wait . . . hold on," Ejii said. She needed a moment to savor the fact that this was the beginning. Onion humphed and began to walk and then trot.

"O . . . okay," she said, smiling. "Let's go then."

At her words, Onion began to move faster. Hours passed. All around her was nothing but sand. In another twenty-four hours or so, she had to somehow reach civilization. "Oh, Allah, what have I gotten myself into?" she mumbled.

"One step at a time," Onion said.

Ejii looked up at the sky. Kwàmfà was a solar-powered town but it didn't need much. Even with the celebrating, the streetlights were dim because everyone knew where everything was. But the dim light was still enough to block out some of the stars above. Out here in the silent nighttime Sahara, the stars burned like tiny suns and falling stars shot about like insects. Movement on the ground caught her eye.

"Look," Ejii said, pointing. "A desert fox!"

Onion merely humphed as the tiny, white creature yipped a few warnings to its comrades and skittered over a sand dune. There were bound to be much bigger and more deadly creatures about. Especially at night. If some dangerous animal comes along maybe I can talk to it now, she thought. Only once had she clearly communicated with an animal. She recalled her experience with the sand-dune cat and shivered.

It had been last year when she walked out into the night, going about a mile from town, the farthest from Kwàmfà she'd ever been. Sammy and Arif had told her about how they had these random strong urges to walk out of town and explore the land, but this was the first time she'd experienced one. She'd simply put down her schoolbook and quietly left the house. She walked past the last mud brick building, where her school was, and kept going till she was in the desert. All that day she'd felt a little under the weather, and it was the headache she experienced as she walked that made her finally sit down and decide that she'd gone far enough.

She'd sat down in the soft sand and rubbed the sides of her head as she looked around. It had been strikingly silent. So silent that the sound of the shadows around her was amplified. This night, they sounded like a man blowing on ashes, low and whispery, like ghosts. She was terrified of her actions. To be out alone like this was dangerous.

As she'd sat there, the shadows did something strange. They pulled in close, and she could feel them press against her cheeks and linger at her forehead. Then it was as if they were massaging her temples. She was so absorbed in this strangeness that she didn't notice the big sand-dune cat approach her. It must have been walking near the bottom of a dune. The cat was the size of a large dog and had a wide, furry, sand-colored face and large triangular ears pointing almost horizontally. It was standing right next to her, staring with its brown eyes, when Ejii finally noticed it. For a few seconds, they just stared at each other. Then the cat spoke, but not as Onion did.

"Sweet sinewy flesh and succulent cords of entrails. All packed in. This one I will chew on slowly. I'll sip her blood like warm milk."

The shadows had made it so that she could hear it speaking in her head. The cat's voice was so strong that it made her ears itch. However, she kept her hands where they were, afraid to make any sudden moves. She briefly wondered if the voice was male or female. But what's "male" and "female" for sand-dune cats' voices? Ejii thought.

"Don't eat me," she psychically replied.

It abruptly stopped talking to itself and narrowed its eyes. Ejii blinked with surprise. With the animals in the market, she hadn't been able to talk back to the few she understood. She could only hear their conversations and morbid musings.

"I've never come this close to a human that I didn't eat," the cat finally said.

"Have . . . have you ever spoken to a human?" she asked. Its sandy fur blew in the breeze and she could see that it was very soft. It slowly walked a circle around her, sizing her up. Ejii inhaled and pulled her belly in, trying to look skinnier.

"You humans have made a mess of things," it said, sitting next to her.

"My ancestors were arrogant," she said.

"And you think you're any different?"

"Yes," she said. She'd broken into a nervous sweat and her skin began to itch along with her ears. *"I can talk to you, can't I?"* She paused. *"And one night I put my hands to the Earth and could hear its heart beating. . . . There was more than one rhythm."*

"Ah, the other places. They're close now," the desert cat said. It sniffed Ejii's knee and licked its chops. Then it looked deeply into Ejii's eyes. It growled low in its throat and stepped back. *"You're worth keeping alive."* It began to walk away. Then it

stopped. Ejii didn't move as it walked up to her, and she didn't make a sound as it swiped her arm with one of its claws, though it hurt dearly. She bit her lip and her eyes watered.

"Now my people will recognize you," it said. Then the sand-dune cat walked into the night. Once it was gone, Ejii ran home to disinfect the small but deep wound the way her mother taught her to. Over weeks, the wound healed and became a straight blue line on her bicep. Her mother hadn't noticed it because Ejii usually wore clothes with sleeves. Now, a year later, Ejii was much farther from Kwàmfà than she'd been that day, and who knew what she'd encounter. She was leaning forward to relieve her back when something in the distant east caught her eye.

"What *is* that?" she whispered to herself, knowing that Onion wouldn't be able to see it yet. It had to be about five miles away. "Onion, stop for a moment."

She climbed down for a better look. She could see clearest when she was very still and concentrated. It looked like an enormous purple-blue hole sitting on the desert floor.

"Allah protect us all," she whispered.

The hole was about a fourth of a mile in diameter. All around it was the early morning sunshine. Inside it, however, was a strange purple-blue nighttime with stars in the sky and a field of lush green grass and a few trees on the ground. Jaa was right, Ejii thought. This is a result of the great merge! Is this place Ginen?

Above her head a flock of green parrots flew by happily squawking to each other. Ejii frowned. The birds could have easily been from wherever that hole led to. Maybe they aren't even birds, she thought. Quickly, she mounted Onion.

"The air smells strange here," Onion said, working back up to a fast trot.

"That's because you're probably smelling air that has never been on earth before," Ejii said. She kept her eye on the hole until she could no longer see it.

The sun was climbing into the sky when she and Onion arrived at the fat, wide baobab tree. Ejii was ravenous. Ravenous to the point of feeling ill. Up to now, she'd been afraid to stop Onion so that she could get something to eat. That hole really scared her and thankfully they hadn't seen any more. She jumped off of Onion and immediately dug out a handful of dates from her camel bag. She shoved them into her mouth. They tasted marvelous. She ate another four handfuls, two patties of flat bread, and some roasted goat meat before she felt more like herself. She groaned. Now her temples had started to throb. "Oh, Onion," she said, "I think I'm really exhausted."

Working hard to ignore her headache, she pitched her goat-hair tent underneath the tree. Her tent was treated with weather gel that cooled the air inside it. It was made to use during the hottest part of the day, which was fast approaching. She made sure the opening was facing downwind so that sand wouldn't blow in. As she worked, Onion walked off to look around. He returned with a chunk of bright red cactus in his mouth.

"Wild cactus candy. This place is good, undisturbed," he

said, poking his head into the tent and dropping it on her tent floor.

"Well, that's good to know," Ejii said, breaking off a piece. She picked out the thorns as she listened to Onion settle down next to the tent and munch on his piece, thorns and all. She took a bite and smiled. Juicy and sweet. She ate the whole chunk and it made her feel much better, her headache finally retreating. She brought out her e-legba and said, "Akwukwo, tomorrow's weather."

"Tomorrow night will be dry and comfortably cool, N.I.U.F.," her e-legba said. Not Including Unpredictable Factors.

When it came to news and local information, the *Nigerian Net* and *Old Naija Times* were the only big publications still able to post online. The members of the famous Obidimkpa family who owned and ran both publications were not even sure why they were still in business. No one knew why the Internet kept working without power or maintenance. The "immortal" Internet wasn't the only technological anomaly. In some towns electricity simply wouldn't work. Ejii had read an in-depth news story about a Niger town called Akidi where nothing electronic worked, even portable devices brought from somewhere else. Before the Great Change, Akidi had been up and coming. Now it was a dying rural town of corncobs with too many spaces between the kernels and angry cows who tried to attack travelers.

And everyone in Kwàmfà knew of sparkling lizards. Rumor had it that these lizards were made of pieces of lighting. If a sparkling lizard came into your house, you could turn off all your power for days and still have appliances work. Its favorite place was next to the house's greatest electricity-consuming appliance. The only drawback was that that plagued the home with heavy static. Ejii had never seen a sparkling lizard but Arif's family had experienced one. Arif said the lizard was a few inches long and purple-white and glittery.

"If you look at it too long, it loses shape right before your eyes!" he said.

No one could explain digital ghosts, either. Digital ghosts haunted entire networks and personal computers. They did the opposite of what a computer virus did. If you found your computer operating at a faster speed or found some kind of wonderful expensive software that you'd always wanted installed on it, you probably were being haunted by a digital ghost. Unfortunately, digital ghosts liked to talk and nag and reminisce about past lives, so if your work computer was haunted, you had a problem.

There was always the threat of digital ghosts when one went online, but Ejii wasn't worried. Digital ghosts tended to haunt sophisticated computers and her e-legba was cheap and outdated. Her e-legba couldn't even make calls or get the news unless she was within Kwàmfà's borders. She tried calling her mother, just to see if she could.

"You are out of range, Miss Ejimofor Ugabe," her e-legba said. When she tried to access the news channels, she got the same response. Her e-legba was now just a journal and weather forecaster. "Okay," she said to herself as she put it back into her bag, ignoring a pinch of panic. She heard the rustle of tree branches.

"What's that?" she said, poking her head out of her tent. She'd made sure that there were no monkeys in the tree before she approached it. To be attacked by a tribe of monkeys when alone was more dangerous than being robbed by human beings.

Onion opened an eye. "Owl," he said and closed his eye.

She looked up into the tree and was reminded that the baobab tree was heavy with monkey-bread fruit. The owl had brown-red plumage, like the color of the kola nuts the elders always broke and distributed before starting an event. Its frowning eyes were black as it perched on a large monkey-bread fruit near the top of the tree. It looked down at Ejii and then dug its claws through the fruit's hard woody shell, and took off with it.

"Owls don't eat monkey bread," she said, going back into her tent.

"Nobody's really sure of anything, anymore," Onion grumbled, his eyes still closed.

✛

CHAPTER TEN

AEJEJ

Eᴊɪɪ and Onion had to leave the baobab tree a little earlier than planned.

She woke at about four p.m. though she could have slept another hour. She could have used another fifteen minutes to saddle Onion and to gather some of that cactus candy that had made her feel so much better. And she could have used another twenty minutes to eat something. It was still hot outside, not good for traveling. But something was happening to the baobab tree. It was the snapping and cracking that woke her.

Then almost immediately, she felt it and tried to pinpoint exactly what *it* was: a moldy, warm sadness, an ancient frustration, a calculating cunning, an insipid meanness, a hungry hunger; she couldn't quite put words to it. But she understood that she had to get away from this place.

"Onion?" she said, sticking her head out of her tent, avoiding looking directly at the tree. She knew if she did, she'd be paralyzed by fear. Onion was getting up and roaring as he stretched. "Are . . . are you all right?"

He shook himself out, spraying dust and sand about. Without a word, Onion walked off. Ejii frowned and went back into her tent to gather her things. She was rolling up her blanket when she heard Onion return. She couldn't ignore the noise anymore. She finally looked at the tree. She was speechless. The bark was snapping and pulling into the tree's yellow wood and the roots that had peeked above the ground were gone. The tree's branches that had been fanned out were all facing the sky, as if made of steel and the sun was a giant magnet. And slowly, the tree was pulling itself underground.

"The cactus candy has gone bad," Onion said. "Something is coming."

Moving quickly, she put on a long indigo dress made of porous material and took several feet of indigo cloth and wrapped it over her head and face Tuareg-style. She touched the amulet from her mother. She'd slept wearing Arif's silver earrings. She rolled up her tent, saddled Onion, tied her burdens onto Onion's back, and they were off.

They traveled south. They were about a day away from Agadez if they continued through the night. A mile later, the terrain went from desert to meadow. Two miles later, they were on sand again. It was terribly hot and Onion's sweat dampened his fur. Whatever had been approaching back by the tree was close, and they couldn't afford to slow down. For two hours neither Ejii nor Onion spoke.

"Onion," Ejii said breaking the silence. "Do you think we'll outrun it?"

"No," Onion said.

Ejii nodded. "Let's go up that dune," she said.

When they got to the top, she saw two things. The first was that there was a small village of sand brick houses about a mile away. From what she could see, many of the houses were falling apart; a ghost village. The second thing she saw was a wall of sand churning into the sky, a violent sandstorm. It was about ten miles to the north and heading right toward them. She felt wetness on her upper lip. When she touched it, her hand came away red with blood. She wiped it on her clothes.

"That's an Aejej!" Ejii said.

"What's an Aejej?" Onion asked. Ejii had never heard him sound so afraid.

"Giant storms that are . . . alive," she said. The Scribe had talked about them in her book, *My Cyborg Manifesto*. Ejii knew the passage well:

> The Aejej's whirlwinds of rage and confusion and sand and air sound like a thousand women screaming. They may be mad, but they're also *very* conscious. Too conscious. It's human life they seek to destroy, but only those in small numbers, alone in the desert, most vulnerable. Again, I'm reminded that it is never safe to travel unaccompanied. I wonder if they're afraid of cities.

"See that village?" Ejii asked.

Onion responded by breaking into a sprint. When Onion wanted to run fast, he was faster than any horse. Ejii glanced to the side and saw that the Aejej was still coming, churning up huge clouds of sand as it moved. She could already hear its screeching.

"We'll make it," she said into Onion's ear.

The roads between the houses were narrow but large enough for Onion to run through. Most of the houses had caved-in raffia roofs. Ejii looked around, frantic. Whatever place she chose would be the place where they would either live or die.

"There," she said, pointing to the house that still had all four walls and a roof. She jumped off Onion and pulled down her burdens. "Hurry!"

"Will I fit?" Onion asked, following her in.

"Bend low, suck in as much air as you can." As she spoke, the sun was blocked out by the approaching storm, dressing everything in shadow. The camel tried to squeeze in and was soon stuck.

"Come on," Ejii shouted, tears coming to her eyes. The screeching grew louder, now accompanied by the roar of wind. "Push!"

Onion groaned with pain and Ejii feared that the building's walls would crumble away. If the wind hit and Onion was still stuck, the exposed part of his body would be grated away by the wind and sand. She grabbed the fur around his neck and pulled. He roared as sand started to beat at his exposed rump. "Ejii, get back," he said. "I'm lost."

Ejii looked into his blue eyes. She grabbed his fur again. "Push, Onion! Push!"

As they both strained, he suddenly came through the door,

sending Ejii tumbling back. She slowly got up on shaky scratched legs. Onion's head grazed the thatched roof but otherwise he fit. Inside the hut was even darker than outside. There was no time to look around. Ejii didn't consider the possibility of scorpions in the corners or giant venomous wall spiders stretched over the ceiling. She looked instead at the doorway, listening as the Aejej closed in. It *did* sound like thousands of women screaming. When the boy in the corner stepped out from one of the hut's corners, *she* almost screamed.

"What are you doing here?" he asked, skittering to the farthest corner. He spoke in Igbo. He looked about her age and had a large dusty Afro. He switched to Hausa, the language most people in Niger spoke. "I see your eyes! You're one of those evil people who can see into people's souls and then you steal them!" He hooted in terror.

"I can't see into people's souls," Ejii said, running to look out the window. She shielded her eyes against the wind and flying sand.

"You're a jinni, then! Oh, Ani, God, Chineke, Allah, I'm finally done for! How did I end up so *doomed, kwo*? I don't like camels. Especially ones that talk."

"Shut up!" Ejii shouted in Hausa. "It's coming!"

"You think I don't *know* that!" the boy said, wild eyed. "You think I just got here? I've been trapped here two goddamn DAYS!"

"What exactly is it?" Ejii asked, starting to panic.

"It's our deaths, thanks to you," he said.

Onion backed into a corner and hunkered down. The boy wore what probably used to be white pants and a short shirt, but were now closer to rags. He had a beat-up satchel slung over his shoulder. From the center of his temple to the tip of his nose was a thick, blue line with dots on both sides of the line. The mark of a slave.

The Aejej's howling suddenly grew much louder and there was a drop in air pressure that made Ejii woozy. Then everything went dead silent.

"Get down," the boy whispered, grabbing her arm and pulling her to the floor.

Then the noise came. The sound made Ejii gnash her teeth. It was shrill and so piercing the she thought her ears would bleed. The house shook and sand flew in through the open windows and doorway. The sand pelted their skin like needles and Ejii's eyes watered with pain.

"It's found me!" the boy shouted. "You've led it right to me!"

Ejii closed her eyes and tried to muster up calmness. Next to her, the boy was screaming and cursing with terror.

"Stop it!" she shouted. There was blood from the whipping sand dripping down the side of her face, and more blood coming from her nose. "I need to think."

"What is there to think about? I happened to be resting here when I saw it tear four people apart out there! The only reason I'm alive is because it didn't know I was here! We're done for! *Chineke*, protect us, *kwo*!" Then he cursed some more.

The house shuddered on the brink of blowing away. She

tried to hear the Aejej's voice. Chaos. The Aejej was like a bundle of string that she couldn't unravel. I'll never see Mama again, she thought. Kambili's shadows were right. Why did I leave!? But then she paused, her brow furrowing as she listened.

There it was again.

Keeping low to the ground, the boy moved closer to Onion for protection. The house creaked, dangerously.

But there it was again.

She slowly got up and peeked out the window, hanging on to the windowsill and shielding her eyes as much as she could. The sand bit at her hand. At first all she could see was whipping sand. She couldn't even see the houses across the street anymore. But now . . . was that a face?

"Allah is punishing me for sure!" the boy shouted, before covering his head again.

"Shut up!" Ejii cried. The boy's panic was starting to make her panic. The house was shaking more vigorously, the walls starting to crumble. It *was* a face that she saw outside. The Aejej had lowered its stormy body onto the house and was looking inside. Inside the sandstorm, Ejii saw two light-green, glowering eyes and a gaping black mouth that seemed to lead into a million miles of shadow. It could have swallowed them into its screaming mouth of infinity . . . if it wanted to. But something was giving it pause.

"What do you think it wants?" she asked the boy.

"To kill us!" he said. "Its belly is full of sand and wind but it's still hungry."

"That's because it's . . ." Ejii blinked. "It's probably not eating the right food." She remembered something Mazi Godwin said: *When one is starved enough of anything good—like food, love, praise—he or she almost always grows angry.*

"Don't move," Ejii shouted to Onion and the boy. She wasn't sure if they had heard her above the noise, but neither of them moved when she started for the door. For a moment, the wind's velocity threatened to slam her against the wall, but it calmed, as if allowing her to approach. Ejii had no idea what she was going to do. As she made her way outside on shaky legs, she felt a moment of panic. There was suddenly nothing between her and the sweeping power of the Aejej. She stood there in the now calm but volatile wind. Sand lightly whipped against her face, threatening and warning.

"Hey! What the hell are you doing!?" she heard the boy shout.

I don't *know*, she thought. Then she looked up and faced the Aejej, and it happened almost automatically. She reached out to the great shadow caused by the Aejej and listened to what it told her. Doing this was so easy this time that she was only vaguely aware that she was doing it at all. As her subconscious mind spoke with the Aejej's shadow, her conscious mind tried its best not to panic, not to scream, not to cry.

A pocket of calm air surrounded her; any moment the Aejej could decide to take it away. The sand would kill her before the strength of its winds. It would tear the flesh away from her bones within seconds. She couldn't even see a foot above her head, let alone the sky. It was like standing in a bubble under muddy water. Suffocating. And the air felt warm and moist as if she were standing inside a whale's belly.

She held her head high and stood up straight, shoulders back. She took a deep breath and spoke in the language that she thought the Aejej would best understand.

"What is it that pains you, Great Creature?" she shouted in Arabic.

Mazi Godwin had also taught her that one responds best when addressed with respect. But she didn't need an answer to know what pained the Aejej. Its shadow had answered her question already: the Aejej couldn't remember its own story.

"I rage," she heard it say. Its voice was not a voice. It was a shift in the winds, a hiss of the sands. *"I was calm and then humans caused me to rage. I need peace."*

"Peace doesn't come . . . peace is not something . . ." She stuttered as she tried to talk to the Aejej. She couldn't find the words that she wanted. She tried again. "Sometimes, peace is not something that just comes. Sometimes you have to actively search for it."

The Aejej was *listening*, its ghostly face hovering before her. The face was the size of two houses.

"I am not saying to forget that man has harmed you," she said. "But you have forgotten what exactly he did. Maybe it is time for you to put it to rest. Maybe it is time for you to *calm down*. Make your own peace. Create it yourself." As she spoke, the Aejej *was* calming down, but then her last words must have caused it to feel a sharp pang of rage and a whip of wind sent Ejii flying. She slammed against the wall of the house. The air was knocked out of her chest and she tasted blood in her mouth. Everything went black.

✤ ✤ ✤

Pain. Sand and blood in her throat. Heat on her skin. Slowly, she returned to herself, opening her eye to a blue sunny sky. Everything was gone. The boy was roughly patting her cheek and Onion was licking her other cheek.

"Ejii," Onion was saying softly in his monotonous voice. "Please wake up."

Ejii could hear a soft chirping sound close to her ear. When she turned toward it, she met the boy's eyes. He stared into her eyes and gasped. Then he just stared.

"My shoulder," she groaned, sitting up. Her mouth was gritty with sand and she coughed up sandy red saliva. She gasped and frantically felt her hip pockets. She started to panic. When she felt the hardness of the egg stone, she let out a great sigh of relief.

The boy handed her a cup of water. "Hope you don't mind, I had some too."

Ejii only grunted and drank deeply from the cup. Her clothes were also filled with sand. And her face and hair were covered with it. Onion and the boy were equally drenched. When she looked next to the boy, she softly gasped. The owl standing next to the boy ruffled its feathers and clicked its beak again.

"Is that the same owl from . . . ?" she trailed off trying to catch her breath. She looked around. From horizon to horizon, there was only sand. The sun was starting to move deep into the west. "What happened? Where's the . . ."

"It all got buried," the boy said. "Whatever you . . . were you speaking to it?"

Ejii nodded, rubbing her shoulder and standing up. All of them, even Onion, had stinging, bleeding abrasions from the sand. "Oh, Onion, are you okay?" she said when she noticed the red patches on his sandy brown fur.

"I'm more worried about you," Onion said.

"Who's this?" she asked, looking at the owl. "And why's it awake?"

"This is Kola," the boy said.

Ejii smiled weakly. "Like the kola nut."

The boy nodded. "She's a day owl, I guess. She sleeps when I sleep."

"I saw her yesterday, I think," Ejii said. "She flew off with a monkey-bread fruit."

The boy smiled sheepishly. "When the Aejej killed those people, she got really scared and flew away. The Aejej lurking about has kept her from me," he said. "I like monkey-bread fruit, so she must have hoped to eventually present it to me."

Ejii wanted to ask more about the bird—she'd never been able to speak with birds—but her shoulder was aching too much. She closed her eyes and sighed again.

"We saw you standing before it," the boy said. "I thought you'd lost your mind. Then *WHOOSH*!" He dramatically flung his hands in the air. "Its wind threw you against the house! We

106

couldn't see where you landed! I thought we were all done for, *kwo*!" He frowned. "I jumped up and was about to try and help you. But your camel grabbed my shirt with his teeth and held me back. Right after that, everything just stopped! All the wind . . . everything. The sand just froze in the air. And there was this rosy smell. My mother used to say that the smell of roses meant something had been freed."

He took a deep breath. Ejii waited for him to continue. His story was so fascinating and he told it so well that she momentarily forgot the pain in her shoulder.

"Then something flew off, couldn't see what it was, and the sand began to fall! All that sand the Aejej had been filling itself with just fell! Sounded like rain. Shhh! Your camel ran out and found and grabbed you by your dress with his teeth. I hung on to his tail and we started walking. We could have easily been buried!"

"What did you say to it?" Onion asked.

"Um . . . I . . . I told it that it needed to create peace," she said.

"Well in making peace, it fell to pieces," the boy said, helping Ejii stand up.

She smiled. She cocked her head looking at the blue markings that ran down the bridge of his nose. "So it's true?" she said.

"What's true?"

"They make children work in the north, in Assamakka?"

The pained look that crossed his face made Ejii want to take back her words.

"What's your name?" she asked.

"Aren't you supposed to *know* things like that?" he replied, raising his eyebrows. He looked afraid again, letting go of her arm.

"I can't go into your mind like it's a computer," she said, stretching her shoulder. She didn't think anything was broken. "And if I could, I'd only do it when I needed to."

The boy narrowed his eyes at Ejii. She didn't have to consult her shadows to know he had trouble trusting people.

"Relax," she said. "You're taller than I am and you're . . ." She was about to say he was a boy. She shook her head. "I can't do anything to you."

"But you have that camel," he said.

Onion humphed.

"Onion?" Ejii said. "He's sweet as cactus candy. He'd never hurt anyone."

"How do I know that?"

"If he was going to hurt you, he'd have done it a while ago," Ejii said. "He could have kicked you when you were hanging on to his tail. Instead he led you to safety. You said so yourself."

The boy bit his lip and glanced at Onion. Then he looked at Kola. She puffed her throat in and out and screeched. "Okay," he said. "Dikéogu, my name is Dikéogu Obidimkpa." He pronounced his first name "DEE-keh-aw-goo."

"I'm Ejii Ugabe," she said, holding out a hand. He slapped the back of his hand against the back of hers three times. The handshake of friendship. "And this is Onion."

He held his hand out for Onion to sniff.

"Where were you coming from?" she asked.

"From nowhere, and that's where I was going," he said, looking away. He wouldn't say any more than that. "You?"

She crossed her arms in front of her chest and sucked her teeth. Her eyes wandered to the markings on the bridge of his nose again, and she felt bad about asking him where he'd come from. She'd been thoughtless. "I'm . . . do you know of Sarauniya Jaa?"

He smiled and Ejii felt a little better. He reached into his dusty satchel and brought out a book. Ejii grinned. It was a beat-up copy of *My Cyborg Manifesto*.

"Jaa was my favorite character because she was kidnapped and still became a leader," he said. He sighed and looked at his sandals.

"It's Jaa that I'm following," Ejii ventured.

"You *know* her?" he shouted.

She hesitated and then nodded.

"How?"

She paused again. They had been through an adventure together but he was still a stranger.

He raised a hand. "Don't tell me if you don't want to," he said. "You never know who you can trust. That I know."

"No . . . I . . . I'm from Kwàmfà," Ejii said.

"You're kidding," Dikéogu said.

"No. Jaa works very closely with my . . . She executed my father."

Dikéogu shrank back. "You're . . . Was he the chief of Kwàmfà?"

Ejii frowned. "How . . ."

"I know you. I mean, I know *of* you. Everyone saw it happen on Naija Net. I was nine or ten years old. My mother tried to cover my eyes. I remember that. Horrible."

"Yeah," Ejii said.

"I'm sorry," he said.

"It was complicated. . . . I'm not after revenge or anything." Dikéogu looked at her suspiciously. She laughed and shrugged. "You want to come with us?" she asked. She didn't know what else to say. It didn't make sense for them to just go their separate ways, not after what they'd just been through together.

Dikéogu looked at Kola. She clicked her beak. "Maybe," he said. "For a little while . . . just to see Jaa."

✦

CHAPTER ELEVEN

SHALLOW WATERS

THEY walked well into the night, the best time to travel because it was cool. Ejii lent Dikéogu her thick burka to keep warm. According to her e-legba's map, they were only a half day away from Agadez. But Ejii's body was aching.

"Do you think we should stop tonight and camp?" she asked.

"How should I know?" he asked. "You're the one who knows the way."

"Well . . . I shouldn't be making all the decisions," she said. She didn't know many boys who liked to be led. It's not right for me to lead, she caught herself thinking. She frowned. The ideas of her father, again. What of Jaa? She leads everyone, she thought. And Dikéogu doesn't seem to mind me making the decisions. And I *do* know the way.

Dikéogu gave Ejii a strange look and said, "I'm fine with you making the choice."

"Okay . . . we should go an hour longer and then camp,"

she said. She held herself from glancing at Dikéogu for his approval.

"If you say so," he said.

"Then, if we make faster time, we'll make it there by morning," she said.

As she walked next to Onion, Dikéogu trudged beside her, his arms across his chest as he looked up at the sky. The owl was perched on Onion's hump. Ejii was very aware of walking next to Dikéogu instead of a step or two behind him, but she said nothing, quietly preferring it this way. She was glad for Dikéogu's silence. She wanted to let her mind relax; that way she'd be less likely to have nightmares when she slept. The image of the screaming, angry Aejej was still fresh in her mind. She touched her Cross of Agadez and wondered what her mother would think had happened. Then she remembered that she'd left without her mother's permission, that her mother had said not to come back if she left.

"Let's camp here," Onion said when they arrived at a cluster of palm trees with a small pond and some green stalks growing around the palm trees. It was the first thing he'd said in seven hours. The sun would rise in four hours. Dikéogu used his flashlight to see what the green stalks were.

"Wild onions," Ejii said. Onion was already digging and pulling out the bulbs.

"That pond will probably be gone in the morning," Dikéogu said, sitting down. Ponds, sometimes even huge lakes, were known to appear one day and disappear the next. For the moment, this pond was shallow with clear water. Ejii

112

saw that there were several fish occupying it. Some were long and golden and others were flat and brown. She stared for a moment longer, suddenly feeling the urge to look closer. For a brief moment, she thought she could see tiny, tiny, tiny creatures in the water. Microscopic organisms? she wondered. Then she gasped as a deep aching tore into her temples.

"The . . . the water is all right," she said, closing her eyes for a moment. When she opened them, she felt better.

"What do you mean?" Dikéogu said.

She picked at her sand-encrusted, sweaty dress. "I don't see any danger," she said.

"How do you know?" he asked.

Ejii sighed. "Stop asking me that. You know how I know."

Dikéogu tried to see her face in the dark. "Do you think I trust you so much that I'd go into a pond I can't even see?" he asked.

Ejii groaned. "Let's build a small fire and . . . I'll go into the water, first," she said. "I need to bathe anyway. You gather the palm fronds and I'll light it with my lighter."

Ejii watched Dikéogu gather the fronds as she sat next to Onion. "He doesn't trust anything or anyone," she whispered. "I wish I *could* read minds."

"You could ask the shadows what they know," Onion said in between crunches. "Or you could ask him."

Once the fire was burning, Ejii flipped off her sandals and walked into the pond with all her clothes on. Her clothes needed washing just as much as her skin did. The water soothed her wounds. "See. It's fine!" she called to Dikéogu.

Dikéogu still hesitated. But only for a moment. Then he

laughed and flung himself into the water. The two swam about for a half hour, despite the cold. When they got out, Onion decided to go in. Dikéogu took his only change of clothes and went behind the palm trees where the firelight didn't reach. Ejii changed in her tent. She'd have to wear her wool coat to sleep because her weather-gel-treated tent was made for using under the hottest sun.

"I have to gather water," Ejii told Dikéogu. "I don't think that pond water is good for drinking. Onion can drink it but not us."

"I'd give you some of my water but I had to drop everything to outrun that Aejej," he said, looking guilty.

"It's all right," Ejii said.

There was an awkward silence.

"I would have died there. . . ."

Ejii looked away. "But you didn't. And I have a portable capture station." She brought out the smooth, shiny metal box from her pack.

"Nice. Let me see," He turned it over in his hands. "It's not the best but this is a good one." He looked at her. "I know your father was no good, but the rest of your family must be okay. Why did you run away?"

"I *didn't* run away," she said. "Not really." She brought out her e-legba, clicked on the *walkabout* definition and handed it to Dikéogu. As he listened, she looked up at the sky. It had thickened with clouds and there was a distant rumble of thunder.

"I don't understand why anyone would leave his family to tramp through the desert on purpose," he said, handing her e-legba back to her. He looked up at the sky and cringed. "Why didn't you leave *with* Jaa?"

"I guess I didn't make up my mind fast enough and . . . what's the matter?"

Dikéogu was staring up at the sky again. "I'm a little afraid of storms," he said, laughing nervously and stepping back toward the trees.

Ejii frowned. These days, storms didn't produce much rain, so they didn't really have to worry about getting soaked. Dikéogu seemed as if he would be afraid of his own shadow. She laughed at the irony that she was a shadow speaker.

"It's not funny," he said.

"I'm not laughing at your fear of . . ." She stopped. That was exactly what she was laughing at. "Anyway, it's best to try and collect some water before the storm moves on. We can put the capture station just past the trees, so that it doesn't make us too cold tonight."

They walked some yards away from the small oasis. Ejii unfolded the fiber bag, yet another mysterious item from Ginen. It was made of a kind of plant fiber that weighed practically nothing, but could stretch to hold a thousand gallons if it had to. This capture station would need to produce only four gallons of water. Ejii and her classmates had had the capture station's history pounded into their heads in school. Invented decades ago by a Nigérien scientist named Dan'Azumi Afer, it was Niger's pride and joy well before the Great Change. It was hard for Ejii to believe that Niger was once a desolate country dying of thirst.

Capture stations came in small personal sizes to accommodate a few people and large ones that could irrigate whole fields and keep whole cities awash in clean water. And before the Great Change, in the dry desert lands of Niger, water was life. The capture station sucked the atmospheric humidity from the clouds and then cleaned, cooled, and condensed it into drinkable water.

Enriched uranium, Niger's greatest resource, was the ingredient that allowed the nuclear-powered capture station to be so powerful yet so small and reasonably priced. Niger's presidential administration immediately saw the enormous potential. Instead of making small fortunes exporting uranium, the government decided to make use of its own resource for once. This turned out to be a great decision, for after the Great Change, nuclear weapons and nuclear power plants were no longer being made because the science that had made them no longer worked. This was another result of the Great Change. Capture stations, however, worked and sold well, not only in Niger, but also all over the world where clean normal water had become scarce.

Along with being a wonderful way to produce water in the Sahara desert, when capture stations pulled humidity from the sky and cooled it, they produced a wide perimeter of cool air. In Ejii's village, it was during the hottest part of the day that people turned on their capture stations. On cool nights, it wasn't very pleasant to be too close to an operating capture station, even a small one like Ejii's.

She attached the fiber bag to the capture station, making

sure the tiny metal vial at the bottom for collecting the trace amounts of nuclear waste was secure.

"We should get a lot of good water," she said, looking up at the fat clouds.

"Can I flip it on?" Dikéogu said, scuttling over, keeping his head low. "I've always wanted to, but my father never let me. It was always the 'servant's job.'"

"Servant? I thought you were a slave."

"I was," was all he said. Ejii stepped aside so he could flip the switch on the side. Then they both stepped back some more. The capture station wasn't even close to as earsplitting as the Aejej, but it was noisy.

"Praise Allah," Dikéogu whispered with a grin, seeming to temporarily forget his fear of storms. "I've always wanted to just stand and watch this."

The white funnel of spiraling air rose from the silver box and slowly extended into the plump clouds above. It was like a ghost's delicate finger. The air around them cooled as the spiral grew thick with condensed water.

"That's good water," Ejii said. "I'm glad I . . ."

Ejii felt it first, from the ground. Like gossamer spiderwebs softly blowing up from the earth and tickling the hairs on her legs, arms, face. She heard and felt the short hair on her head prickle. Her eyes met Dikéogu's just before it happened. His eyes were wide with fear and his lips were pressed together as if he were bracing himself. Then . . .

PhhhBAM!

The bolt of lightning flashed down from the sky, a jagged

ribbon of neon blue and white. She had a moment to see it zip right for Dikéogu, and then it was as if she were on a cloud of charged dust. She wasn't thrown violently. It was more like being picked up and carried several feet away and then put heavily onto the sandy earth. She slid back a few more feet and then came to a stop. She could hear the shadows whipping around her, whispering, touching. She strained to understand. *He is not from the desert.* Then they, too, grew quiet. Over and over, she thought, How is it I'm alive? How is it I'm alive?

Silence. Then the padding of Onion's hooves. He looked down at her. He sniffed her face, seemed satisfied with what he smelled, and then walked over to Dikéogu.

Silence.

"Ejii!" she heard Dikéogu shout as he ran over, Onion in tow. "Are you all right?"

She lay there, still in shock. How is it I'm alive? How is it he's alive and fine? When all she continued to do was stare at him, Dikéogu did the only thing that he could probably think of. He slapped her.

Ejii scrambled to her feet and so did Dikéogu. They stood staring at each other.

"I'm sorry," he said.

"What?" she said, still breathing hard.

"Are you okay?" he asked.

"Do . . . I . . . look okay?" she said, starting to hyperventilate. She'd seen him slammed with lightning. He should have been some feet away, dead. *She* should have been dead. Onion trotted over to her and pushed his hide against her. She leaned

118

on him and soon her breathing slowed. She glared at Dikéogu. "Is something . . . *wrong* with you? Has someone cursed you? Is that why you're all alone? Is that why the Aejej was after you?"

She felt bad as soon as the words were out.

"It's better if we talk under the trees," he quietly said.

As they sat at the fire, despite all that had just happened, Ejii's stomach growled. Without a word, she got up and went to her supplies. She looked back at Dikéogu, who sat with his back against the palm tree looking into the fire. As she unpacked a plate, her hands shook. She closed her eyes and took a deep breath. She brought out another plate and put fried plantain, dates, bread, and some hunks of salted goat meat on both of them. She stood up, walked to Dikéogu, and put a plate of food before him.

"It's over a day old," she said, sitting down, aware that her voice was hoarse. "But it's okay. Just check the bread for mold; bread doesn't last long."

Dikéogu looked at the food with wide, hungry eyes. Ejii leaned over and pushed the plate closer to him. "Take."

Dikéogu hesitated, glanced at Ejii, and then said, "Thank you."

She nodded, placing another piece of goat meat on his plate. They both looked up when Kola left her tree, her powerful wings not making a sound.

"She sees a meal," Dikéogu said, looking cautiously at Ejii. "She can always find food, no matter where we are." He paused. "She saved my life a year ago. . . . I must not be meant to live if my life has to keep being saved and the sky keeps trying to kill me."

"Where are you from?" Ejii asked. "All the shadows tell me is that you're not from the desert, not originally."

"They're like a sixth sense to you?" Dikéogu said.

"Huh?"

"The shadows."

"Oh. No. I can't control them."

"Hmm," Dikéogu said. "Can they tell you the wrong thing?"

"They don't lie," Ejii said. "Dishonesty's a human habit, they say. But enough about me, I want to know . . ."

"So you were born . . . like that?"

Ejii sighed. "Yes. Dikéogu, just tell me what hap . . ."

"I will," he said. "I just need to . . . Where do your shadows say I'm from?"

Deciding to go along with him, she tried to hear an answer if they gave one. Dikéogu looked around as the shadows gathered and the darkness around them deepened.

"Relax," she said. She smiled as she herself relaxed and realized the ease of hearing them. She was getting better at it. Then she shrugged. "You don't want them to tell me, they say," Ejii said. "All they tell me is that you're not from the desert."

"Does that happen all the time?" he asked.

"Huh?"

"Just then," he said. "When you were listening to the shadows . . . you got all black. Your skin. I mean, you're pretty dark already, but you got darker. Then you looked normal again. Or maybe it's just the firelight."

Ejii looked at her arms, thinking about how Mazi Godwin said that travel strongly affected shadow speakers. Maybe this was an example, as was her increased ease at hearing the shadows.

"Well, it's good that they won't tell you everything," Dikéogu said. "No one should know everything." He paused and said, "Okay, I . . . I was born in Arondizuogu. That's a village in the southeast part of Nigeria."

"Are you Igbo, Yoruba, or Efik?" she asked. "Igbo, I'd guess, by your name, but your mother could be something else or you could be New Tuareg."

"I'm Igbo. And you're New Tuareg. You father was Wodaabe, right?"

"Yes, and my mother is New Tuareg; her mother, my grandmother, started off Igbo. She and her sister migrated from Nigeria to Niger to join the New Tuareg. Dikéogu, tell me what happened to you. Please."

Dikéogu distrustfully eyed Ejii. He took a big bite of his goat meat and chewed and swallowed and said, "It's a long story, Ejii."

"Well, I think I deserve to know. I almost just died because of you."

"How do you know it was because of me?" Dikéogu asked. "Is that what your stupid shadows told you?"

"Will you just tell me?" Ejii snapped.

He took another bite of goat meat, chewed, and swallowed. When he spoke, he didn't speak in Hausa, the language they'd been speaking in since they'd met. He spoke in his first language, which was Igbo. "All those rumors and news stories about child slavery in northern Niger are true . . ."

✝   ✝   ✝

"Assamakka is the center of it. You always have this feeling that stuff like that can't happen to you. Some of us there were only five, others seventeen. We were slaves. My group worked on cocoa farms. They had us rub ourselves with weather gel, so the heat wouldn't kill us . . . not too quickly at least. Weather gel isn't even for human skin!

"I remember one of the slavers in particular, a light-skinned man who always wore white. He was so evil. They fed us only bad fruit and old meat. The capture stations that irrigated the fields gave us clean water. But this evil man would sit there eating chocolate bars as we worked. Sweet, smooth, delicious chocolate, thick blocks of it, every damn day. There was a girl who always cried whenever she saw him eating it. He'd beat her for 'wasting time.' Then he'd bite into his chocolate bar and laugh with his chocolate-smelling breath, his tongue brown like he'd swallowed mud.

"We carried sacks that were too heavy, planted seeds, pulled dead leaves in the hot sun, and dug holes in the hard dirt. They beat us when we got tired. Sometimes they killed us. Even covered in itchy weather gel, it was so hot. It really *was* like being in hell. The plantations were surrounded by miles of desert. Who knows how they got the soil that the cocoa plants grew in to this desert-surrounded place. Probably more of Earth's weirdness. Whatever the reason, it was a perfect place to hold us captive. Most of us, at least.

"All the other kids were too scared of dying in the desert to try to escape. I'd been there for months and I felt like my very soul was drying up in the sun. I couldn't stand the thought of being there all my life. There were teenagers who'd been there since they were five! So I ran off. I'd rather die in the desert than die from too much work with that chocolate-tongued man watching and laughing at me.

"I waited for the next new moon, when it's the darkest. There were guards but they always fell asleep by midnight. When I left, it was nothing like when *you* left. I didn't have supplies or a camel to talk to. And I wasn't leaving a happy place. I had nothing but my satchel with my book, my own two feet, and the tattered clothes I wore. I walked for days! If I thought about dying, I might have died. I came across a monkey-bread tree and two spontaneous ponds. They saved my life, at least for those days. During that time, I was actually happy. I was more alone than I'd ever been in my life. But I was happy.

"I read *My Cyborg Manifesto* over and over. Have you ever read while walking? I walked miles with my head in that book. It made me feel like what I was going through was normal. In the story The Scribe tells, Jaa was kidnapped . . . but she still made something of herself.

"The ponds eventually disappeared and soon I was baking in the day and freezing at night. At some point, I passed out. I remember the sun was near setting. I was walking and then I fell and the world went black.

"I woke up to the smell of mangos. I thought I was dead. But right in front of my nose was a mango and an owl. Kola. That was the name that came to me when I saw her. By the time I was done eating the mango, she had returned with an orange from who knows where. Eating it stung my cracked lips, but it was so so good. She brought me more fruits and even coconuts filled with water. How an owl can even *grasp* a coconut is beyond me! Kola brought me back from the dead. And since then, she's been with me. Sometimes she leaves for a day or so, but she always finds me.

"With her help, I made it to Biafra City where I did some petty work for food, clothes, and travel things. At first I was trying to make it home but . . . it's been over a year now. I've changed my mind."

✝   ✝   ✝

". . . If anyone tells you that my story is not true then he's full of camelshit."

Ejii glanced at Onion who only humphed and said, "Why not human shit?"

"But . . ." she hesitated. "Dikéogu, what about the lightning?"

"I'm not telling you about that," he snapped. "I don't know you. I can say that I'm . . . relatively safe to be with. How often do storm clouds gather? Not often at all." He hesitated looking angry. "If you want to part ways now, then . . . fine!"

Ejii was so angry that she almost jumped up and kicked

sand at him. But then his story touched her heart and she held her anger back. She balled her fists and sat back down. "So, how did you end up in Assamakka in the first place?" she asked.

But Dikéogu only sucked his teeth. "That's more camelshit. Doesn't matter."

"Ah, you're so . . . ugh!" she got up and walked into the darkness, away from the capture station's coolness. As she looked out at the quiet, calm desert, she tried to consult the shadows, but they remained silent. This was her decision to make. His story was easy to guess. He'd probably run away from home for some reason he now regretted and then been picked up by the slavers. . . . But that didn't explain the lightning. Maybe he's some sort of metahuman, she thought. But if he was, why would he be so secretive about it? Especially to her?

By the time she returned to the fire to tell him her decision, he had curled up under a tree, laid his head on his satchel, and fallen asleep. Who knows if he'll still be there when I wake up anyway, she thought as she climbed into her tent. Most likely not.

✛

CHAPTER TWELVE

CITY OF BURROWS

"**E**JII, wake up," she heard Dikéogu say. It felt as if she'd just closed her eyes.

For a moment she lingered in her strange dream of Dikéogu getting struck by lightning again, the sparks nipping at her arms as she shielded her face. The strangest thing was that in the dream it all happened backward. Instead of the lightning striking him, it shot from him into the sky. She'd tried to shout to him, but her words came out backward, too, and all she could think of was that backward meant away from Jaa.

"Ejii, get out here," she heard Dikéogu say again.

"Huh?" When she touched her face, a painful spark popped from her finger.

"Come out. Hurry," he said, from outside. "Uh . . . we have visitors."

She quickly wiggled into her long draping indigo dress. She emerged from the tent, slowly, very slowly. No fast moves. There were at least fifteen, all lined up in perfect formation before her tent. Sand-dune cats, all as large as the one she'd met back at home. The sun was just thinking about rising. Only two or three hours had passed.

"Must be the whole tribe," she whispered.

Dikéogu nodded. Onion stood next to him, Kola perched on his hump.

"Can you talk to them?" Dikéogu asked.

"Me?"

"Yes, you!" he hissed. "Who else?"

"I . . . I don't know," she said.

She let her shoulders slump as she relaxed her body the way Mazi Godwin had taught her. Silence. Beads of sweat formed on her brow. She could hear Dikéogu nervously shifting from one foot to the other. Then she heard something else.

"Your skin. It's happening again," Dikéogu whispered.

She glanced at her arms. Indeed her normally dark-brown skin looked black as beetle wings. She started to hear things. It was as if they were coming from the back of her head. Slowly, the chatter grew louder, moving to the forefront.

"We should eat them."

"I enjoy camel meat."

"We won't be able to catch the bird."

"The male human makes my hair stand on end. You feel that?"

"It's bad luck to eat humans that aren't fully adult."

"Their people may come after us."

"They are almost adult."

"That one has eyes like ours."

Ejii just stood there in awe. The shadows felt as if they'd

become a part of her, as opposed to whispering to her or giving her a sort of access to the voices of the cats as they had last year. It was a strange frightening sensation. For a moment, she listened to the soft guttural purrs and soft grunts, more musical than any human voice.

"I hear you," Ejii said with her mind. She braced herself for the cats to jump at her. To hear and understand her speech would be a shock to them. They didn't attack. Instead, all chatter ceased. *"Excuse us,"* Ejii said to the cats. *"Are we trespassing?"*

"We've been following you," said a cat from the back. Ejii wasn't sure how she could tell which was speaking, but she could. The others cleared the way as this cat sauntered up to her. Unlike the others who had pale-yellow to gray-brown coats, this cat was more robust and its fur was a deep black. It had a white star-shaped patch of hair in the middle of its forehead. *"We had no intention of hurting you."*

Ejii frowned. This cat was lying.

"A shadow speaker?" it asked.

Ejii nodded, but then realized the cats might not understand such a human gesture as Onion or Kola did. *"Yes, I am,"* she said. *"And you all were going to eat us."*

The sound of the cat's laugh was unpleasant, a series of low growls. The others chuckled too. *"I am Star Cat, Priestess of the Airensis Tribe. This is our land,"* the cat said. The others purred for emphasis.

"What'd it say?" Dikéogu asked.

"She," Ejii said. "I think she's a 'she.' Her name's Star Cat and the rest are her tribespeople."

"Well, introduce us, too," he said anxiously. "They might be less likely to kill us if they know our names!"

Ejii turned back to Star Cat. *"I'm Ejii and this is Dikéogu, Onion, and Kola. We're coming from the South. We're sorry for trespassing on your land. We're on our way north to Agadez. We have no time to waste."*

"We allow only our own people to go that way," Star Cat said.

There was an irritated growl from beside Star Cat, as one of the cats ran its paw over its face producing a crackling sound. *"These children are infested with prickly forces,"* it said. Several of the other cats agreed.

"You won't let us pass?" Ejii quickly asked, wanting to change the subject.

"Why are they all meowing like that?" Dikéogu asked.

"Let her talk," Onion said.

Ejii didn't know what else to say. These cats could easily kill even Onion, there were so many of them. From her village to Agadez was less than sixty miles. Jaa probably made it in a half day, she thought. We're running out of time. It suddenly dawned on her what she should do. She quickly pulled up the sleeve of her dress.

"I am *a member of your tribe,"* she said, turning to them so that they could all see her scar. *"I was given this marking last year by one of your people."* The cats purred loudly and Ejii smiled. They were impressed. And even better, they stopped complaining about the static in their fur, which was probably caused by Dikéogu.

"Ah, she is one of us," one cat said.

"Who initiated her?"

"I knew she was one of us. Look at her eyes."

"You say you're from the human town of Kwàmfà?" Star Cat said.

"Yes."

"I know who gave you that," Star Cat said. *"My brother. He likes to wander those lands. You must be the first human he has gotten so close to without eating."*

Ejii smiled with relief. *"That's what he said."*

"Come, then."

Ejii translated everything for her friends. Dikéogu narrowed his eyes. "How do you know they don't just want us to go to their village so they can eat us?" he asked. "It's easier to make your kill close to home and not have to drag the meat. . . ."

"She seemed sincere," Ejii said, cutting him off.

"Seemed?" he asked. He looked at the sky. Ejii followed his eyes with hers, noting the location of the sun. They didn't have much time.

✝   ✝   ✝

"So many of them," Dikéogu said.

The sand cats that they'd met were a tiny fraction of the tribe. The city of burrows spanned at least two square miles. The ground was pockmarked with hundreds of tunnels; each housed several cats. Here and there were clusters of dry look-ing trees, their roots serving as burrow entrances. As Star Cat led them through the city, cats peeked out.

"Onion," Ejii said looking behind her. "How are you doing?"

The camel was having a difficult time stepping around all the burrow entrances.

"I'll be all right," he said. Kola landed on Onion's hump. She'd been flying high above as they walked.

"Dikéogu, do I still look pitch black?" Ejii asked, looking at her arms.

"No," he said. "It lasted only a few seconds. Is something wrong with you?"

"Nothing unexpected, I suspect," Ejii said.

They were led to a large tree in the center of the city where two burrows were dug into the tree's trunk. A brawny white cat with red eyes and tufts of fur covering its paws stepped out of one of the burrows.

"He must be from high in the mountains," Ejii said.

"Maybe," Dikéogu said. "Or maybe he's just a big albino cat."

"This is Snow Cat, Priest of Airensis and my mate," Star Cat said. *"Snow Cat, the female human is initiated."*

"You're kidding?" Snow Cat said.

"Show him the tribal marking," Star Cat said.

Ejii did so.

"You can understand us?" Snow Cat asked, after stepping up to Ejii and looking at the marking. He came up to her hips.

"Of course I can," Ejii said, trying to sound confident.

"Sit. We've never gotten to hear of the human world from a human."

"He says to sit down," Ejii told Dikéogu and Kola. She

131

translated the rest of what had been said. "Dikéogu, don't give me that look. If they wanted to eat us, don't you think they would have by now?"

"You assume they behave like humans," he said. "I don't feel comfortable here."

"You don't feel comfortable anywhere," Ejii snapped.

"I didn't get this far by keeping my eyes closed," he grumbled, looking around as if he expected something to jump on him.

They sat down in the tree's shade. Onion folded his legs and plopped down. Kola flapped to Dikéogu and perched on his leg, mindful not to scratch him with her sharp talons. Dikéogu's frown softened as he stroked the bird's feathers. She clicked her beak and puffed out her throat. Then she flapped back to Onion and landed on his hump.

"Why do you like being there so much?" Dikéogu asked, annoyed. "You might be hurting Onion with your claws."

The bird looked at Dikéogu and clicked her beak, remaining where she was.

"I don't mind," Onion said.

"Fine," he said curtly.

Two cats dug shallow holes in front of Ejii and Dikéogu and two cats dug a deeper hole in front of Onion. Then two mangoes were placed in Ejii and Dikéogu's holes. More cats dragged forth leaves heavy with red and yellow cashew fruit, monkey-bread fruits, cactus candy, piles of grass, and a dead mouse and lizard each. Ejii realized that the holes were like bowls.

It was a feast, except for the stalks of grass, the mouse and lizard. A mouse was left next to Onion for Kola. She flew down, snatched it up, and returned to Onion's hump. She inspected the mouse and then began to eat it. Ejii figured it must have been fresh because owls only ate things that they had killed themselves. Several cats dropped wild onions in Onion's hole.

"Ask them how they knew he liked those," Dikéogu said.

"Dikéogu wants to know how you knew Onion liked those," Ejii asked.

"Why else would a camel have such a name?" Snow Cat said.

"His name," Ejii told Dikéogu. "They can't read our minds or anything."

"You don't know that," Dikéogu said.

"Well, if they could, I think they'd be laughing at you," Ejii snapped.

Star Cat and Snow Cat sat next to each other in front of their burrows as two other cats dropped a jackrabbit and a mouse before them. *"Before we eat,"* Star Cat said, *"we must thank the Cat of the Land for providing this food. Close your eyes."*

"Shut your eyes," Ejii told Dikéogu and Onion. "He's going to say a prayer of thanks."

"How original," Dikéogu said but he closed his eyes.

Onion closed his eyes, and Ejii was surprised when Kola did the same.

"Oh, Gracious Cat of the Land who bestows abundance at our paws,

We thank you for this food and will always honor you with awe.
We take this offering into our bellies and we will remain strong,
And hope you give these travelers good luck, for their journey will
be long."

Ejii quickly translated for Dikéogu, Onion, and Kola.

"Our journey will be long?" Dikéogu said. "How does he know?"

Ejii only shook her head and rolled her eyes. They ate and talked for about an hour. Around them, cats walked about, some of them complaining about the static, some carrying babies in their mouths, others with fresh kills. Many played or lazed about. Quite a few gathered to listen to Ejii talk and translate Dikéogu's words. Onion had fallen asleep after his big meal of onions, and Kola had taken to the sky.

Dikéogu had to admit he enjoyed the monkey-bread fruit. They were very starchy, just the way he liked them. Then the cats that had gathered started in with their questions. They asked about Ejii's and Dikéogu's villages. Ejii showed them her e-legba and told them what it did. Dikéogu told them about his escape. They were especially interested in how he met Kola.

"It's rare that an owl will help a human or any other creature," Star Cat said.

"Maybe she's his kindred chi," the one named Eve Cat said. She sat next to Ejii.

"What's a chi?" Dikéogu asked. Ejii translated his question.

"The twin of your inner spirit," Eve Cat told him. *"I believe*

that the more you are around the owl, the more you'll communicate and see into each other's minds."

Ejii thought about the fact that the owl seemed to understand human speech and Dikéogu seemed to understand the owl's form of speech. It made sense.

It was Jaa that they talked about most. *"She's a human whose soul is constantly dancing and fighting and killing,"* Star Cat said after Ejii explained where she was going and why. *"We have known of her since she became what she is."*

"A group of our strongest people fought her and her people once," Snow Cat said. *"We lost terribly."*

"We always keep a great distance from her now," Star Cat added.

"You're connected to her, Ejii," Snow Cat said. *"Be careful. Jaa should be careful too. Maybe it's best you stay away from each other. You've already risked so much."*

Star Cat purred in agreement. *"You've risked everything. You have my greatest respect. Only true warriors will sacrifice their lives for a quest."*

Ejii felt embarrassed. *"My travels have been dangerous, but nothing required me to sacrifice my life,"* she said. Except walking into that Aejej, she thought.

"You're a shadow speaker and you left home. That's risk enough," Star Cat said.

Ejii frowned. *"What do you mean?"*

Dikéogu was growing bored. He yawned, "What're you all saying?"

"Shhh," Ejii hissed, her index finger to her lips. Dikéogu scowled but was silent.

135

"A shadow speaker who travels must be mature. You don't look old enough. Is your taste for greatness so strong for your age?" Snow Cat asked.

"Greatness?" she asked. "The shadows told me to go with Jaa. So I am."

"Don't you know the significance of travel to your kind?" Star Cat asked. "Don't you have a teacher? Don't you know the facts of your life?"

"I . . . sort of left without consulting my teacher. . . . It's complicated," Ejii said.

The two cats gazed at her for a moment and then purred deep in their throats. Star Cat spoke slowly, "For a shadow speaker to move away from home, for a shadow speaker to travel is to court death and greatness."

"Death?" Ejii said frowning deeper. "You mean I could die?"

"Or achieve greatness," Snow Cat said.

"The farther you move from home, the closer you move to death," Star Cat said. "At any time, the strain, the growth of your ability could become too much for you. You could just wither away. Several of us have come across the freshly dead bodies of your kind, humans with eyes like ours. Always open in death. The eyes of your kind don't rot with the rest of your bodies when you die."

"Your teacher must have been protecting you from this news until you were ready," Snow Cat said. "A noble thing, but he was assuming you would be mature enough by this time to talk to him before leaving."

Ejii turned to Dikéogu. "I think I've made a terrible mistake."

"What do you mean?"

"They say that I might die," she said.

"What?!" he screeched, jumping up.

"They say that when a shadow speaker leaves home, she risks death." She thought about how her abilities had been increasing and changing since she'd left. Even now, the way she was speaking to the sand cats was something she had never experienced.

"Well, how do you *not* die?" he asked.

Ejii was about to ask the cats when Snow Cat asked, *"Does he know what he is?"*

Ejii blinked at the unexpected question. *"I . . . I don't know. He's something."*

"Yes, a rainmaker," Star Cat said, using her paw to wipe her face. *"And he is discomfort to all creatures with luxurious fur."*

"Oh," Ejii said, glancing at Dikéogu, who was looking at Star Cat as if he hoped to understand something. *"I don't think he has any control of the weather."*

The two cats chuckled their guttural chuckles. *"Do you still intend to continue on your quest?"* Snow Cat asked, as he nuzzled against Star Cat. Their black-and-white fur crackled and now stood on end.

"The shadows tell me that I'll help prevent a war," Ejii said. *"But only if I go."*

"Humans," Star Cat said.

Snow Cat growled.

"Do you know something of it?" Ejii asked, leaning forward.

"Nothing. Humans are warlike, no matter where you come from," Snow Cat said.

Ejii wanted to press the issue but they were cats, large cats. And there was something in the way they said "humans," that made her uneasy.

"The sun moves and our fur sparks," Star Cat said. *"It's time for you to go."*

CHAPTER THIRTEEN

✛

THE DESERT MAGICIAN

DIKÉOGU bit into a mango and juice squirted onto Ejii's neck.

"Hey! Watch how you eat that," she said.

"Sorry," Dikéogu said, using his shirt to wipe her neck.

She was playing her favorite hip-hop files on her e-legba and the music sounded clear and crisp. Onion's ears were turned away from the sound. He preferred Arabic music. Kola had flown ahead to Agadez and Ejii and Dikéogu both rode Onion. Initially, Ejii hadn't wanted to; she thought the two of them would be too heavy, especially in the heat. But Onion had insisted. "You're no heavier than the owl," he'd said.

They were making good time and Ejii could see Agadez about ten miles away.

"Can you see Jaa?" Dikéogu asked.

Ejii wanted to smile at Dikéogu's joke but couldn't. With each step Onion took she feared that something in her body would go haywire.

"No," she simply said. "I can't see her."

The city was huge. How was she supposed to find one person there? Even someone as flashy as Jaa?

"But I can see the mosque," Ejii added.

At any other time, Ejii would have been whooping with excitement. Her mother often talked about the famous Agadez Mosque. Built in the sixteenth century and rebuilt just after the Great Change, when it crumbled to the ground. Shaped like a pyramid and made of glass, it was the highest and most glorious building in Agadez. At its top were sand bricks embedded with solar cells that produced all the energy the building needed. At the stroke of midnight lovely periwinkle daisies sprouted near the base of the building. They made all of Agadez smell sweet for one hour before withering into dust. No one knew why this happened. Every morning a crew came to sweep up the dust, which was later sold as a healing powder.

"It's going to be dark soon enough," Dikéogu said. "It won't be safe."

Ejii nodded. "She's probably staying in a hotel. I hope we're not too late." She took a breath. "Listen Dikéogu . . . if, if anything happens . . . to me, I want you to go . . ."

"Shut up," he said, leaning over her shoulder to see her face. "Nothing's going to happen to you. Have some confidence."

She nodded. "Dikéogu, I'm scared," she admitted. "If I'd known, if I hadn't been such a baby, I wouldn't have done anything this stupid! If I die, how will my mother . . ."

"Some things have to happen, I think," he said. "For the sake of other things."

They were silent for a while. How was she supposed to tell him that the shadows hadn't felt the same since leaving the sand-dune cats? That now, aside from her skin getting really dark when the shadows spoke to her, the shadows felt sticky on her skin, as if they had melted in the sun and were blending with her flesh? That neither sand nor water washed them off, and if it weren't for her already dark skin tone, she'd look as if her skin were stained? Could all this be a sign of her fast-approaching death or at least some shadow speaker illness? She tried to focus on other things.

"Do you know how to rent a room for the night, if we have to?" she asked him. "I've never . . . really done that sort of thing." She sighed, feeling uncultured.

"I've seen my parents do it," Dikéogu said. "It's easy."

About a mile later they came to a crossroads. Since they'd first come across paved roads some miles back, they'd been avoiding the busier ones leading into Agadez. Onion didn't like the smell of car exhaust. But this crossroads seemed to suddenly appear out of the desert haze. A large Bedouin tent sat on one of the road's corners. Onion slowed his walk. No motorbikes or camels came from any of the four directions.

"You think anyone's in there?" Ejii whispered, turning down her music.

"Of course," Dikéogu said, looking worried. "Why else would it be there?"

The tent was a shiny metallic pink and Ejii could hear things clicking inside. Above the tent's opening hung a sign that said, ENTER AT YOUR OWN RISK.

Dikéogu cursed under his breath. "Something's not right here," he said.

"Stop being paranoid," Ejii said, trying to hold down her own escalating unease.

He came shuffling out of his tent just as they were passing. Ejii frowned. Yes, she thought, he's a man . . . or at least shaped like one. Just very small. A little person, a midget. He had long, long dreadlocks that reached all the way to the ground. The tips were encrusted with sand and they grew 360 degrees around his head covering his face. His large potbelly pushed up his long red caftan through his dreadlocks. Dikéogu took one look at him and screamed. Ejii had turned around to yell at him for being so childish when Onion suddenly reared up. They tumbled off his back.

"It's a jinni!" Dikéogu shouted, grabbing Ejii's hand and running.

"Dikéogu! What . . ."

"It's our only chance," he gasped.

"Quick thinking, boy, but not quick enough," the small man said, reappearing in front of them. Dikéogu stopped, turned around, and pushed Ejii to start running back toward the crossroads. The midget reappeared again in front of them.

"You think you can outrun the Desert Magician?" he said with a snicker. "Follow me, if you have any sense." He walked past them, moving quickly for a man with such short legs.

They stood there for a moment, breathing heavily.

Maybe I can get some information from him, she thought.

In all the stories she'd heard from the storyteller, mystical creatures, even the mean ones, always knew things. Maybe this one would know about what she could do to stay alive.

When they got to the tent, Onion was standing in front of it looking as worried as a camel could look. Still, no one passed on the roads. Ejii could see Kola circling high above.

"Don't you even think about spitting at me, beast," the man said, stepping past Onion to stand at the entrance of the tent. He turned to Dikéogu and Ejii. "Welcome to my humble abode, stationed strategically at the crossroads, my favorite spot to place my toes." He motioned to the sign above. "As it says, you enter at your own risk."

"Do we have a choice?" Dikéogu asked.

"Nope," the man answered with a laugh, going inside. "But it's still your own risk."

Ejii felt the shadows drag against her skin and start to whisper. She almost screamed with relief. They would know what to do.

"Uh-uh," the man said, over his shoulder. "None of that, cat eyes. This is *my* territory. You play by *my* rules."

Ejii ignored him and steadied her mind, the shadows clinging more closely to her. She saw her skin and everything around them darken. But before she could understand anything, the shadows were torn away and scattered in every direction like bits of paper in the wind. Ejii gasped. The shadowy earth spirits had always been with her. Now everything seemed too bright. She frowned, trying her best to keep her mind from a complete shutdown.

"What's wrong?" Dikéogu whispered, pushing her forward. Ejii couldn't answer.

The tent looked much bigger on the inside. The floor was carpeted with a red, velvety rug. In one corner were bunches of the kind of leafy greens used for stew, a white bowl filled with shelled peanuts, a large glass jug of what looked like honey, several bottles of whiskey, piles of wrapped candies, and other foodstuffs. In another corner were a large woven mat and a fan that blew cool air. There were amulets made of metal and cloth and tiny bells hanging from the ceiling. They clicked and clacked in the circulating air. Incense burned from somewhere, and soft drum-heavy Yoruba music played.

"Remove your sandals, dirty children," the man said.

As they did so, Dikéogu kept looking at Ejii. "*Say* something!" he whispered.

"The shadows . . . I can't feel them at . . . at *all*! Gone!" she said.

Dikéogu cursed. The cool rug would have felt wonderful under Ejii's feet if she weren't so bewildered.

"Sit," the man said, motioning to three wicker chairs around a wicker table. As they sat down, he stepped over to his stock of food and returned with three glasses on a tray. The glasses were decorated with intricate white drawings. He filled two with tea from the blue kettle he took off a metal bowl filled with hot coals. He filled the last with whiskey. "Drink and we'll talk," he said, sipping the whiskey.

Her mind blank, Ejii began to reach forward. She felt empty and alone. Dikéogu grabbed her hand. "No disrespect, sir," Dikéogu said, still holding her hand tightly. "But our parents taught us not to take drinks or food from strangers."

The man smiled. He reached into his caftan pocket and brought out a sharp-looking dagger with geometric carvings on the shiny blade and painted black lines on its silver handle. He nonchalantly put his elbows on the table and picked his nails with the dagger. Ejii held her breath. He may have been a small potbellied man but, even without her shadows, she could sense his enormous strength.

"What kind of games are you playing?" Dikéogu asked, his fear replaced by annoyance. He stood up. "I'm taller than you and I've been through a lot. You think we're just two stupid kids lost in the damn desert? You couldn't be more wrong."

The man grinned, putting the dagger back in his pocket. "Three tests passed, destiny gained," he said. He stood up. "I've decided not to chop you up." He walked over to a red e-legba that sat on the straw mat in the corner. He turned up the music. Ejii thought his e-legba must be very state-of-the-art to produce such clear sound.

He danced a little dance, his hands on his hips. Even in her fear, Ejii found herself very annoyed. She didn't like the way he kept pointing his toes. His feet were strange, inhuman in some way. They looked like the feet of a man who spent most of his time lying around. His toenails were perfectly manicured, even polished with clear gloss. Ejii could tell that the man was getting on Dikéogu's nerves too. The man turned the music down and, breathing hard, faced them. He smoothed out his long white caftan and bowed.

"I am the Desert Magician," he said. He turned to Dikéogu. "And I am not a mere jinni. Think, boy, do I look made of fire? Like a pinch of salt could send *me* away? I *could* make my eyes vertical, but that's not how I prefer to see the world." He laughed. "Who I am is none of your beeswax, but if you must know, I'm a god, a supreme being, Allah's best friend, Legba's alter ego, Abassi's uncle, I am Jesus's general!"

Dikéogu and Ejii jumped back when the tiny man suddenly grew into a very tall, dark-skinned man in an olive-green military uniform that clicked with medals. A red beret capped his long face-covering dreadlocks. His head reached the ceiling. Then just as quickly, he shrunk back to his short self. He giggled and said, "I have a thousand names for a thousand reasons. What I am has always been and will always be. What you silly children need to worry about is that you've walked into my territory." he paused, obviously enjoying himself. "Have you heard of Ginen?" he asked, as he sat back down.

"Yes. The other world," Ejii said, somehow finding her voice.

"One of them, anyway," the magician said. He looked at Dikéogu. "Smart irritating boy. First you ran, then you refused drink, then you stood up to my dagger. I could have killed you for such stupidity. Well done."

"Uh, thank you," Dikéogu said quietly.

The magician grinned devilishly. "You see that I'm small, but you understood that I'm not weak. Things aren't always what they seem." He jumped and did a little dance around his chair then sat down. "But sometimes they are. Your camel has

146

a long neck," the magician said. "He must have incredible stamina."

Ejii had no idea how to respond to this, so she didn't. "Mr. Magician," she said. "If it's not too much to ask, do you know how I could . . ."

"It's too much to ask," he said. His dreadlocks shook as he laughed hard. Ejii grumbled, frustrated. The magician leaned forward. "So, are you brother and sister?"

They shook their heads and the Desert Magician grinned. "Runaway young lovers, then? One of you obviously has a death wish," he said, giggling harder. "Will you, boy, take your life after the strain of travel takes hers? Romeo and Juliet of the African Sahara. Oh, how sweet and tender."

Ejii's cheeks grew hot and she gnashed her teeth in anger.

"We . . . we're traveling companions," Dikéogu said. "We *travel*. And Ejii will become the greatest shadow speaker in the world. So will you please just let us . . ."

"Watch your tone, boy," the magician said, suddenly growing serious. "I am small and playful, but I look down from my high mountain and I can barely see your great-great-grandmothers! I'm older than time, slave boy. Remember that."

Ejii winced at his words. She could almost feel the flash of Dikéogu's anger.

"I am *no* slave," Dikéogu shouted, standing up. "I don't care *who* you are! I am no slave!"

"Oh, that's right. You're the son of the Obidimkpa's. The one and only offspring of the great journalistic duo of the *Old Naija Times* and *Nigerian Net*," the magician said. He looked at

Ejii and said in mock secrecy, "He's practically royalty, this one. You sure know how to pick 'em. It's always best to marry for money instead of love."

"What?" Ejii exclaimed, turning to Dikéogu. She found it hard to believe anything the magician said, but at the same time, she didn't like the look on Dikéogu's face.

"Maybe he's doing a news story on you," the magician said. "You know, like his mother did on that poor woman living in the bush in Imo State? Your mother pretended to be such a good friend to that sad woman when all she wanted was to write the best investigative news story of the year. These days, who can you really trust, hmmm?"

"That's camelshit!" Dikéogu shouted.

The magician laughed as they stared at each other. Ejii didn't want to believe the magician but . . . she knew of that news story. She'd found it depressing but couldn't stop reading.

"Mhm," the magician continued. "You know they have fake tribal markings made out of latex? They probably have fake slave tattoos, too."

Dikéogu looked as if he were about to explode. Ejii just rubbed her forehead, afraid, confused, angry, and unsure which direction to aim any of it.

The magician held up a hand, "Hee hee, okay, okay, I made all that up. I can be a real goat's ass sometimes. But it remains, you two need to talk. You, young lady, need to know who you travel with. Even his parents didn't want him. It's why he is a slave."

"Shut up!" Dikéogu screamed.

The magician feigned terror and then laughed loudly. "If you're not a slave, then you shouldn't care that I call you one." He grew serious. "Sit down."

"Uh, Mr. Magician," Ejii said, feeling tired. "You have our respect . . . but, please, don't say such things to my friend. He's been through a lot. He deserves respect, too." She glanced at Dikéogu. He wouldn't look at her but he did sit back down.

"Your respect for mine," the magician said. "I like that. A shadow speaker without her shadows still has insight. So, where is it that you two are going?"

Ejii put an arm around Dikéogu, hoping that it would calm him. She was hesitant to tell this creature anything. But I'm sure he can find out if he wanted to, she thought. "Agadez," she said. "We're going to see Jaa."

"Ah, the Red Queen," the Magician said. "Lovely woman."

"She is," Ejii said.

"You and this boy have a long journey ahead," the magician said. "As I've pointed out, it'll be better if you know a little more about each other."

"We really need to be moving along," Ejii said. "We don't have . . ."

"Time for a tiny bit of truth," he said, bringing out his dagger. "I won't meddle too much but I can at least break the ice." He pointed his dagger at them and swiped horizontally, cutting the air. The smell of peanuts wafted into the tent. "Peanuts go well with entertainment," he said sitting back. "Ejii, tell Dikéogu a little about yourself."

Before Ejii knew it, she was speaking. "Well," she said,

looking at Dikéogu. "I can't stand eating cauliflower because of the nasty sound it makes when it crunches, and sometimes I fart when I laugh." She gasped and slapped her hands over her mouth.

Dikéogu burst out laughing.

"Dikéogu, your turn," the magician said, grinning. Dikéogu instantly stopped laughing and said, "I once saw a man fall into a ditch by the side of the road and I laughed at him before I went to get help!" His grin turned to a look of mortification.

Ejii tried to keep her mouth shut but the magician's spell was too strong. "My mother . . . buys bras for . . . me but I hate wearing them because they're uncomfortable and I don't think anyone will notice." She crossed her arms over her chest.

The magician laughed with glee and looked at Dikéogu.

"I used . . . to . . . wish . . . I looked like the son of a white British family living in my neighborhood," Dikéogu said, straining to control his words. "Arrrrrah! STOP IT!" He grabbed one of the cups of tea and threw it at the magician. It knocked the dagger from the magician's hand and immediately a breeze flew threw the tent, rattling the ceiling amulets, jingling the tiny bells, and blowing the smell of peanuts away.

The Desert Magician sat back in his chair smirking mischievously. "You broke my juju," he said. He held a hand to his dagger and it flew back into his hand. "For your little act of violence, I'll let you go. The good part is right around the corner. I enjoy a good story and the longer I keep you, the slower it gets."

Ejii pushed his confusing riddles out of her head. All she

wanted was to be away from him, he was nothing but trouble. As the Desert Magician shoved a bag of shelled peanuts into each of their hands and herded them out of the tent, the shadows returned to her, enmeshing themselves deeper into her skin. As they walked off, the magician said, "Don't you want to take this?" he held up the egg stone.

Ejii's eyes grew wide as she thrust her hand into her pocket and felt nothing there. "Please, I need that," Ejii said, but she was growing angry with frustration.

"Please, I need that," the magician mocked. "Wah, wah. I know you're a girl, but get some balls. Stand up tall and say, 'Give it to me or I'll kill you with my bare hands!'"

Ejii threw down her peanuts and started to stride up to the magician.

"Ejii," Dikéogu and Onion said.

She ignored them, hoping that they knew not to try and stop her. They did. The magician laughed when he saw her coming and threw the egg stone into the sand when she was only a few feet from him. Ejii glared at the magician.

"You have a foul mouth," she said. Then she snatched the egg stone from the sand, turned, and marched back to her friends.

"*That's* more like it!" he said from behind her. "Must I teach you everything?"

✢

OLD NAIJA

"**STUPID** camelshitting magic man," Dikéogu grumbled as he walked next to Onion. "Calling me a slave. I'll show him."

Ejii looked back. They'd only walked about a half mile and, out of nowhere, they found themselves in civilization—roads, people with camels, and vehicles running noisily all around them. Already even she could barely see the Desert Magician's tent.

"You shouldn't let him get to you," Ejii said. She smiled at her own hypocrisy.

"You haven't been through what I have!" Dikéogu said, waving his hands about. "You have *one* good parent. I almost died to escape slavery. How dare he call me that!"

"You're . . . you're overreacting."

"Overreacting?" His voice was even louder than the motorbikes and cars passing them.

"Yeah, overreacting!" Ejii shouted back, her nerves frayed. "There are worse things than being called a slave!"

Dikéogu blinked and looked at Ejii. Then he looked at Onion, who had turned both his ears toward his head. "Sorry," Dikéogu said, wiping sweat from his brow.

"Why get angry over something that's not even true?" Ejii said. "You think the Desert Magician *really* thought you were a slave? He was just trying to get your attention." But she wasn't sure if she believed this.

"Dumb idiot Desert Magician," Dikéogu grumbled. "He's lucky he was the one with the dagger. I'd have skinned his neat little feet like yams and . . ."

"No, you wouldn't," Ejii said.

"Yes, I would," he said.

"Okay, maybe you would have," Ejii said. "Maybe I would too," she said. "But, Dikéogu, what . . . what happened with your parents?"

"Just know that I'm not a slave," he said.

"Then who are you?" she said.

He sucked his teeth. "You heard him. I'm the son of the great goddamn Obidimkpa duo, West Africa's bringers of news and entertainment." He paused. "But I'm not doing some stupid exposé story on you. That remains my mother's territory."

"So how'd you end up in Assamakka? Please," she said. "Tell me."

"I *hate* them," he said, baring his teeth.

Ejii felt she hated them, too and she didn't even know why yet. A truck zoomed past them, dangerously close. "Onion, stop for a second," Ejii said. She climbed off and looked up at Dikéogu. "Come on."

They walked to a group of palm trees for shade. Onion groaned as he bent his legs so he could sit down and rest. Ejii and Dikéogu stood in the shade facing each other. Ejii waited, her arms across her chest.

"What happened is weird," he said, giving Ejii a worried look.

"I'm familiar with weird," she said.

"We . . . we lived in a big house with servants, had five cars, which I always thought was stupid. Fuel is expensive. I don't know why my parents felt they had to always show off. Anyway, there was always a lot of noise and activity around my parents. They own *Old Naija Times* and Naija Net. Yeah, yeah, they're famous and influential, but they're awful parents. You probably know my mother's face because she's often the anchorperson on Naija Net.

"Ever since the Great Change, all the villages in south-eastern Nigeria have gotten really tightly knit. The elders have got this stupid attitude. They pretend everything is the same as it used to be. They keep calling for a return to 'ancient times.' That's why my parents called the newspaper the *Old Naija Times*; they want to appeal to stupid people who think like this, all stuck in the past. 'Naija' is slang for Nigerian and the newspaper's slogan is: 'News for the *true* Nigerian.'

"Never mind the permanent forest that sprung up between Arondizuogu and Aba that people refuse to go into because of the weird noises coming from it. Or the fact that a lot of people in the swampy Delta region have turned into pink dolphins. Or the birds that fly backward all the time. My parents cashed in on this denial.

"So, this was the village I was born into. Imagine if you'd been born there! They'd have taken one look at your eyes and some goat's ass would have stolen you from your mother and thrown you into that weird forest, like they used to do with one of each pair of twins long ago. I heard more than once that someone did that with a metahuman baby. Anyway, for most of my life, I was like everyone else; pretending not to see what I saw. It was all I knew. So I wasn't as horrified when the lightning started coming."

"So what happened at that pond, that wasn't the first time?" Ejii asked.

"Ha! Not even close," he said. "I was about eight years old the first time. I was in my mother's garden, my favorite place because it was so peaceful and green there. A thunderstorm was coming. It was rainy season, so I didn't give it much thought. I was just standing there looking at the yams when *BAM!* My mother saw it happen from the kitchen. She came running. My clothes were a little burned and I had a headache, but otherwise I was fine. My mother told me to just forget that it had ever happened. So I did.

"But something bothered me about the way my mother looked at me, even back then. The moment she knew I was okay, she kind of pushed me away. Like she didn't want to touch me. The second time I was struck was when I was ten. Same year that I saw Jaa . . . do what she did to your father. During rainy season again. I was walking down the street on my way home and *BAM!* My mother told me to forget about this too, but this time she told my father. He came to my room that night angry as hell! He was cursing and sweating and breathing heavy like a man five times his weight.

"'It never happened, you understand? Goddamn you!' he shouted. I should have cursed right back at him. But I just nodded and set my mind to forget about it again. By this time, I also had to forget about the static in the house and the sparks that popped when I walked too fast. The third time it happened couldn't be ignored. And by then I had a reputation. Someone with a big mouth had seen that second time. Probably the old lady across the street, Agnes. She never has enough to do. People were calling me 'the boy that God hates.' They said that I was sick. Slow in the head. Who could get struck by lightning and not have brain damage?

"My friends stopped talking to me and teachers punished me for nonsense. My parents were embarrassed. My father kept saying, 'Get a hold of yourself, damn it! Control it. You can be normal if you try.' To him it was all my fault. He thinks everyone can control everything with a little effort. In this day and age, how crazy is that? I would squeeze my eyes shut on stormy days and try my best to not get struck. I'd ask the sky not to rain until I was inside. I was almost thirteen when the third time happened.

"I'd had a bad day at school, mean teachers, stupid classmates. For goodness' sake, that second time had been three years ago! Why couldn't people just forget it? I was walking fast because the sky was quickly growing dark. I didn't know what else to do. I didn't want to take cover in any of the neighbors' homes. They'd just talk about me more.

"I was passing Mr. Chidi's house when *CRASH!* It came down with such force that I fell to my knees! It smelled sweet and felt like warm, soft water. Ejii, I didn't do anything wrong. I knew boys who had stolen, beaten people up, were involved in secret societies that committed huge crimes. It's not fair, Ejii!

"Mr. Chidi was bringing in some stuff for a party, some goats, yams, palm wine, beer and such. He's always having parties because he's some sort of stupid, shady politician. The explosion burned Chidi's goats to a crisp, fried his yams to charcoal, blew up his palm wine bottles and beer, and burned the back of his car! He lost his eyebrows too; they were burned off in the blast. He was lucky to be alive! But he was angry as hell, especially at the loss of his stupid, expensive he-goats.

"The rain began to fall in big, fat droplets and I ran home. After that, everything happened fast. Mr. Chidi had a lot of friends and he convinced them all that I was a demon and should be torn to pieces! I was at home when I heard them coming. My mother started crying and my father shouted and cursed at me to get out before they burned down his precious house! With one satchel of things, I ran down the street.

"I don't remember leaving my parents behind . . . or them leaving me. A friend of my father's, Segun, came driving up, splattering mud on me. He told me to get in. I remember falling asleep in his car, thinking over and over how my parents hadn't protected me. It was Segun who took me to Abuja and sold me! I'd known that guy all my life! I called him 'uncle.' He was rich and always buying me things. He was the one who bought me my copy of *My Cyborg Manifesto*. Now I know why he is so rich. He was selling children into slavery!

"He dropped me off at some place that I don't remember; it was dark, and I was scared and covered in mud, and hungry and angry. By then, it was almost dawn and getting dry and hot. There were other kids my age and younger in this place, a lot of them crying. I remember that I slept standing up. We were soon packed into another truck that drove through the day and night and another day. They didn't give us anything to eat or drink and the going was bumpy, slow, and sweltering. And that's how I ended up in Assamakka." He kicked at the sand.

"The sand-dune cats said that you were a rainmaker," Ejii said after a moment.

"Ha! Can't they tell the difference between a gift and a curse? Does it *remotely* look like I can control the lightning that keeps striking me? None of this is *my* fault!"

"I didn't say . . ."

"Then don't say it!" he snapped.

A woman riding a donkey passed by, followed by a man riding a camel jingling with bells. The couple was moving away from Agadez.

"So what do you decide?" Dikéogu asked.

"Huh?"

"Do you want to keep traveling with me or not? Another thunderstorm could come at any moment."

"If you're not afraid of my abilities," she said, "why should I be afraid of yours?"

"I *am* afraid of your abilities."

"You're afraid of what you've heard, not what you *know*. Dikéogu . . ." She held her hands up, unable to find words. Then she stepped forward and pulled him into a tight hug. His body stiffened and she quickly let go. Without looking at her, he thrust his hands in his pockets and mumbled, "Let's go. We only have a few hours, right?"

"I admire you," she said, taking his hand. "What you've survived is amazing." She sighed. "Your parents weren't much better than my father."

✛

CHAPTER FIFTEEN

AGADEZ

'M OKAY, Ejii thought as they approached the biggest stretch of human civilization she had ever seen.

It was nearing sunset and Agadez was only a mile away. The desert was crisscrossed with busy paved highways and roads populated by motorbikes, pedestrians, cars, horses, camels, and trucks. There were raffia stalls on the roadside where people sold glass and stone bracelets, jugs of pink gasoline, cheap and costly e-legbas, card PCs, cigarettes, dancing bah-boo toys, spicy kabobs, and more. And then there were the items whose origins no one asked about, but everyone knew were from Ginen, like the tiny lizards that would eat all the insects in your house while pooing out sweet smelling pellets; the solar radios shaped like plant bulbs; the whispering orchids that no one could understand.

Dikéogu and Ejii walked next to Onion. "I hate all this movement, and everything is so damn close together," Dikéogu complained. "Who knows who's hiding behind all the corners and walls? And how's Kola going to find us?"

"Don't worry," Ejii said. "It's all going to be okay."

Dikéogu just grumbled, stepping closer to Onion.

It was dark by the time they entered the city but there was still plenty of activity. Ejii heard several languages; mostly she heard Hausa and Arabic. Agadez was an old Muslim city full of people, from Arab to African, so there were many women wearing veils and burkas. Ejii draped her veil around her head so as not to stand out too much.

She spotted a few children with the slave markings on their faces. Some appeared to be with their families and she wondered if these children, too, had escaped. Onion had grown annoyed when he saw all the other camels tied up and silent. Still, Ejii loosely put a rope around his head and held it so that no one would think he was a wild camel.

"What's wrong with wild camels?" Onion quietly asked.

"I don't think people here are used to free camels," Ejii said.

Dikéogu patted Onion on his muzzle. "You're not a slave," Dikéogu said.

"But the others are," Onion said.

"That's the world," Dikéogu said. "Some of us are slaves, some of us aren't."

Onion angrily chewed his cud as a man passed riding his camel. The camel was decorated with a colorful saddle, a bright blue, fringed saddlebag, and bells and gold decorations on each of its ankles. "He looks ridiculous," Onion grumbled. Ejii agreed.

They stopped at a date stand and Ejii looked at Dikéogu. He shrugged and started to climb off. "No," Ejii said, putting her hand on his shoulder. "I'll do it." She climbed down and walked up to the stand. She plucked one of the wax-lined paper bags and used a scoop to fill it with sweet juicy dates. A short man with white Afro puffs of hair on the sides of his head sat beside the dates listening to Arabic music and watching the news on an e-legba.

As Ejii handed him the bag to weigh, it dawned on her that the man was probably watching the station that Dikéogu's parents owned. The anchorperson talking was probably his mother. Ejii leaned forward to get a good look. She had waist-length brown-black dreadlocks and the same intense look that Dikéogu constantly wore.

"One hundred," the man said.

"That's too much, sir," she said, looking him in the eye. The man broke eye contact quickly. He'd been trying to cheat her, as men often did with women or girls too timid to protest. This now irritated Ejii.

"Fifty," he said. "My final offer. I have to close soon and you are using my time."

"Ten," she said, taking out some money and handing it to him and taking the bag. "These should be about five, so I am doing you a favor."

The man looked at her for a long time. Then he smiled and folded the money. "Did your father teach you how to drive such a hard bargain?" he asked.

Ejii shook her head. "My mother."

"Are you one of those . . . you have the strange eyes," he said, pointing to his eyes.

Ejii smiled as she always did when people were honest enough to ask about her eyes as opposed to making assumptions. "I'm a shadow speaker, yes," she said.

"Most people think you all are evil, but I've never believed that," he said. "I'm a good Muslim. I believe people are people."

"And you are very correct," Ejii said.

"Can you see my future? How to get rich? Things like that?" He leaned forward. "There are many shadow speakers who tell fortunes around here but they are expensive."

"I can only know what they tell me, sir," she said. She listened for the shadows. Silence. Then her temples throbbed as the knowledge came to her as if from deep within her subconscious. She could smell his cologne and the scent of his two children. One liked to leap over the street's gutters and one liked to draw. His wife shouted at him often. They were poor, but she liked good things. Unfortunately, his wife didn't realize that she was married to a good man.

"Kiss your wife more often and . . . pay the high price and buy the sweetest dates," Ejii said, amazed at this new change. It was as if her body had absorbed the shadows and what they could do, as if they were a part of her. Her ability had stretched and changed again, and she'd lived. Thank Allah, she thought, relieved. "You should make more money because that's what people will buy. Not the cheap dry ones."

The man grinned, hugged Ejii, and clapped his hands together. "Thank you!" he said. "All week I've been biting my nails about taking a chance with the more expensive dates! I'll give my wife a thousand kisses tonight!" He grabbed Ejii's bag and scooped more dates in. "For your husband over there," he said, motioning to Dikéogu. Ejii bit her lip hard. There was little point in trying to correct the man. He tied up the bag and gave it to Ejii.

"Thank you, sir," Ejii said. "Um . . . Would you happen to know where Jaa the Red Queen is staying?"

"Ah, the Red Queen. Eh, can you believe it? Here in Agadez? I was reading about her this morning, but I don't think it was mentioned where she was staying," he thought for a second. "Go online and you can replay the speech she made today."

"My h-husband and I are hoping to catch a glimpse of her in person," Ejii said. She was glad that Dikéogu wasn't there to hear her refer to him as her husband.

"She probably left Agadez already. But you could check the two best hotels in Agadez, the Oasis and the Yellow Lady. If she's here, she'd stay in one of those places."

"Which is closest to here?" Ejii asked.

"The Oasis. Just go down the street and make a left," he said. "The Yellow Lady is at the center of Agadez."

Ejii nodded. "Thanks. Oh, one more thing. Did I turn darker as I . . . read you?"

"No," the man said. "You looked as you do now."

What is happening to me? she wondered as she went back to Dikéogu and Onion.

The Oasis Hotel was a green, four-story building. There were motor scooters parked in the front, and Ejii could hear camels in the back.

"You'll be okay, then?" Ejii asked Onion.

164

"As long as there's hay and water," he said. "I will talk to the other camels, too."

She kissed him on his furry muzzle.

"If you plan an uprising, do it in the early morning," Dikéogu said with a laugh.

"Dikéogu, stand in front of me," Ejii said, stepping close to Onion.

Dikéogu quickly understood and moved to block what she was doing from any passersby. She reached into her saddlebag and brought out a bundle of naira notes.

"Here," she said, handing the bundle to Dikéogu. "You're the one who knows how to get rooms at hotels, not me. So *you* hold the money."

Inside the Oasis Hotel, it was bright with pink lights and the air was cooled. There was highlife music playing and several trees growing in large clay pots in the lobby. People frowned as Ejii and Dikéogu passed. Ejii knew how the two of them must have looked in their tattered clothes. Especially Dikéogu. It didn't really matter to Ejii. If she'd been wearing clean clothes people would have probably stared at her because of her eyes.

"Is the Red Queen staying here?" Dikéogu confidently asked the receptionist.

The receptionist, an angular woman with a large beaklike nose, shiny black hair, and lovely dark eyes, looked up from her computer at Dikéogu. She stared at him for a long time, paying special attention to the markings on his face. Then she looked at Ejii.

"I only speak to people who are checking into the hotel."

"How do you know we're not?" Dikéogu asked.

"You can't possibly have digital credit," she said.

"I have cash," Dikéogu said.

"Is she your wife?" she said with a chuckle.

Dikéogu scowled. "Of course not," he said. "This . . . this is my sister."

The woman shrugged. "Where are your parents?"

"Not here," he said. "I didn't ask for an interview. I just want to know about Jaa."

"Who set you free?" she asked with a smirk.

Ejii quickly stepped forward. "Our father," she said. "It was a big mistake. A long story. But it's all straightened out now."

The women sucked her teeth, looking at Dikéogu a bit longer.

"Is it really *any* of your business?" he asked, with a clenched jaw.

"One thousand francs, then," she finally said.

"Oh please, woman," Dikéogu said. "We weren't born yesterday."

We don't even have francs, Ejii thought with despair. She didn't think anyone would change money at this hour.

"We don't want a room, madame," Ejii said. "We just want to know about Jaa."

"Then go find a newspaper," the woman snapped, looking down her pointy nose at them. "Where are you two traveling from?"

There was something about the woman that bothered Ejii. She reached into herself and there it was, the knowledge. Not everything. Just enough. This woman lived well. Her husband owned the hotel. She was the third wife. She didn't like her co-wives. Ejii frowned at this information. This type of toxic union would not have been allowed in Kwàmfà or in any other predominately New Tuareg community. All had to agree to the marriage; in this woman's case, the husband had taken more wives without getting approval from the wives he already had.

Her husband's rich from the hotel business but . . . oh no, Ejii thought. He made much of his money dabbling in child slavery. This woman would do a lot of things to please her husband. Anything to make him like her more than the other wives.

Then something happened to Ejii that she couldn't control. She was sucked into this woman's . . . *pain*. Terrified, Ejii fought not to scream. The pain was going to swallow her. Slowly it dawned on her. The woman was in pain because of the relationship she was in. *It was sharp, red, and black.* It filled Ejii's entire being. This woman was capable of murder; anything to make the pain better. Ejii began to sweat and feel nauseated as the woman looked at her with too much curiosity. She was going to call the authorities, both out of fear of Ejii and for her own gain. The authorities would learn that she and Dikéogu were alone, then this woman would have them sold.

Ejii did everything in her power not to collapse. All she could manage was a slight shake of her head to Dikéogu. *Don't tell her anything.* She was sure that he wouldn't understand her gesture.

"Oh, our parents aren't far," he said loudly. "We have an

aunt and uncle and cousins here in Agadez. We're just fans of Jaa."

Ejii focused on the floor, trying to get a hold of herself. Thankfully, the horrible sensation was subsiding.

"Oh," the woman said, looking disappointed. "I was about to say that Jaa isn't here but I could have someone take you to her."

"Thanks, but we'll just be on our way," Dikéogu said, he took Ejii's hand and pulled her with him out of the hotel. "Are you all right?" Dikéogu asked once outside.

"I don't know what happened."

"Did it hurt?"

"Yes! But not . . . I don't know what happened," she said. "Things are changing with me, Dikéogu. I can't explain it."

"In a good way?"

"I don't know," she said.

"That woman was creepy," Dikéogu said after they'd gotten Onion.

Ejii only nodded. "We should get out of here fast." Dikéogu didn't need to know about that woman's intentions and her child-enslaving husband.

They asked an Arab woman sitting on a bench for directions to the Yellow Lady. She was a metalseeker, and Ejii had no bad feeling about her. As Ejii stood before her, she could feel her silver amulet and earrings being gently pulled toward the woman. From what the metalseeker said, it would be a half-hour walk.

Riding Onion, they took in more of the city. Agadez's

buildings were decorated with intricate tile artwork. Outside on the streets were multicolored festival lights. Many of the larger buildings had flat, shiny black parabolic reflectors on their roofs that collected solar energy during the hot sunny days. Smaller homes had smaller reflectors and brick-size black solar cells were embedded in their roofs. As was the case in Kwàmfà, almost all of Agadez's power was solar. The city was a modern, ancient metropolis.

"Dikéogu," Ejii said. "What if we've missed her or we find her tonight. Will you still leave me?"

He didn't answer for a long time. "Yes," he finally said.

"But . . . why?" she said. "Where will you go?"

"Don't know."

Sighing, Ejii brought out her e-legba and checked the weather.

"It is 8:12 p.m.," it announced. "Tomorrow will be hot and dry. Over a hundred degrees, N.I.U.F. There is a heat advisory. Travel at night. There are also reports of a rather nasty Aejej north of Djado and a dense forest has sprung up south of Agadez. Do not eat the coconuts from these trees. They are reported to be filled with brown, biting worms."

"We must have just missed that spontaneous forest," Dikéogu said. He looked at Ejii and began to say something. Then he changed his mind.

Along the way, they walked through a market. There were pyramids of cashew fruits, groundnuts, and beans. There were trays of brown dates and sticky hard candies. Meat, used motors, cooking oil, dried fish, goat and cow milk, palm wine, cloths, jewelry, and some strange Ginen items like fast-growing plants that changed color each day and e-legbas shaped like green plant pods with screens. Ejii found herself for the first time thinking about how the Ginen items were never anything too complicated, as she'd heard Ginen technology could be. It was as if those who brought things from there were told not to bring any of the really revolutionary items, whatever those things might be.

One woman sold a sort of green, glowing grasshopper with thick legs that she kept in a glass container. She boasted that these "phosphor bush hoppers" could jump all the way to the sun and their strong legs were a "nutritious delicacy." Ejii and Dikéogu saw one escape, and it had indeed shot into the sky like a shooting star in reverse.

People rode motorbikes on the narrow roads running through the market. There were almost as many camels, goats, sheep, and horses moving about as there were people. The smell of incense and camel and goat dung dominated the air. Dikéogu was not happy with any of this, and Ejii had to work hard to keep from making eye contact with people, for already many were staring at and even avoiding her. She wished she were wearing her burka instead of her veil.

When they passed a man selling sunglasses, including pairs made of a clear material that molded to your face, Ejii couldn't resist. She'd had enough of the staring. One woman carrying a baby in her arms had even run away from her, protectively clutching her child. The date-seller was right, people here didn't like shadow speakers. She chose a plain pair that was tinted blue. The moment she put them on, she felt as if she'd donned a costume. Because it was nighttime, most likely people would think she was blind, which was still better than being treated as if she were evil.

Ejii gave Dikéogu some money to buy a new shirt and pair of pants, which he slipped into an alley to change into. At the end of the market, something caught Dikéogu's eye. A dagger that looked like the one the Desert Magician had with its silver blade and geometric shapes and symmetric design.

"Go ahead and buy it," Ejii said, pushing him toward the sellers. "My gift to you for coming with me all this way. Just hurry."

The two sellers spoke Hausa but with a strange accent. She frowned as she noted their wares. Podlike e-legbas, "always inking" pens, bush hoppers, and some sort of potted plant that wildly undulated when touched, all Ginen items. Were these merchants from Ginen? Ejii was too preoccupied with more urgent worries to give it much thought. As Dikéogu had a brief discussion with the seller and bought the dagger, she looked at the clear night sky, closed her eyes, and prayed to Allah to *please* let Jaa still be in Agadez.

The Yellow Lady Hotel was easy to find. Not only was it the second tallest building in Agadez—the Agadez Mosque being the first—but it was built with marigold-yellow bricks. They stood across the street from the hotel. There were motorbikes heavy with polished chrome, and even jewels and sleek cars that looked more like tiny airplanes pulling up to the front, dropping off expensive-looking people.

"Look, even the inside is yellow," Dikéogu said. "I hate this place. These people remind me of my parents."

"And my father," Ejii whispered.

"I don't want to go in there," Dikéogu said, sitting on the curb, his arms across his chest. Ejii sat next to him, wrapping her arms around her knees. Her belly fluttered. She had no idea why but suddenly she felt like crying. Maybe because Dikéogu was silently shedding tears.

"What is it?" she asked.

He didn't answer. He only sniffed.

"Dikéogu?" Ejii said. He didn't answer. "Dikéogu?"

"What?" he grumbled.

"Come on. Let's go in," she said. "You're not cursed. You know that."

"I *won't* forgive them!" he said. "Do you know what I've been through? They've stayed in this damn place. I used to hear them talking about it all the time, as if it was the best place on earth. The Yellow Lady, this, the Yellow Lady, that. They came here for business meetings while they left me at home with the servants. I have Yellow Lady Hotel pens from my dad. I've seen the small goddamn bottles of Yellow Lady Hotel shampoo and lotion in the bathroom at home. They've probably been here since they drove me off. I'd rather burn that place down than set foot in it." He dropped his voice. "Then I'd go home and burn that place, too."

Very carefully, Ejii said, "Would you like to go home . . . some day?"

"No," he said quickly. "They don't want me."

"You said things happen for a reason. That applies to you, too."

He sucked his teeth but said nothing.

"You never know." She stood up and held out her hand. "Come in with me."

He paused for a long time. Then he said, "Why?"

"Because."

He scratched at the ground and then looked up. "Okay. I . . . I've got a plan then."

As they opened the doors, Ejii put on her sunglasses. Dikéogu walked close behind her. "Be ready," she said, remembering the receptionist at the Oasis.

Inside, the air was cool and the people milling about were even cooler, looking at Ejii and Dikéogu with condescension. They walked up to the front desk where the receptionist was looking at a computer screen embedded into the table. He didn't look up.

"Hello," Dikéogu said.

The receptionist continued to ignore them. Ejii huffed and puffed, trying to appear extremely impatient. She pushed Dikéogu closer to the receptionist desk.

"Excuse me?" Dikéogu said, a little louder.

Still the receptionist ignored him.

"EXCUSE ME, SIR!" Dikéogu shouted angrily, pounding his fist on the desk.

People passing by looked at Dikéogu; those sitting on a nearby couch stopped in midconversation. The receptionist looked up. "What?" he asked.

"My mistress would like your service," Dikéogu loudly demanded, motioning to Ejii. "Is this the way you treat all your customers?"

"That's the way I treat children who cannot pay," the receptionist said.

"If I can *afford* my slave here, then I can afford this stupid place," Ejii said, stepping forward. "We're looking for the Red Queen." She had no idea if they could pay for a room, but as she tried to fake it, her mother's words popped into her head: if you act like you know what you're talking about, people will treat you that way.

"How old are you?" the receptionist asked, as if his words tasted like rotted fruit.

"What's it matter?" Ejii said. She looked at the people on the couch. "Did he ask any of you rich people how old you were when you checked in?"

Ejii stood tall, took off her sunglasses, and leaned forward so that the receptionist could see in her eyes. She was surprised at how much she relished his shock. She turned and looked at the people who had stopped to watch the spectacle and the people on the couch. Several of them gasped. Ejii was disgusted. Who knew what rumors and urban legends circulated here about shadow speakers. And who cares? she thought. These people know nothing about who I am, what I risked to get here, and the war that hangs over all of us. She turned back to the receptionist, looking into him without a thought about falling into a well of pain again. Then she spoke.

"I'm ten years older than your son! But I'm sure even a four-year-old will be ashamed that his father lost his job for being so *rude*!"

Dikéogu laughed hard. "Good one, Ejii," he said, grinning.

"I doubt I'll be fired from here," the receptionist smugly said, reclaiming his composure. He glanced at the couple standing a good distance behind them waiting to be helped. "Anyway, I'm not to give out information about our guests, especially that one."

"So she's here?" Ejii asked.

"I didn't say that," he snapped, avoiding Ejii's eyes.

"Give me a room," Ejii said. "I'll be a customer and then you can tell us."

"You're underage."

"Did I tell you how old I am?" Dikéogu asked.

"I don't *care* how old *you* are, slave boy," the receptionist snapped.

"I rented a room at the Oasis Hotel just fine," Ejii lied.

"Well *this* is the Yellow Lady, *not* the Oasis," the receptionist said haughtily. He leaned to the side to address the waiting couple behind them. "I'll be with you in a moment." Then he looked disdainfully at Ejii and said, "I've notified security."

Ejii and Dikéogu were about to run for the door when a man came from behind and grabbed them both by the arm. He was beefy and wore a yellow uniform. Dikéogu tried to snatch his arm away, he even tried biting. Ejii looked frantically around and then up at the man, hoping to catch his eye, but he refused to look at her.

"Not here," the receptionist told the guard, motioning toward the waiting customers.

"Come with me," the man said, dragging them down the hallway.

"We don't want trouble!" Ejii said.

"Is that so?" the guard said smiling.

"We just . . . is the Red Queen still here? We came for her," Ejii said, speaking fast. They were marching toward a small doorway that led outside.

"Please don't throw us out," Ejii said quickly. Dikéogu was spitting curses at him and the man laughed. The door was only a few yards away. Ejii could think of only one thing to do. She relaxed and concentrated. The man slowed his walk when he noticed that she'd stopped fighting. Then he began to suddenly walk faster, afraid.

She smelled cigarette smoke and heard the clack of an old computer keyboard. His small cramped "office" was a terminal in a Net café where they still used the large bulky computers. So different from his large home in Agadez. His code name was Sir Edmond Slate and he'd scammed many. He was a highly wanted 419 scam artist, an especially clever and uncatchable type of con man whose work tools were the computer and Internet. This security guard job was part of his cover. When Ejii pulled back from the guard, her fingertips ached as his did from all the typing.

"I know who you are!" she said quickly. "It's . . . it's bad and I can make you go to jail if you don't take us to Jaa!"

The man shoved them both against the wall. He'd knocked the air out of her but she quickly took in more to speak. She spoke fast. "Your code name is Sir Edmond Slate and if authorities find you, they'll throw you in jail forever. You'll get the sentence worse than death, the one where they digitally wipe your brain with that machine from . . . from Ginen. You'll be a zombie servant of the state."

The guard looked horrified.

"Take us to her!" Dikéogu demanded.

Sweat ran down the guard's face. "I could kill you both right now."

Ejii said, "Try it. Try and see what happens when you attempt to harm a shadow speaker. Show me how stupid you are." She was shaking now, but she held her head up.

"Come on," he said. Violently grabbing them, he took them back down the hallway in the opposite direction. He walked fast and they had to jog to keep from dragging on the floor. They passed the hotel shops and restaurants. They stepped into an employee-only elevator and went to the seventh floor. He shoved them into a large elegant office, with an entire wall that was a window. There was a wide, shiny, red wood desk with a bright yellow chair in front of it.

"Sit," the guard said, shoving them each into chairs facing the desk. "I know how to find people, even pathetic street shit like you." Then he slammed and locked the door.

"One day I'll be big enough to knock the heads off men like that," Dikéogu said.

Ejii rubbed her sore arm. "We shouldn't want to 'knock the heads' off anyone."

He got up and tried the door. "Whose office do you think this is?" he said, giving the locked door a kick.

"Not his," Ejii said.

"We have to get out of here," he said.

"We have to find Jaa," Ejii said.

"We don't even know if she's here," he said, picking up one of the brochures that sat on the table between their chairs. On one side of the office were pictures of celebrities, politicians, and other important people who had apparently stayed at the hotel. On the other, lined up in rows, were pictures of smiling African men and women. Ejii put her sunglasses back on.

"Wow," Ejii said, looking at the brochure. "Looks like presidents from many different countries have stayed here."

When the door opened they both stood up. The woman that walked in was an eyeful. She was over six feet tall and curvy like the statues of fertility goddesses sold in the market. She wore a long, long, bright yellow dress and had her hair in a large Afro with a yellow flower tucked in the side. There was a necklace with a silver Cross of Agadez pendant resting on her very ample bosom.

"What are you two doing here?" she asked. "Isn't it past your bedtime?"

"The security guard . . ."

"Oh yes, my son mentioned some altercation that he called security to handle, but you two were to be thrown out, not in here."

The receptionist was her son? Ejii thought.

"Looks like I need to talk to some people about how to take orders," the woman said, going to her desk and picking up a folder. She sat down. "How old are you?"

"Sixteen," Ejii said at the same time that Dikéogu said, "eighteen." They looked at each other and then looked away.

She chuckled, "Which translates to about fourteen or fifteen. Don't lie to me." She motioned to the numbered pictures on the wall, "I have more children than the number of years either of you have been on earth. I can always tell when a child is lying."

Ejii glanced at the pictures. They couldn't *all* be her children? She noticed a grinning picture of the receptionist.

"Names?" the woman asked.

They looked at each other, unsure.

"Names," she said, loud enough for them both to jump.

"Dikéogu Obidimkpa."

"Ejii Ugabe."

The woman looked at Dikéogu. "You can't be related to . . ."

"I'm . . . I'm their son," he said.

She frowned deeply, her eyes on the tattoos on his face. Ejii took the brief moment to read the woman, being careful to keep her mind on the surface. *Marigold, perfume, the sound of laughter and children, and she never told lies.* Ejii relaxed. This was Yellow Lady.

"They never brought me along whenever they came here," he said. "Most people outside of my village don't know about me. . . . I've been through a lot in the last year."

"So you've come all the way from Arondizuogu?" she asked.

He nodded. "I . . . took the long way."

"And you?" she asked Ejii.

"Kwàmfà," Ejii said.

Yellow Lady sat thinking for a moment. "Relationship?"

"Huh?" Dikéogu said.

"Are you two m—"

"We're *friends*, traveling," Dikéogu said.

"Mm-hm. I can always tell. If not now, soon enough," she said. "And did you get those markings on your face by traveling?"

He frowned. "I'm Mrs. and Mr. Obidimkpa's son. Don't you believe me?"

"Maybe," she said. She looked him over. "You look a lot like your mother. Got the same forceful look and you've got your father's nose. I was just . . ."

"Look, we don't want to stay here," Dikéogu interrupted. "We want to see Sarauniya Jaa. Is she still here?"

Yellow Lady blinked and was about to speak when the phone rang. She held up a finger and answered it. "Yellow Lady speaking," she said.

As she talked on the phone, Dikéogu leaned over to Ejii. "She's so full of herself," he whispered to Ejii. "And she's got the biggest melons I've ever seen!"

"At least she's not a criminal like that security guard," Ejii said with a laugh.

"Like one of those fertility goddesses!" he said.

"Shhh!" Ejii hissed.

Yellow Lady put the phone down. "You two know who I am, no?"

"You're Yellow Lady," Ejii said.

She nodded. "My name was Patience Okonkwo, but I've since *lost* patience with it." She leaned back in her leather yellow chair. "My meeting has been postponed, so I have some time to waste on you two. Tell me why you want to meet Jaa. No, first tell me what you're doing here."

They told Yellow Lady of their adventures. She wasn't a passive listener; she asked questions and wanted details. Neither of them gave away the security guard; Ejii had given him her word, even if it had been forced out of her. By the time they were finished talking, an hour had passed. "It's been a long time since I've met children like you," Yellow Lady said, grinning. "Adventurers."

Ejii liked the sound of that.

"Now, Ejii, are you feeling well? Do you need any pain killers or special . . ."

"I feel fine," she quickly said.

Yellow Lady nodded. "Dikéogu, it's awful what your parents did. They were here two months ago and they seemed happy enough." Dikéogu bristled. "If you'd like me to give them a . . ."

"No," he said.

"Okay," she said softly. "About Jaa. Yes, she is still here." Both Ejii and Dikéogu gasped with relief, sinking into their chairs. "But I don't know if she'll see you." She stood up. "Come, I'll have a room prepared for each of you. That's the least I can do."

"I don't need a room," Dikéogu said. "Just a balcony."

This delighted Yellow Lady even more. "Ah yes, you hate being enclosed. Okay, one room with a balcony, then. You two must be exhausted . . . and some new clothes."

"Thank you so much!" Ejii said.

"Dikéogu, do you mind if I tell a friend about you? Ali Mamami is the head of Timidria, a sect of the Nigérien Bureau of Investigation. I think he'd like to take a look at the plantation you told me about."

Dikéogu looked as if he'd die of happiness. "No, Madam. I don't mind at all."

As they followed Yellow Lady out, Ejii remembered something. "Will our camel be okay downstairs?" Ejii asked. "He is a talking camel named Onion."

"He'll be bathed, brushed, fed, and lavishly bedded," Yellow Lady said with a flick of her wrist.

"Thank you," Ejii said. "Tell him that Ejii said it's okay. And please don't let anyone put a rein on, or rope around him."

Another of Yellow Lady's sons showed them to their rooms. He wore bright yellow pants and a red shirt and walked very fast. He laughed a lot like his mother, and by the time they got to their room on the eighth floor, he had Ejii and Dikéogu laughing too. "We'll bring you some clothes in an hour, okay?" he said. "I suggest you both take long, hot showers. Make sure you smell nice and look stunning because Sarauniya Jaa, Gambo, and Buji are having a late dinner and they may agree to see you."

✛

THE GHOST ROOM

"**LOOK** like camelshit," Dikéogu said. "Do these pants have to be so white? I feel as vain as my father." He looked at himself in the mirror again and grimaced.

"Relax, you look very stylish," Ejii said. "I like the sand bead necklace, and the caftan is well made. You look like you come from Kwàmfà."

Ejii wore a green *rapa* and a matching top and head wrap.

"Your outfit's . . . okay," Dikéogu grudgingly. "That's what all the *shakara* girls in my village who think they're so beautiful like to wear."

An hour earlier, yet another of Yellow Lady's children named Chinwe had taken them downstairs to see Onion in his new stall. Chinwe was even taller than her mother and she was far from voluptuous, all angles and thin as a rail.

"How many brothers and sisters do you have?" Ejii asked Chinwe.

"Twenty," she said matter-of-factly, as she turned left.

✛ ✛ ✛

"I'm so nervous," Ejii said, sitting on the bed as they waited for yet another of Yellow Lady's children to come get them. Everything in their room was blue and expensive. It even had a wall-size netvision set; neither of them was interested in watching it. She put her sunglasses on. "What if she doesn't like me?"

"Why wouldn't she?" Dikéogu said. "She wanted you to be her successor."

"Yes, but this is a different situation."

There was a knock at the door. "Call me Innocent," the short, dark skinned man said when they opened it. He wore all black and a blue bead necklace.

"Are you one of Yellow Lady's . . ."

"Yes," Innocent said. "The third son."

She thought of her own father. How many children would he have had if he'd lived? "Will we get to meet your father?" she asked.

Innocent laughed and shook his head. "Doubtful, nor any of the others'," he said.

They were quiet in the elevator and as they walked through the lobby of the hotel. "The dinner will be in the Ghost Room," Innocent said as they passed two guards standing in front of a hallway. The guards both carried machine guns. They looked long and hard at Ejii and Dikéogu, but didn't say a word. The hallway was shaped like a round tunnel sheathed with gold wallpaper. Soft drumbeats played as they walked.

"Ghost Room?" Dikéogu asked.

Innocent smiled. "It's Jaa's favorite room and she insists on having her meetings in it. She and her husbands are anxious to meet you." He inserted a large yellow corkscrew-shaped key into a hole next to an elevator.

"*Ina wuni?* Innocent?" the elevator greeted in the Hausa language.

"*Lafiya lau*, Mgbeke," Innocent said.

The doors opened. Inside, the walls and ceilings were decorated with yellow cloth, the floor made of red marble. They stepped in. "The thirteenth floor," he said.

"My pleasure," Mgbeke the Elevator said.

"Just be yourselves. And Ejii, take those silly sunglasses off," Innocent said, quickly plucking them from her face.

She looked at her feet, embarrassed. Innocent folded the glasses and put them in his pocket. Ejii knew she'd never see them again.

The elevator doors opened to a large room with lush blue carpeting. In the center was a large table. The walls were made of glass, providing a 360-degree view of Agadez. Incense burned somewhere and ambient music played. Innocent showed them to their seats, which were directly across the table from three empty thronelike chairs.

"Stand up when they come in," Innocent said. "Let them speak first, and mind your manners when you eat."

Ejii and Dikéogu were quiet after he left. The room had an eerie feel to it. They scooted closer to each other as they looked around. "Dikéogu," Ejii whispered. She didn't know why she was whispering. "It's cold in here or . . . something."

"Not cold, but . . . I wish they'd come. Feels like someone's watching us."

"Yeah," Ejii said. "That's it. It feels like . . ." She gasped. It was an icy blue substance slightly more substantial than haze. It undulated from side to side as it came toward them. Dikéogu cursed under his breath. The closer it came, the more substantial it grew. By the time it was a few feet away, it was a tall, lanky man. He wore indigo cloth from head to toe, his face covered with a turban veil. A piece of cloth around his waist held a shimmering sword.

Dikéogu jumped up and ran to the other side of the room, yelling, "Ghosts! Get them away from me!"

"One of the Blue People," Ejii whispered. She'd seen pictures of them in her e-legba's encyclopedia. The Old Tuareg were called the Blue People because of the indigo they dyed their clothes with. The dye tinted their golden skin. These were the people that had enslaved Ejii's ancestors on her father's side. She stood up tall, determined to represent her ancestors well. There must have been others around the room because Dikéogu was running back and forth, swatting at his head, as if pursued by wasps.

"Good evening, sir," she said to the ghost standing before her.

The ghost spoke Tamarshak, the language of the Blue People. Ejii's mother spoke it but Ejii had never learned it.

"Young man, if you'd stop being afraid, you'll see that they're quite beautiful," a voice said from behind them in Hausa. A red flower fell and bounced off of Ejii's shoulder, another missed Dikéogu's head. Dikéogu stopped running. Jaa, her two husbands, Yellow Lady, and one other woman stepped out of the elevator.

Ejii experienced a storm of emotions: awe, fear, resentment, excitement. She'd made it. She'd found her. Her eyes grew moist with tears.

"Yes, they're ghosts," Jaa said in her high-pitched voice. "But you'd be surprised at how the looks of things change with your attitude." Today Jaa was wearing red pants, a long red close-fitting silk top, and her usual sheer burka over her head. Her wooly black hair was braided into many thick braids. One of the ghosts floated up to her. She bowed her head and laughed. The ghost flew a circle around her, causing her burka to flutter.

"They've haunted this room since the Great Change," Yellow Lady said. A ghost standing next to her nodded. She wore attire much like Ejii's, except it was yellow. "There was a battle here long ago. These men were killed. They come and go, now."

"So they won't . . . hurt us?" Dikéogu said. There was a tickly sound of faraway laughter, like many tiny bells. The ghosts found Dikéogu quite amusing.

"Not if they don't want to," Gambo said. He wore brown pants and a brown tunic adorned with red beads and copper rings. Several silver-and-leather amulets hung from his neck. Dikéogu slowly walked over and stood next to Ejii.

"Dikéogu, Ejii," Yellow Lady said ceremoniously. "Sarauniya Jaa the Red Queen, Gambo, son of the Sand and Wind, Buji son of Ooni, and my oldest daughter, Wanga."

"Good evening," Dikéogu and Ejii said.

"Ejii, you've traveled far to see me," Jaa said. "Why?"

"Well . . . I . . ."

"Let's have dinner first," Buji said, whisking his dreadlocks back. Around each of his wrists were bracelets made of what looked like green plants. He looked at Dikéogu. Then he reached out and touched Dikéogu's forehead and ran his finger down the blue-line-with-dots tattoo. Surprisingly, Dikéogu didn't move away. "Did it hurt?"

Dikéogu nodded. "I hate it," he said. "Everyone who looks at me knows."

Buji pushed Dikéogu's chin up with his fingers. "We all have warrior marks and they always hurt when we get them. You'll collect many more as you grow older." He stepped around the table and sat down across from Ejii and Dikéogu.

"Ejii," Jaa said, sitting down. "You've grown since the last time I saw you."

Ejii looked at her with a shaky smile as she sat down. When Dikéogu sat down next to her, she felt a little more composed.

Men and women dressed in yellow shirts, pants, and sneakers quickly brought in the food. There were dishes from both her home and Dikéogu's. There was: *egusi* and *edi ka kong* soup, both made with greens and chunks of stockfish, chicken, and goat meat; *miyar dankali*, a tasty potato soup; *waina* rice patties; fried plantains; red tomato stew with large chunks of goat meat, beef, and chicken; and a large bowl of pepper soup with big shrimp floating in it. Everyone was poured a milky glass of palm wine.

Ejii noticed that many of the ghosts had settled near the window, listening, though many of them were having conversations and arguments that she couldn't hear. After Wanga blessed the food, everyone dug in. For a while, the only sound anyone made was the occasional grunt of approval.

A ghost walked up to Jaa and whispered in her ear. She smiled. "I love this room," she said, popping a fried plantain slice into her mouth. "These ghosts have priceless knowledge of war. The strategies they've taught me have been more than useful in the past. I hope they will be useful in the future." She paused as another ghost stood next to her with his hands on his narrow hips and spoke to her in Tamarshak. Gambo threw his head back and laughed hard. Buji smiled, shaking his head. Jaa looked at Ejii.

"These ghosts' human lives were long ago, as is their way of thinking," Jaa said. "They feel I have no business carrying a sword. And this one is complaining about my burka. He reminds me that burkas are meant to *cover* my face."

Ejii had to smile. She could easily see Jaa's face right through the red sheer cloth.

"I have to keep reminding them that things have evolved," Jaa said. "Women are still women but we are also many other things."

Behind Jaa, Buji, and Gambo, Ejii saw one of the ghosts ride by on an elaborately decorated camel. The camel ran toward the wall. Then there was a flash of light that made Ejii and Dikéogu jump. The ghost man and camel were gone. "That one just crossed into the wilderness," Yellow Lady said.

"Some stay for years, others pass through to the wilderness after a few hours. One leaves, another always comes and replaces it."

"That's what they call the afterlife in *My Cyborg Manifesto*: the wilderness," Dikéogu said, as he spooned hot pepper soup into his mouth.

Yellow Lady nodded.

"You've read it?" Gambo asked.

"Oh yeah. It kept me from going crazy in that plantation and after I escaped."

"Yellow Lady told us about you two," Buji said, dipping a ball of gray doughy gari into his egusi soup. "You met an Aejej and you lived to tell about it. That's rare."

Ejii looked to Dikéogu to answer, but he was suddenly too busy trying to eat a rice patty and several plantain slices at once. "It almost killed us," she said. "Dikéogu was trapped in a deserted town for two days hiding from it! I . . . I ended up speaking to it."

"And what did you say?" Buji asked.

"I told it to let go of its anger and pain," she said. "It couldn't even remember what it was angry about."

Buji exchanged a look with Gambo. Jaa chuckled to herself.

"Did I say something wrong?" Ejii asked.

"No," Jaa said. "You see, Gambo used to be an Aejej, too."

"What?!" Dikéogu said, dropping his spoon. Ejii grabbed his shoulder. The ghosts came and settled around Gambo.

"I'm over five hundred years old," Gambo said. "My parents, sister, and I were slaves to an Arab family. We lived somewhere between what is now Chad and Niger. When I was seven, they took me from my parents to travel the salt roads with our master. This made me so angry.

"One night, during our travel, our camp was hit by a great sandstorm. I ran into the storm to escape. Death was better than being away from my family. The storm was not normal. It was haunted. Even back then, centuries before the Great Change, there were such things. The sand fell on me and it fed off of my anger and I grew. I lost myself. I became an Aejej. I forgot my family, who I was, what I was. Over the centuries, I must have eaten thousands of vulnerable travelers.

"Until I met a woman traveling alone on camelback." He looked at Jaa. "I went after her, intent on tearing her to pieces. But she shouted at me in a high voice that penetrated all my noise. Her voice was so lovely that flowers fell from the sky and so did I. I was human again. For days, I wailed and sobbed. But when I lifted my head, my mind was clear, and the woman was still there. Jaa taught me control. She brought me to her first husband, Buji, who taught me about the world and showed me how much things had changed. Soon I was shrinking and taking on his characteristics. These two keep me whole."

Ejii felt odd. Jaa was able to do the same thing she'd done. Except, Jaa had shouted, where Ejii had spoken softly. Did the Aejej we encountered turn into a human being? she wondered. Dikéogu had said something about something flying off just before all the sand began to fall. Maybe not human, but something, she thought. The elevator doors opened and three servants brought in the desserts. A double-layered chocolate cake and small bowls of caramel cream with hard, melted sugar tops.

Dikéogu scowled. "I hate chocolate," he said, rubbing his tattoo. Ejii handed him a bowl of caramel cream. She took a bowl for herself, but she barely tasted it. The click of Kola's talons on the windowsill as the owl landed broke the silence. Everyone turned.

"That's my friend," Dikéogu said getting up. "Her name is Kola."

Kola hooted and Dikéogu laughed. Ejii was glad for the interruption. Gambo's story was unsettling. For centuries he'd been raging and killing. Yet Jaa had saved Gambo, given him a chance to change his ways. Funny that he was now Jaa's husband. Shouldn't Jaa have cut his head off instead?

"This is the owl that adopted you?" Gambo asked, getting up to see the bird.

"She saved me," Dikéogu said.

Ejii glanced at Jaa who gazed back at Ejii with narrowed eyes. Ejii quickly looked down at her plate. She didn't have to look at Jaa to know that she was smiling. Always smiling. Even the bloodiest things in the world amuse her, Ejii thought angrily, thinking of how Jaa had smiled when she'd executed Ejii's father.

"Why did you leave your home and risk your life to cross the desert?" Jaa asked.

"I didn't know that I could die," she said. "The shadows told me to go, they said there was going to be a war and that I would help to prevent it."

Jaa smiled knowingly and shook her head. "There will be no war," she said. "There's going to be a meeting. The Golden Dawn. I'll settle everything there."

A ghost dressed in yellow robes and a blue veil and turban sat in Gambo's empty seat to listen to Ejii and Jaa. All Ejii could see of his face were his gray eyes.

"Why'd you have to kill him?" Ejii finally asked. Her chest tightened. For so long she'd wanted to ask Jaa this. She looked at Jaa's left hand, the hand that had carried the sword that beheaded her father.

"A great philosopher, Frantz Fanon, once said, 'Violence is a cleansing force,'" Jaa said. She stood up and held out a hand. Ejii only looked at it. Jaa's fingers were small, the nails cut neatly as always, the palm rough. Ejii shook her head. Jaa took her hand back and stepped past Ejii to Yellow Lady, who was loudly telling Buji how Agadez was on the verge of becoming greater than Rome.

"We're going to the top floor," Jaa said. Yellow Lady dropped a key in Jaa's hand and continued talking. Dikéogu was still standing with Gambo, Kola on his arm. He caught Ejii's eye.

"It's okay," Ejii said. Dikéogu nodded.

"Come," Jaa said, stepping into the elevator. It took them to the top of the hotel. When the doors opened, Ejii was looking over the city of Agadez. To her right was the mosque, which reached a little higher than the Yellow Lady Hotel. The top of the hotel was carpeted with grass and several potted palm trees and flowering bushes. The air smelled of lilies, and

Ejii could hear the sound of crickets and katydids. It was as if she'd stepped into a pocket of paradise.

"Lovely, isn't it?" Jaa said.

Ejii nodded.

"Yellow Lady's a good friend," Jaa said. "But she's not the only reason I come to her hotel."

Ejii walked to the edge of the forest in the sky. As she walked, her feet grew damp, the grass seemed to have been freshly watered. Jaa stepped up next to her. For a while they stood that way. Ejii could see beyond the city's limit. A caravan of what looked like traders was just arriving from the desert.

"My father was bad," Ejii said after a while. "He was murderous, greedy, destructive. He turned Kwàmfà into a place of fear. He was ruining my life. But . . . why did you have to kill him? If he had lived, he might have ch—"

"He wouldn't have changed," Jaa said.

"Gambo did," Ejii said.

"Gambo was a *child* when he became an Aejej," Jaa said.

Jaa looked at Ejii with such force that Ejii couldn't help reading her. It rushed into Ejii's mind like blood. Red and warm and alive. *Jaa, born Fatima, had been a smiling young woman who loved romance. She'd been studying to be a doctor, on vacation with friends, when she was kidnapped, a day before the Great Change. Her past was as the book described. After the Great Change, she herself went through a great change. Something awoke in her, she realized the power within her and that power was amazing.*

Jaa was a madwoman and the sanest individual Ejii'd ever met. She was so sharp in mind that she hadn't *had* to think before beheading Ejii's father, so sure she was of her actions. She knew exactly what she was doing, Ejii thought. And she regrets none of it.

"Eh, what? . . . Don't do that," Jaa snapped, stepping away from Ejii.

Ejii shook her head. "I . . . I didn't mean to . . ."

Before Ejii could finish what she was saying, lightning fast, Jaa drew her sword, threw off her burka, grabbed the neckline of Ejii's dress, and with incredible strength, shoved Ejii into the wall next to the elevator.

"Ugh!" Ejii groaned. She whimpered as Jaa pressed her clear-green-tinted sword to Ejii's neck. Jaa snarled, her upper body muscles swelling beneath her close-fitting red silk top. She looked deep into Ejii's eyes. "I've wondered about you," she hissed. A rose fell from the sky and bounced off the sword. Ejii felt the sting as the sword drew blood.

"Wondered what?" Ejii screamed. She shoved at Jaa's arm, moving the sword from her neck. Then she pushed Jaa some more. She was suddenly so angry and she didn't know why. The two stood glaring at each other. All Ejii knew was that if Jaa came at her again with that damn sword, come what may, Ejii would fight. With my bare hands, she thought. She glanced at the spot of her blood on Jaa's sword's edge. Even as she watched, the spot grew smaller and smaller, as if the sword were drinking it up.

"Well?" Ejii daringly said.

"If I'd wanted to, I'd have taken your head off before you even thought to push me away," Jaa said, stone-faced.

"Why didn't you?" Ejii said. "You're obviously threatened by me, as you were by my father!" She covered her mouth, looking at Jaa with eyes wide. All the fight that had balled up hot and ready in her chest, cooled and dispersed.

Jaa lowered her sword and sheathed it. Then she walked to the wall and looked over its edge. Ejii remained where she was. Her legs had started to tremble. What was I doing? she thought. But no matter how she looked at it, she'd been ready to fight, take on Jaa by any means necessary, damn the consequences.

"I've been a warrior for too long," Jaa said, her back to Ejii.

"Maybe," Ejii said. From behind, Jaa looked like a child, she was so tiny. Only the sword that hung at her side hinted at her great potential for violence.

Jaa turned to Ejii. "Come." Ejii hesitated. She didn't like the idea of standing next to Jaa in front of a three-foot-high wall that ended in a drop of over twenty stories. Jaa laughed. "I won't throw you over the edge," she said. "Not today, at least."

This didn't comfort Ejii at all. She touched the thin cut on her neck and the amulet that hung just below it. Slowly she walked over, all her senses on guard.

"Let me see this 'box' that the shadows told you to bring," Jaa said.

Ejii hesitated again. She decided to bring it out while watching Jaa very closely. If she saw one weird twitch in Jaa's eye, she'd put it right back in her pocket and prepare to defend it. When she held it up, Jaa looked at it blankly. "What is it?"

Ejii found herself laughing. "I have no idea."

Jaa grunted and turned back to the edge. Ejii put it back in her pocket.

"I didn't mean to . . . do what I did," Ejii whispered, leaning on the wall and grasping the edge. "Lately when I'm too close to someone, I just sort of fall into them."

"Did you learn what you wanted to know?" Jaa said.

Ejii only looked at her hands. She knew better than to respond.

"I don't like being out of control," Jaa said. "That's what it felt like. Like someone probing into my mind's artillery without me being able to stop it."

"I'm sorry."

Jaa waved a dismissive hand. "It's this way with every talent. You'll get to a point in your life when you'll wonder if you're controlling it or is it controlling you." She turned to Ejii, leaning back. "You have a problem with me. I have a problem with you. You are your mother's daughter, thank Allah. But your father . . . he is in you, too. I'll forever *hate* that part of you. But there's something else to you that bothers me." The breeze blew a braid in her face and she pushed it away.

"I'm not a queen in the traditional sense. I don't *rule* anyone. I'm just a woman, a person, a creature. After the Great Change, things could have gotten very bloody. In my heart, I knew what needed to be done. I knew. And I did it. Sometimes it must be this way. People deserve to be allowed to be who they are, nurture their talents, dig up and eat happiness, fail at things they try. I know of places like your friend's plantation. I've dedicated my life to making things better. But to make things better, you can't fool yourself. You can't always be soft. Sometimes you *have* to use your sword."

"I don't agree with that," Ejii whispered.

Jaa smirked. "What of your fight with your brother, Fadio?"

Ejii was so thrown off by this question that she couldn't respond.

"Mm-hm," Jaa said, letting Ejii off the hook. "So what *do* you believe?"

Ejii thought for a moment. Her thoughts wavered when she realized she was actually having a conversation with Jaa. "I . . . I believe . . . I've come far to find you," she said. "I left home with just my camel and supplies. No gun, no sword. There's been danger, but there was always a way around violence."

"If someone accosted you with a sword, what would you do, Ejii?" Jaa asked.

"I would talk to him. Ask him why he wanted to kill me."

"What about at gunpoint?"

"Same thing."

"What if your town was surrounded by an army?"

"The night before the attack, I'd disguise myself as a civilian and walk into their camp. There I'd talk someone into letting me see their leader."

Jaa sucked her teeth and shook her head. "You've never seen war. People don't think before acting," Jaa said. "And I don't believe you. I look at you and I see a warrior just like me. When challenged, you always eventually fight."

Ejii looked away. "But fighting is what caused the Great Change in the first place."

Jaa stared at her for so long that Ejii began to feel uncomfortable. It was the same look Jaa had given Ejii's mother right after she beheaded Ejii's father. "Your ideas are silly and idealistic," Jaa said. "But I've always been impressed by the wisdom beneath it all. And your passion. Honesty, passion, and conflict." She paused. "I've had you on my mind the last few years. One day I'll grow old. It's a good time to start grooming a successor."

Ejii held her breath.

"I approached your mother but she feared for you," Jaa said. "She felt you were too young to risk a shadow-speaker death. Yet here you are alive in Agadez, changed."

"I didn't know the risk when I left," Ejii said.

"It's best that way," Jaa said. "Now that you have earned the right to make the choice yourself, will you be my apprentice?"

Ejii frowned and stepped back. "But you killed my—"

"Yes. But is it so simple? And what will you be if not my successor? Most likely my eventual enemy. Look deep within yourself. What will you become, Ejii?"

Ejii didn't know what to say.

"Before you answer, know that to say 'yes' would mean that you would come with me to the Golden Dawn Meeting in Ginen," Jaa said. "I don't know what traveling to a different world will do to even the strongest shadow speaker." Jaa chuckled to herself as she walked a few steps away to give Ejii room to think.

Ejii looked over the city and then shut her eyes. Her heartbeat slowed as she relaxed and called for the shadows. Silence. She was herself now. But they are in me, she thought. Part of me now. But this didn't help either, for it still meant that the only voice in her head was her own now. What'll I do if I don't go? she thought. Go home? And then what? Read in the papers about the war I didn't help to stop? Or maybe I won't even make it home. Maybe I'll die a shadow speaker death along the way. I'd die a failure.

"O . . . okay," she said, turning to Jaa.

Jaa came back over, a solemn look on her face. "A true hero honors sacrifice," she said. "We leave in the morning. I hope your interesting friend will join us."

Ejii hoped Dikéogu would come, too.

✦

CHAPTER SEVENTEEN

EJII EVOLVES

WHEN Ejii and Dikéogu returned to their rooms, they were too exhausted to stay up and talk about it all. Plus Ejii didn't really want to think about the risk of traveling to Ginen. She'd talk to Dikéogu about it in the morning. Still, she slept poorly that night, plagued by thoughts of pain and death. When she did finally fall asleep, she was besieged by nightmares in which she melted, bled, and screamed. It was about a half hour before sunrise when she woke up feeling unrested and anxious.

"Dikéogu?" she said, rubbing her eyes. He froze in front of her bed. He was fully dressed, his satchel slung over his shoulder. He looked very guilty. "What are you doing?" she asked. Then she realized, "No!"

"I just . . . What do you expect . . . ?" he said with a sigh, sitting down on Ejii's bed.

"Why?"

Outside, the morning prayer blared through the streets and Ejii felt a pang of guilt. The last few days had been so hectic that she hadn't kept up with her prayers. Kola was standing on the balcony rail watching them. She began preening, flicking light, broken old feathers into the air with her beak. They floated into the room. Dikéogu's blanket still lay on the balcony floor where he'd slept.

Dikéogu shrugged. "I don't like good-byes."

"*Why* are you leaving?" she asked. "For what reason?"

"Do I *need* one?" he said. "I can go whenever I want. I'm not your slave!"

Her eyes stung but she held her tears back. "You know, you're a camelshitting coward sometimes. Why can't you just face what has happened to you? What you *are*?"

Dikéogu looked as if he were about to say something, but then closed his mouth. He jumped to his feet. "You can't force me to stay."

Ejii only stared at Dikéogu, her legs still under the covers. She glanced out the window, past Kola, miles and miles into the desert. A spontaneous forest had sprung up overnight. She could see a monkey perched in one of the trees picking out the seeds of what looked like a pomegranate and popping them in its mouth.

"I'm not forcing you," she said slowly. "I'm *asking* you. We're about the same age, almost the same height. I saved you from the Aejej and you saved me from the Desert Magician. Aren't we friends? Don't you want to see Ginen?"

He looked at his feet. "I didn't . . ."

"Jaa asked me . . . *us* to come," Ejii said.

"How come you didn't tell me last night?"

"I was going to tell you everything this morning."

"Or maybe you weren't going to ask me in the first place," he snapped.

"What?"

Kola launched herself into the sky, blowing more old feathers into their room as she took off. Dikéogu watched her fly away and then said, "It's morning and I'd like to get an early start. Hurry up and tell me what Jaa said."

Ejii closed her eyes for a moment. She'd only known Dikéogu for a few days but he was like a brother to her already. She'd never had a brother. They'd been through so much. Now he was leaving. To wherever. What would happen to him? When she opened her eyes, she found Dikéogu was watching her closely. "I didn't read you, if that's what you're thinking," she said. "I hate how you don't trust me."

He looked away. "As if *you* can fully control your ability, either."

"Jaa said . . . well, she asked me to be her apprentice," Ejii said.

He said nothing to this.

"We talked about things," she continued. "As it works out, she is taking me to the meeting. So it is as the shadows asked. I'll be there to do whatever I have to do."

"Well that's *great* for *you*," he said. "It's always you. You're always so lucky and privileged and . . . and . . . you had one good parent and you left her!"

"It's not that simple!" Ejii said. "Think about what I'll be risking by traveling to another world. If it were only about me, I would not be going!"

"You shouldn't go," he worriedly said. "It's not our fight, we're not adults."

"Whatever happens will affect us all," she said. "My hometown is probably one of the places that the people of Ginen will attack first if there's war. I saw an opening to another place only a few miles after I left home!"

"Why are you so self-righteous?" he asked. "You and that egg stone. What makes you think you can stop a war between worlds? What if you die while trying to get there? You'll have sacrificed yourself for nothing."

"It's what the shadows told me to do," she insisted. "And the shadows don't lie. I have faith." And though she was afraid, she realized that she did. Plus, you only die once, she thought. Why not make it for a good purpose? It was a light thought, but it felt very heavy. Having faith didn't mean one was fearless.

Dikéogu grabbed his satchel. "What if I don't want to go?"

"You don't have to go," Ejii said.

"She won't come after me or anything?"

Ejii shook her head.

"Gambo and Buji won't track me down?"

Ejii shook her head again.

Dikéogu rubbed his coarse hair. Ejii held her breath. When Dikéogu headed for the door, her stomach dropped. He opened the door and, without a word, left.

For the first time since she'd left home Ejii desperately wished her e-legba could call home. She needed her mother. If she didn't talk to her mother soon, she'd fall apart. But she couldn't call her mother. At least not with her e-legba. She was too far away. She'd gone too far. Ejii's legs felt weak, so she couldn't get up to find Yellow Lady and ask to use her phone. She pounded her fist on the bed and dug her nails into the bed-sheets.

What had that camp done to Dikéogu to make him act that way? Or maybe it was the betrayal by his parents. Ejii thought of how her father once told her not to look at him with her "demon eyes." How he insisted that girls were most useful as a man's wife. How he never came to see her. Yes, she thought. Cruel parents can create all kinds of side effects. Dikéogu couldn't trust and was afraid to care about anyone.

Ejii grabbed the first thing her hand touched, a bag of dates. She threw the bag with all her might at the wall, and it burst open, scattering dates on the floor. She was wiping the tears from her eyes when the door opened.

"Some shadow speaker you are," Dikéogu said, stepping back in. "You didn't even know that I'd come back." He threw his satchel down. "I *was* standing at the elevator. I *was* going to go. But then a ghost appeared and refused to let the elevator doors open for me. She looked like a palm tree pushing through the floor. I guess she was the ghost of a tree that used to grow there before the hotel existed. She said, 'A friend is like a source of water during a long voyage. Without water, you'll wither away.' Then she shook her leaves and disappeared. Even the damn trees are nosy."

"But you believed her?" Ejii said.

He went to the balcony. Ejii got up and joined him. For a

while they stood side by side. Ejii could see Kola a few miles away, high in the sky. "When you went to talk in private with Jaa, Buji and Gambo took me aside," he said. "They asked about my parents, about all those times of getting struck by lightning. Buji said I was meant to leave home. How can some-one be meant not to be with his family? What does that make me?"

"Life's complicated," Ejii said.

"Yeah," he said. "Gambo asked me to come along."

Ejii frowned and looked at him. "Then why were you . . . ?"

"*Because*," he said. "Just because. My family was bad. I don't want a new one."

"Dikéogu," Ejii said putting her hands on Dikéogu's shoul-der, turning him to her and looking him in the eyes. He fid-geted and she waited for him to look back into her eyes. When he did, she asked him a very important question. "May I read you?"

She didn't know she was going to ask this until she asked it. She was asking to be allowed to see his past and present, to see the times where he was weakest and most humiliated. She was asking him to trust her. They stood like that for a while. Eyes locked. Then ever so slightly, but not too slight for Ejii to miss it, he nodded.

She closed her eyes and it was like she fell in. Suddenly everything around her began to move very slowly because Dikéogu's mind moved so quickly. In this way, he was like Jaa. *Back in his village, he'd always been sharp in mind. His mother used to rely on Dikéogu to remember anniversaries, birthdays, and deadlines. There was a sweet sensation, and the smell of copper and incense when Dikéogu was struck by the lightning. The day he'd had to leave home devastated him. Ejii felt his pain as the truck took him farther and farther from all he knew.*

Then Ejii could smell chocolate, but it didn't smell yummy; it smelled evil. It reminded her of helplessness and fury. On the plantation. A slave. He'd slept in a shack during the day with many other children. The sting of the ink-filled needle on his forehead, down the bridge of his nose as they held him down and marked him forever. Like stabs of a scorpion's tail. So painful that he had thrown up when they were finished.

And a boy named Adam was his partner in crime. Adam was skinny and dark-brown and talkative, as Dikéogu was. He was the only one who liked to eat the little black bugs that were always in the garri the children were given. But he managed to convince everyone else to eat them, too. "It's good for you," he said. "Protein."

Dikéogu never asked Adam how he ended up a slave. Dikéogu and Adam had tried to organize the children to run away. And they might have succeeded if Adam hadn't suddenly fallen sick. Many were sick; every day when the sun came up, there was always someone who had died or was ill. One day, one of the dead was Adam.

Ejii took in more but then had to pull back. Lying on the hay, Dikéogu's friend had looked simply asleep . . . except for the black beetle that came out of his nose.

"Oh, poor Adam," Ejii whispered.

"They brought a doctor to see him," Dikéogu said, staring off. "They acted like they really cared. They promised to take him to the hospital and . . . Ejii!"

She shook her head, tiny drops of blood dribbling from her eyes and nose. She had to sit down on the floor. She felt light-headed and nauseous. Dikéogu looked down at her and then sat down, too. "Are you all right?" he asked.

"No," Ejii said, breathing heavily. "I'm not. I . . . I don't know what's happening to me anymore." She got up and ran to the bathroom and threw up everything in her stomach, which, it being morning, was mostly bitter bile. She wiped her mouth with toilet paper and sat with her back against the toilet. She felt cold and started to shiver.

Dikéogu's pain sat heavily on her chest, making it difficult to breath. Gradually it was retreating like a nightmare. Dikéogu moistened a towel with warm water and wiped her face. He pulled the sheet from Ejii's bed and wrapped it around her. He filled a glass with water. "Try and drink this," he said, handing it to her, his hand shaking.

She sipped slowly, her eyes stinging with each blink.

"Do you feel better now?" he whispered.

She shook her head. "I . . . I'm losing control," she said. Even as she spoke she felt her eyes going haywire. One minute she was looking at Dikéogu's face, the next she could see each skin cell of his face. She shut her eyes. "I think I'm changing," she said.

He nodded. He frowned. "What's the matter with your eyes?"

"I don't know," Ejii said, her eyes still closed.

Dikéogu ran more warm water over the towel and patted her face again, wiping her bloody tears. It was soothing and

Ejii relaxed. She stopped shaking and felt the heat return to her body. She heard him close the bathroom door and turn the lights off.

Still, she couldn't open her eyes. She was descending into the darkest part of herself. The last place she wanted to be. Deeper and deeper. Where her father was alive and well and where Jaa swung her sword about with dangerous bravado. Ejii stood in the corner while these two figures faced off. Her first reaction was to curl herself up, tighter, for more protection against them both. Fear. Helplessness. Ignorance. Shame. Then Ejii remembered how far she'd come and why. She stood up, eyes steady and focused.

"Ejii?" Dikéogu's voice sounded as if it came from far, far away.

"Yes," she whispered.

"Please, try opening them now," Dikéogu said. "Not too fast, but just try."

Slowly, she opened her eyes. She found that her vision had stabilized. But something felt different. She took a sip of water.

"Better?"

"Yes," Ejii said. The dark of the bathroom was soothing, unlike the dark of her self-doubt. She looked at Dikéogu. "Your friend Adam . . ."

"I saw him die," he said, sitting down next to her in the dark. "They knew of our plan to escape, so they made an example of him. When he got sick, they let him die."

"Tell me what happened," she said.

As Dikéogu did so, Ejii realized that his spoken version was different from the one he'd let her see. There were several details that he didn't speak of, like the fact that he'd slept next to Adam all that night before he died. That he'd had so much hope in the other children and that now all he thought about them was that they were lowly, faceless cowards. That Adam had spoken one word during that feverish night, "Go," and this word had given Dikéogu the courage to do just that after Adam died.

Dikéogu's telling of what happened was not as honest as his knowing of what happened. Just like the shadows, true memories—the ones people buried deep in their subconscious for safekeeping—didn't lie.

"You and I are both cursed and gifted," Ejii said.

"More cursed, maybe," he said with a chuckle.

"Maybe," Ejii said. "Dikéogu, make me a promise. Let's both make a promise."

"Of what?"

"That above all things, we do what has to be done to make things better," she said. "That we leave this earth having made it better than when we came to it."

"I promise with all my soul," Dikéogu said. "For Adam."

✛

CHAPTER EIGHTEEN

WILDNESS

THEY traveled east at a moderate pace. As the camels trudged under the waning sun, Ejii leaned forward and lay on Onion's mane. Before traveling, she'd given him a thorough bath. Then she'd brushed his fur. Even after five days of travel, it was still fluffy and sweet smelling. Without trying, she slipped into Onion's being.

He was thinking about how the onions would taste in Ginen. Sweet, crunchy, perfect, they would be. His only concern was to feed himself and protect Ejii and maybe try a Ginen onion or two. He liked Dikéogu and Kola and would protect them too. He remembered having siblings and a mother, but he didn't remember where they were, and this was okay. Ejii gave Onion a hug, feeling a deep love for the camel who had brought her so far. She touched her eyes, no blood. She felt only slightly nauseated.

"You grow," Onion said. "But I fear for you. Ginen is another world."

"I know," she said, petting his fur.

"Your grandmother and mother would both approve,"

Onion said. "You are all adventurous ladies."

So far, Ejii was okay, though she'd had a few moments. Once, her eyes had focused so sharply that she could have sworn she could see the molecules rotating in the powdery blue petals of a flower she'd picked. Afterward, her eyes bled a few drops. Then there was the second night when they'd camped. She'd been trying to sleep when she suddenly became aware of something beneath her. She focused her eyes on the dry earth and found herself reading a giant wormlike creature tunneling some distance below. *Eight days, eight grains of sand, I will eat eight roots, and then I will be strong enough to bear eight babies. Life is good. One, two, three, four, five, six, seven, EIGHT!* The number eight was the creature's God.

Ejii didn't know when she passed out. And neither did anyone else because it was night and everyone was asleep. When Ejii woke up, she had a terrible headache and her cheeks were encrusted with dried blood that had run from her nose. All of this worried her. She wondered if each time she bled, something was rupturing or weakening inside her. Or maybe after one of these moments where her ability stretched, she'd just keel over and die. Still, she kept most of this to herself.

On the sixth night, the moon was high in the sky, lighting their way as they traveled. The clear night sky was easy to navigate but the sand was soft, so the camels moved slowly. Buji said that in the past going this way would eventually take them south to Jaa's hometown of Tahoua. "But these things aren't so simple, anymore," he said. "A straight line is no longer a straight line."

Ejii asked Onion to walk up next to Buji. Dikéogu, who sat behind her, had been trying to sleep. He woke as Onion began to move faster to catch up to Buji.

"Is Ginen the only other . . . world out there besides Earth?" Ejii asked Buji.

He looked at Jaa.

"Tell her," Jaa said. "Dikéogu? Are you listening? Wake up."

"I'm awake," he grumbled, smacking his cheeks.

"There are five worlds in all," Buji said. "We haven't been to the others. But that will change. You see, before the Great Change, there were few places where you could pass from one world to another. These places were hidden and kept secret. Two of the five worlds are protected by guardians . . . immortal creatures with their own agendas. You can leave these two worlds unhindered, but you have to convince the guardians to allow you back into them. Ginen is one of the guarded worlds, Earth is not."

Ejii frowned at this, feeling oddly insulted.

Buji continued. "When the Peace Bombs were dropped on Earth, the Great Change affected all the worlds, though not nearly as much as the Earth. My grandfather said that Earth was the only place where there was such strong denial of magic. In Ginen and the other places, the mystical was normal. My grandmother was one of the few who were allowed by the guardian to travel freely back and forth between Earth and Ginen. She saw Earth as problematic, but she never imagined what you people would do to yourselves.

"Now with the great merge, people from different places will soon begin to migrate on a larger scale. It's inevitable. And as I said, the guardian has its own agenda. It won't necessarily keep trouble out of Ginen. I think it actually enjoys trouble. And as people love to search for new and better places, the ones that refuse to migrate will hate strangers. On top of this, Earth people have a certain way of doing things. Combustion, exhaust, pollution. We know for a fact that to bring this type of technology to Ginen is to bring poison to the land. This is why the chief is considering war against Earth.

"The Golden Dawn is a meeting of masters; a gathering of wise people from all five of the worlds. It was called by Ginen's Chief of Ooni himself. The masters can be sages, oracles, prophets, hungans, mambos, seers, chiefs, chieftesses, sorcerers, witches, wizards, shamans, witch doctors, priestesses, or living books. The last Golden Dawn Meeting was over two hundred years ago when there was a serious conflict between the worlds of Lif and Agonia. Ancient history."

"So it's a little like the United Nations from the early twenty-first century?" Ejii asked. "Except on a grander scale?"

"Yes, Ejii, just like that," Jaa said.

"What's the United Nations?" Dikéogu asked, yawning.

"It was a group with representatives from all over the world that helped in keeping peace and maintaining relationships between countries," Ejii said.

"It fought hard to prevent the nuclear war and failed," Jaa said. "We will not."

Ejii remembered Jaa's conversation with her mother that

night, "I'll cleave that man's head in half!" Jaa had wildly said. Now Ejii understood. Jaa meant to turn a meeting of peace into one of assassination. She looked behind them at Gambo. He'd been quiet. He wasn't listening. He was looking at the sky as he hummed to himself.

"Tell us about Ginen," Dikéogu said. "I don't really know anything about it. I didn't even think the place was real."

"Ginen is a planet, like Earth," Buji said. "But it's bigger. We are going to the Great City, which is inside the Ooni Kingdom, a four hundred mile stretch of human civilization. It is the only place in Ginen where human beings reside in large numbers. There may be a human family here and there outside Ooni, but as far as we know, all large groups like villages, towns, and cities are in Ooni. Most are close to the Great City."

"So there are no places except that?" Ejii asked.

"No *human* places," Buji said. "But there are other types of cities out there. Ginen is full of all kinds of intelligent peoples. But human beings are definitely the best at cultivating complex structures and marrying them with technology. Now, you'll notice when we get there, that the people look like us: dark-skinned, thick lips, and wide noses; they look like black Africans and their cultures are similar, too."

"Why? And why no other kinds of people?" Ejii asked.

"They're the way they are because they chose not to explore the rest of Ginen," Buji said. "On Earth, the first humans left Africa and explored other places. Earth people have explorers' blood. The different environments and demands gave them different outside features, ways of thinking, cultures. So there were some with blue eyes, others with brown eyes, dark skin, light skin, woolly hair and silky hair, big noses, thin noses, brawny bodies, sinewy bodies. Africans resemble Ooni people because, according to Ginen history, long ago many people migrated from Ginen to Earth through openings that led to parts of Africa. No one knows which exact parts."

"Oh," Ejii said. ". . . Really?"

"So what's the *rest* of Ginen like?" Dikéogu asked. "Are there airplanes? Cars?"

"In Ginen, plants, trees, and bushes rule, not humans. The Ooni Kingdom is close to a million years old. We have ourselves. Why go elsewhere?"

"Why not?" Dikéogu grumbled. Ejii elbowed him in the ribs.

"There have been a few human explorers that have seen most of Ginen. These people have been windseekers," he said.

"Flying people," Ejii said with a grin.

"Yes. Because windseekers can fly, they have an insatiable urge to travel. Certain abilities beg for travel," he said, looking from Ejii to Dikéogu. "A man named Sunrise is the most-known living explorer. We're hoping he'll be at the meeting."

"Are you from there or something?" Dikéogu asked Buji. Ejii was wondering the same thing because of the way Buji referred to himself as one from Ginen, not Earth.

"Yes," he said. "I'm one of the Northeastern people; the people that live on the northeast side of the Ooni Palace. My people specialize in botany and architecture." Ejii looked at his green bracelets. So they *were* what she suspected: plants. How far from home he must have felt with his wife and co-husband in the Sahara?

Suddenly there was the sound of hooves pounding on the soft sand. Jaa turned and met Ejii's eyes and in that moment, Ejii felt them connect. Ejii's mind was immediately filled with images of when Jaa cut down her father. *The sound of camel hooves as they leaped onto the stage.* The images shifted. *Hooves pounding sand. Jingling bells. Screams. Male voices shouting. Gunfire.* Ejii dragged her eyes from Jaa's, and her head whipped backward as if Jaa had literally thrown Ejii from her past back to Ejii's present.

Then Ejii saw them. Men, dressed in skintight blue pants and blue shirts, with pink skin, like unripe cactus candy. White men dressed in Western attire; their pants were called jeans. They were coming over the sand dunes on horses. They had torches and guns and they shot several rounds. The last shot made Onion jump and roar.

"Easy, easy!" Ejii said, as she and Dikéogu fought to stay on.

Several of the men fell off their horses, wounded. Bullets no longer obeyed their masters. Everyone knew that. Ejii wondered why these men didn't. Several of the horses tumbled down the sand dune with their riders. These men don't know how to ride in the desert, either, Ejii thought. "Kill them!" one of them shouted.

"Onion, kneel," Jaa said. She paused, looking at Onion. "Ejii and Dikéogu, stay with Onion. These men are lost and confused. They'll kill you first, and feel guilty later."

"I'll keep them safe," Onion said to Jaa.

Ejii looked at Jaa and saw that her face had changed. She flinched when Jaa glanced at her. Jaa's eyes were wild, her nostrils flared; this was the Jaa from the moment of her father's death. Buji and Gambo were already riding their camels fast toward the men who were now trying to flee. More shots rang out and more of the men were felled by wildly zigzagging bullets. A bullet zinged by not far from Ejii, sending up a small puff of sand a few feet away. She understood some of what the strange men were shouting. She'd learned the English language during her obsession with the United States years ago.

Jaa turned her camel and was gone before Ejii could think of anything to say. Ejii huddled beside Onion as she watched Jaa run toward the wild men with her green sword held high. Jaa took on two men who'd brought out knives, and both men went tumbling from their horses. With each swipe of Jaa's green blade, Ejii's world went metallic and she felt a terrible sting and oozing nausea. It was a sensation Ejii had experienced before, when Jaa had beheaded her father. She gagged and held her belly.

Another man tried to use his gun as a blunt weapon against Gambo. He ducked, and with a swipe of his sword, the man went limp, falling off his horse. Suddenly, Jaa and Buji turned their camels and started back. They'd left Gambo surrounded by nine men brandishing axes, knives, and clubs with nails.

"Oh!" Ejii moaned. "This can't be!"

"What's going on?!" Dikéogu shouted. He couldn't see much in the moonlight.

"They've sacrificed him!" Ejii said. "Jaa and Buji left Gambo and are coming back to us!"

Gambo remained still as his camel first bent his front legs, then his back legs, to sit in a submissive position. Gambo climbed off. Ejii stared in horror, unable to avert her eyes. As the men approached, Gambo's face was calm and he looked down. When the men were only a few feet away, he looked up and then shot into the sky.

"Wha . . . ?" Ejii whispered. Then she noticed that Jaa and Buji had dropped to the ground about a quarter of a mile away. Ejii pulled Dikéogu down just in time. The powerful, sand-filled wind blasted over them. She grabbed Dikéogu's arm and linked it with hers and they held on to Onion for dear life. All around her, she could hear Gambo singing in the hiss of the windblown sand. When the sand settled, all the men were scattered about. Only some of them moaned or moved limbs. Many bled. Above, the stars and moon shined as if nothing had happened. Ejii could see Kola circling high in the sky.

"Gambo," Jaa called. She was standing up and looking up. Buji stood beside her, his arm around her waist. "Gambo, return to us, *kwo*," she called again. Then she laughed. Her voice sounded strange in the quietness of the desert. Ejii dug herself out of the sand and got up on shaky legs. She helped Dikéogu up.

"Kola," Dikéogu said, looking around. "The wind got Kola!"

"She's okay," Ejii said "I saw her, and she knows we're here."

"You sure it was her?" he said. "Don't say things just to . . ."

"I saw her," Ejii said, her voice shaky. "Trust me."

Dikéogu squinted trying to see Ejii's face more clearly. He brought out his flashlight and flicked it on her. "You okay?" he asked after a moment.

"Yeah."

"You have survived," Onion said, trying to get up. His legs buckled and he plopped back down.

"Onion?" Ejii said. "What's the . . ." Then she saw the wet hole in his hide. Then another. And then another. All three bled copiously. "How . . . Onion!"

"Ah, ah! He's been shot!" Dikéogu exclaimed grabbing his hair, his eyes wide. He took off toward Jaa and Buji, shouting for them to come.

"Oooh," Onion moaned, resting his head on the ground.

Ejii scooped up sand and started frantically packing it into the wounds. "I'm sorry, Onion," Ejii said, breathlessly. "I'm sorry. I'm sorry!"

"Oh, Ejii," Onion mumbled. "I die today. . . ." then his large body stopped breathing. She dropped the sand in her hands and ran to his head. His tongue had rolled out of his mouth and his eyes were closed. For a moment, Ejii thought, at least he has the luxury of dying with closed eyes. Then she fell to her knees and just stared at him.

"Get her away from him," she heard Jaa shout. "That's the type of thing that will kill her."

Strong hands pulled her back. "No!" she screamed, tearing her arms away from Gambo and Buji, glaring at them with such rage that they stepped away from her. She crumbled to the sand, pressing her forehead to its coolness, Onion's body feet away.

"Ejii," Jaa said softly. "I'm sorry."

Ejii's brain was in a muddle, but somehow she understood that if she stayed near Onion's body, she'd fall into it, falling into death. Jaa had just saved her life. Ejii snatched Dikéogu's flashlight from his hand and stalked away. She was glad when no one tried to stop her; she'd have hit whoever it was over the head with the flashlight. There was sand in her mouth and a grain of sand stung her left eye. Her long blue dress was heavy with sand and her veil had been blown off. She was weak but despair, rage, and nausea made her keep walking. She heard Dikéogu call her but she ignored him.

She walked straight to the closest man. He sat in the sand next to his dead horse. He looked confused but otherwise fine. He had thin lips, hair that was silky like the mane of a horse, and silver eyes like coins. Ejii was momentarily distracted by his eyes. But they were not like hers. They were just a strange color. She flicked on the flashlight and shined it in her face so that he could see her eyes. The man looked horrified.

"What is this place?" he asked.

She understood this but she didn't answer. She looked into his silver eyes some more. Let him see what he must, she thought. A rush of rage flew through her and she kicked him in the side as hard as she could. He moaned with pain. She kicked him again.

"You in desert!" she screamed in her best English. The sound of his groans and the feel of her sandled foot smacking into him was satisfying. She kicked him again. "Why? Why you kill? He my friend! *My mother's camel!* He talk and was sweet, sweet beast! Never hurt anyone!" she stumbled over her English. "We did not try hurt you!"

More sweat dribbled from the man's brow, mixing with the sand that stuck there. Ejii understood most of what he said next but there were gaps. "I don't know," he said, wiping his face. "I'm sorry. We don't know how we got here, we've been— for weeks. Where are we? This place is—It's either kill or be killed."

"We not try kill you!" Ejii shouted. She kicked him again.

This man spoke United States English. It was the only English she knew. Somehow he had ended up here from America. This is because of the great merge, she thought. Not only were the boundaries between other worlds gone, but space that made places far away and close must have also been scrambled. And because these men didn't understand what happened, they decided to kill whomever they encountered!

Ejii kicked sand at the man with the coin eyes and then walked away, every curse word she'd ever heard in her life flying through her mind in multiple languages. This type of thing had to be happening all over. When she got back, she slapped the flashlight into Dikéogu hands. By this time, Gambo had returned from the sky.

It took them hours to dig a grave for Onion. Jaa wouldn't allow Ejii to get close to Onion's body, not even when they put him in the hole. None of them talked as they walked alongside their camels for several miles, leaving Onion's grave and the dead and confused men behind. Then Jaa said that they should stop for an hour.

Ejii walked a half mile away, saying she wanted to be alone. She sat down in the sand and cried. All she could think about was Onion's deep, peaceful voice and his furry hide and the fact that, like her, he was a product of the Great Change and deserved to see a settled world. And he came to protect me, she thought. I could have at least protected him, too. She didn't regret kicking the man at all. She was pulled out of her sorrow when something dropped in front of her. She looked up and couldn't help but smile when she saw the red mango. She picked it up.

"Thank you," Ejii said, her voice hoarse. Kola clicked her beak and flew away.

"She's quite intuitive," Jaa said, coming up from behind Ejii.

Ejii looked up at her and then started peeling her mango. Jaa sat down in the sand next to her. "If it makes you feel better, I'm very sorry about what happened," Jaa said.

"It doesn't," Ejii mumbled, taking a bite into her mango. The mango was sweet. Her mother had always said that mangos had healing powers.

"Fine," Jaa said. She put her hand on Ejii's shoulder. "But you'll have to find a way to stay with us. Don't go losing yourself."

Ejii wasn't in the mood for a lecture from Jaa. She didn't want words.

"I'll leave you with your thoughts then," Jaa said getting up and walking away.

Ejii watched her leave and then gnawed on the peel of her mango. She sucked on the seed and then held it before her. It was the size of her hand, oval-shaped and flat. She stared hard at it, imagining that she held its eyes with her own. She could almost feel the warmth of potential. There was a tiny shadow of life inside. She could perfectly see the tall tree it could become. "Come on then," she whispered to it. She softly gasped as the seed shook a little in her hand, and the bottom of it split just a tiny bit. Ejii turned it over. A light-green sprout had pushed through an opening in the seed.

She planted the mango seed. Then she brought the egg stone from her pocket and held it up. She sat very still and listened. She heard nothing and felt no warmth. She put it back in her pocket. Then she pressed her head to the ground and said a prayer of thanks to Allah. When she stood up, though her eyes stung and a little more blood dribbled from her nose and her head ached, she was ready to move on. And when she returned to her friends, they had the camels ready. Buji would have his own camel, Jaa and Gambo would ride together, and Ejii and Dikéogu would ride the third camel.

✢   ✢   ✢

Ejii saw it before everyone else did but she didn't say a word about it. She wanted to deal with her fear alone. She shut her eyes and calmed herself. The shadows remained silent. If I'm not good enough to live, so be it, she thought. At least I'll have faced what I was meant to face. They stopped when they came to it. Aside from the section of dense forest before them, all around was desert. Kola flew down and perched on the handle of Ejii's camel saddle.

"Pay close attention," Buji said. He moved past Gambo to take the lead.

"Dikéogu," Ejii said, elbowing him. "Wake up! We're here."

"Huh?" he said, groggily.

"Something's about to happen," Ejii said.

"Something's watching us," he suddenly said, straightening up. "Is Kola . . . ?"

"She's right here," Ejii said, softly touching Kola's head. For a moment she expected to hear Onion say something like "More trouble."

They stopped. The stretch of forest began yards away. It was dense, almost solid leaves, trees, bushes, stems, and flowers. It gave off a warm and thick smell. Ejii could see the opening of a path to the right, a tunnel. Gambo, Jaa, and Buji got off their camels, and Ejii and Dikéogu did the same. Ejii's nerves were screaming with anticipation. She grabbed Dikéogu's arm before he could flee, as she knew he was about to.

"Show yourself," Jaa commanded. She laughed after a moment. "Come now. Show yourself, *kwo*. Can't you make a little time for a few travelers?"

"Sir," Dikéogu asked, stepping up to Gambo. Ejii refused to let go of his arm, so Dikéogu pulled her along with him. "Who is she calling?"

"Shhh," Gambo said, watching Jaa.

"She calls the guardian," Buji said. "We need his permission to enter Ginen."

"But aren't there people coming and going from Ginen all the time now?" Dikéogu asked. "Especially since the great merge? Why can't we just sneak in?"

"He can be in many places at once," Buji said.

"Oh," Dikéogu said. He suddenly turned to Ejii. "Let go of my arm!"

"You'll run," Ejii said. "It's not safe to get lost out here."

"How do you know? Did you ask your damn shadow conspirators?"

"No!" she said, flushed with anger. "I wouldn't *do* that to you. I *can't* talk to them like that anymore anyway!"

"Then you don't *know* what I'll do," Dikéogu said, pulling harder at his arm. He was stronger than Ejii and she was losing her grip.

Gambo and Buji looked on, amused. Jaa was still calling for the guardian. A wind shook the trees and blew dust about, and Ejii and Dikéogu forgot about their squabble.

"Red," the voice said. "What do you want?"

Only Jaa laughed. Dikéogu's eyes were wide as he tried to locate the source of the voice; it sounded as if it were coming from everywhere.

"Not him again!" Ejii groaned.

"You know where we're going," Jaa said. "Let us pass."

"These days, everyone is on their way to somewhere," the voice said.

They all turned around. The moonlight made his light-blue robes glow. He walked with his hands behind his back. Dikéogu yelped and Ejii held his arm tighter.

"Can you believe such stupidity?" the Desert Magician asked. "Who goes to a wholly foreign, unfamiliar, alien place? And they wonder why the people of Ginen want to go to war. Hee hee hee!"

He carried a gnarled piece of pointed wood in his left hand and his dagger in the right. Because his long locks draped his face, Ejii couldn't quite see his eyes. She didn't want to. Dikéogu leaned close to her ear. "Can you . . . read anything?" he whispered.

She shook her head. She wasn't even going to try.

"Things just aren't the same, are they, cat eyes?" the magician asked. He stabbed his gnarled staff of wood into the sand and stamped his foot. A pool of water bubbled up. He motioned for the camels to come and drink, and the camels happily obeyed.

"Will you be there, Magician?" Jaa asked.

"I'll be where I'll be, when I go where I go," the magician replied, stepping around the camels. "The doors are open, the lion may sleep tonight but the lioness rears her head; there's more more more. Did you know that in the United States, well what *used* to be the United States, there are riots? What would you do if you were trying to rebuild your fallen cities and suddenly you found a forest in your backyard with people who speak a language you've never heard of but understand? You'd riot! Ha!

"Now, it's about what do you do," the magician said. "But, I'm just a deity. It's not my business, unless I decide to make it so. But you may see me there, a face in the trees, a wall on the fly, an ant in your soup, a scarab beetle on your shoulder."

"Will you let us through then?" Buji asked.

The Desert Magician paused and then said, "No."

"Ah, ah, what is wrong with you?!" Dikéogu exclaimed.

"Dikéogu, be quiet," Gambo said.

"No!" Dikéogu shouted. He snatched his arm from Ejii and strode toward the magician. He reached into his pocket and brought out the dagger he'd bought in Agadez. From above came the rumble of thunder, the sky suddenly heavy with rushing clouds.

"What are you doing?" Ejii exclaimed.

The Desert Magician seemed to wait for Dikéogu.

"Ejii, stay where you are," Jaa said.

Dikéogu stopped in front of the magician, his dagger held before him like a talisman. "You . . ." Then he froze, speechless. When the Desert Magician pulled aside his curtain of hair, Ejii started running forward. Buji grabbed her before she could get closer.

"No!" she screamed. "Let me go!"

A white light was streaming from where the magician's face should have been, flooding Dikéogu's face. Then he dropped his locks and the light went out and a tendril of lightning flashed from the sky, hitting Dikéogu. He stumbled back and sat down hard on the ground, still holding the dagger. Its blade had melted to the handle. The Desert Magician stood there laughing gleefully as Buji let go of Ejii. She ran to Dikéogu.

"Dikéogu?" Ejii said, falling to her knees next to him. She was very aware of the magician's proximity, but she focused on Dikéogu.

"The man I bought my dagger from said that it was the only thing that could challenge the Ginen guardian," Dikéogu said, dazed. "The guardian's tools are his water-finding staff and his juju dagger, the man said. It was all camelshit. . . ." He trailed off.

This made the Desert Magician laugh even harder.

"What'd you do to him?" Ejii shouted. She glimpsed the magician's face behind his hair but she couldn't see it clearly. All that she saw were shades of light and dark.

"Only what he deserved," the magician said. He looked past Ejii and Dikéogu. "Jaa, be thankful that you thought to bring this idiot. He has a certain panache that appeals to me. I can imagine that he'll cause plenty of trouble in Ginen. Because of him, I'll let you all in. Ginen is open to you, make sure you're open to *it*."

He turned and walked into the desert, his hands behind his back. "Buji, say hello to your family for me," he said over his shoulder.

"Come on," Ejii said, helping Dikéogu up. He smelled like smoke. "You okay?"

He nodded, throwing the melted dagger away. They climbed onto their camel and Dikéogu leaned on Ejii's back, exhausted.

Buji led the way and then Ejii and Dikéogu, Jaa, and Gambo at the rear. They had started on a path surrounded by trees and the moon's light was blocked. Ejii looked ahead and saw the path tunneled ahead for about two miles, then it turned. She felt a change in the air and started to sweat. Dikéogu sat up straighter, putting his arms around her waist.

"I won't let you fall off," he said.

You can hardly stay on yourself, Ejii thought.

"Ejii?" Jaa said. "How do you feel?"

"I . . . I'm okay," Ejii said.

But she wasn't. As Dikéogu held her, she shut her eyes. They'd begun to sting and she could feel her focus going haywire again. Even behind her eyes, she saw the tiny veins in her eyelids, then the blood cells, then the universe of molecules in the cells. If her eyes focused any closer, she was sure she'd go mad. She felt her ears pop and then warmth as blood oozed from them. Then it was like the air was squeezing her head.

"Ejii?" she heard Dikéogu say into her ear. His voice sounded tinny and far away. "Lean forward, Ejii. Against the camel's back. She's a peaceful beast."

The moment Ejii did so, it was like she became the wind and fell right through the camel. *Fresh hay, camel dung, contentment. The joy of the walk, the excitement of being in a new place, the taste of water was sweet every time. Water was life. She passed through the camel who called herself Sandapha, and when the winds of Ginen caught Ejii, they spiraled her into the sky where she became one with many. She spread over the lush world of trees, root, stems, flowers, leaves, soil. A land that breathed through its skin. Where there were soily worlds underneath the soil. Moisture, trapped heat, rot, friction, life, death.* See, *a voice said. And Ejii saw. She saw that she had died.*

✛ ✛ ✛

They immediately stopped and spread Ejii's blanket on the forest floor. They laid her out on it. Her body was still, her nose, ears, mouth, and eyes bleeding small rivers of blood. Her shadow-speaker eyes wide open. Gambo knelt over Ejii, his head to her chest, her wrist in his hand. Dikéogu was pressing his hands to the top of his head as he sniffed back tears. "No, no, no, no, no, no," he whispered.

Buji was collecting sticks to build a fire. He needed something to do with himself. Her body is limp and cooling, he thought methodically. He always grew numb and practical in times of crisis and this had served him well during the many battles he'd fought at Jaa's side. To stop here on the border is very dangerous he thought; the wildest creatures live in this in-between place. A fire is of the utmost importance. Heat and light.

But even as he busied himself and focused his mind on what had to be done and why, he knew that Ejii was dead. And though he'd seen many die—the guilty, the innocent, the young, the old, the potential, the waste—he felt deep in his heart that Ejii's death was a particularly terrible loss. The girl had to live for all to be well. For a moment, he resented Jaa for bringing Ejii along. But then he remembered that it was as much his mistake as Jaa's. This is where it really begins to fall apart, he thought with a shiver.

Jaa was pacing, grumbling to herself. Buji was building a fire but that would not bring Ejii back. Dikéogu, Ejii's beloved companion, was at Ejii's side but that would not help. Jaa was disgusted with herself. She'd been so sure about Ejii and when she was sure, she was *always* right. Until now. Guilt and the sting of failure are a terrible combination.

She stopped and stared at Gambo. He looked up at her and shook his head. No pulse, no heartbeat, no life. Jaa cursed loudly, strode over, and dropped to her knees next to Ejii. "Get away from her!" she shouted at Gambo and Dikéogu. She shoved Dikéogu and he fell to the side. He righted himself, glaring at Jaa but staying where he was, at Ejii's side. Jaa looked at Gambo. "Especially you! Don't touch her, Aejej!"

Gambo was about to protest but instead got up. Jaa felt Ejii's face. It was so cool. "Ejii," she said, lightly slapping the side of her face. Then she began to shake her. "Ejii!"

Silence. Jaa threw her head back and screamed a horrible scream that echoed through the forest, sending birds and bats into the air and other creatures running, hopping, scrambling, and digging. A large red flower with hard, red oval petals and a red stem dropped next to Ejii. Jaa picked it up and threw it into the forest. Then she gathered Ejii in her arms and wept. More minutes passed.

Buji got the fire going and Dikéogu saw a thousand shadows retreat from its light. He looked at Ejii's face, into her eyes. What he saw in them moved him as much as it did when she was alive. He closed his eyes. When he opened them, Jaa was glaring at him.

"If you do any such thing, I'll kill you right here," she growled. "Don't you dare take it."

There wasn't an ounce of bravado in her words. But Dikéogu was numb, and so when he reached into Ejii's pocket and took out the egg stone, though his body shrieked with fear, his mind was resigned to the idea that he would die as Ejii's father had, by Jaa's sword. His life was worth sacrificing in order to finish what Ejii had started.

When Jaa made to move, Gambo pressed his hand hard on her shoulder. "Get a hold of yourself, woman," Gambo said, his voice hard.

Dikéogu grasped the egg stone and pressed it to his chest with both hands. He sighed, feeling faint.

✚　　✚　　✚

They love me, Ejii thought. And she loved them. Life was a good place. But still, she turned away. Toward the voice that called to her.

Ejii was no longer herself, she was part of something greater. With relief, she shed her individuality. She was free. Then she joined The Whole, connecting with billions of other winds, waters, lands, and spaces. The Whole was undying, young, old, ancient, constant. One great sigh of love, existence, and purpose. It sang the loveliest, longest song and everywhere that the song touched, thrived or shriveled up, continuing the cycle of life and death and joining The Whole.

When The Whole tore Ejii from its breast, Ejii would have screamed if she had a mouth. For the first time since they'd left her, the shadows spoke to her. Loud and clear and true. No games, no need to concentrate or be still. No need for lessons.

You understand now?

Yes, she said.

Then you're ready.

I am, she said.

Everything had a purpose. Her father. Onion. They'd had a purpose and now they laughed and played within The Whole. Every leaf that the wind blew. Every stone that was tumbled down a hill. Every movement, every lack of movement. It was all one great dance to a music she would never understand. She felt herself thrown and she tumbled into the Ginen sky, downward, toward the treetops. She slammed into the ground and fell through it. Then she felt hands, claws, tendrils, mandibles pulling her up. Up, up, through the rich fertile soil. Into her body.

Warmth surrounded her. Then pain. Her eyes focused but all she could see were blood-tinged, blurred images. She blinked to moisten them. Everything became crystal clear. In the distance she could hear its song, but it was receding. Dikéogu's face was wet with tears. He knelt over her. A fire burned a few feet away. Jaa stood behind him, her back turned. Gambo and Buji were nearby talking quietly.

"Ejii?" Dikéogu whispered, his eyes widening. He scrambled away from her as if he were seeing a ghost. "Ejii?!"

"In the flesh," she said, smiling weakly.

Jaa turned around and Buji and Gambo came running over. And for a moment, they all stood over her, shocked into silence. Then Jaa slowly knelt beside Ejii. "Is this you or some darker juju?" Jaa asked.

"It's me," she said tiredly.

"What is your full name?" Gambo asked.

"Ejimafor Ugabe, daughter of the councilwoman Nkolika and a madman who called himself the Chief of Kwàmfà."

She heard Dikéogu sigh with relief. He took her hand and put the egg stone into it. "This belongs to you," he said.

"You died, Ejii," Jaa said. "You've been gone for a half hour."

"I know."

She knew so much now. She had passed the shadow speaker's greatest test, she now understood. Did all shadow speakers have to die when they embarked on their travels? The sanddune cats had said they'd come across many shadow speakers' bodies in the desert. Were those the bodies of those who did not pass? Oh, she did not wish such a test for her friends, Arif and Sammy. Mazi Godwin certainly must have passed this test, for he had traveled all the way from the United States.

Loud noises in the trees forced them to quickly put out the fire and mount their camels. Though her body ached and her nose still dribbled blood, Ejii otherwise felt fine. They continued on their way.

"Any minute we will cross completely into Ginen," Buji said to Ejii and Dikéogu in a soft comforting voice as their camels walked. "Do you feel okay? Ejii?"

Ejii nodded.

"Dikéogu?"

"I guess," he mumbled, his arms clasped too tightly around Ejii's waist.

Minutes later Buji said, "Ejii, tell me the first thing that comes to your mind."

She thought about it for a moment.

"Don't hesitate," Buji said. "Just speak. It's important."

On both sides of them was dense forest. Palm trees that grew too high, fat trees that Ejii had never seen before. Something was moving in the bushes nearby. "Uh," Ejii said. "I'm so hungry right now. I could eat even the stalest dates."

"Yeah, I'd even eat choco . . ." Dikéogu stopped. Ejii frowned, she heard it too.

"Keep talking," Buji said. Ejii could hear Jaa and Gambo chuckle.

"Pepper soup with goat . . ." She trailed off. "What is happening? Why is my voice . . . why do we sound like this?"

"Can you hear me, Ejii?" Dikéogu said.

She could, but the words that came from his mouth weren't Hausa or Igbo. They were both speaking and understanding a language that Ejii had never heard before.

"It happens when you pass into Ginen," Buji said. "You're speaking Ooni. No matter what language you speak, now that you're in Ginen, Ooni is what comes out."

"You'll get used to it," Jaa said. "Soon you won't even notice it."

They walked for a half hour. Ejii was glad for the monotony. This was the forest she'd seen when she joined with what she could only call Allah. She was born in the desert and now she was right in the middle of the desert's opposite. She could smell the ground, one that was made of black, rich, thick dirt, not sand. Flowers, moss, mold, and moisture. It must have just rained because she could hear water dropping and trickling, the click and peep and drone of insects, and the screeches, howls, and hoots of larger beasts. There must have also been multiplying scarabs about, rolling their balls of dung.

"Never seen trees so tall," Dikéogu whispered. "Look at that one! Square leaves."

"Something's following us," Ejii said. She was able to catch only glimpses of whatever they were. She looked into the forest and tried to read what she could. Instead, she sensed a vastness so enormous and potent that she quickly pulled her mind in.

"Bush cows," Gambo said. "Little thieves. If we'd set up camp, those rodents would steal our food as we slept. Once they see that we aren't stopping, they'll go away."

Buji stopped, holding a hand up, "Wait." Before him, a car zoomed by on the road that Ejii had not noticed. At least she thought it was a car. Another zoomed by. This one Ejii got a look at. It *was* a car; this one flat, blue, and very quiet. She looked more closely at the road. It wasn't paved like some of the roads in Agadez. It was flat, packed dirt.

"Earth cars are *tin cans* compared to Ginen cars," Buji said. "Their engines produce the electricity they run on. They're flatter and faster. Unfortunately, they drive so fast that the driver barely ever sees pedestrians or people on camel or horse-back."

"Allah is great," Dikéogu whispered. Ejii smiled, thinking, Yes, Allah is great.

✛

STRANGERS IN
A STRANGE LAND

'M actually here, Ejii thought. I'm alive and I'm here.

If her mother had a magic quartz shard and could see Ejii right at this moment, Ejii wondered what her mother would think. She'd probably laugh and say, "Look at this girl. My child is crazy, *kwo*!" Though Ejii couldn't see much more than forest, road, zooming cars, and snatches of sky, this place *felt* very different. The air smelled sweet and clean. Buji said the cars produced clean flower-scented air instead of exhaust. And sure enough, each time a car zoomed by, there was a burst of fresh air. The most peculiar thing was that Ejii herself felt like a slightly different person here. Older and wiser.

She turned around to say something to Dikéogu and gasped. "Dikéogu?" she said. "Your tattoo!"

"What?" he said, touching the bridge of his nose. "What about it?"

"It's not blue anymore. And the line is crooked now, like . . . a bolt of lightning."

"Huh?" he said pressing his forehead. "Well, what color is it?"

"The line's red and the dots on the sides of it are . . . white."

"The Desert Magician must have done it." Buji said from the front. "You're now officially a child of Shango."

"Who's Shango?" Dikéogu asked. "What's that stupid magician done to me?"

Gambo's booming voice came from behind them, making Ejii jump. "They call him a god, but to me he is thunder and lightning. His colors are red and white. You know when he's coming. There's noise and light."

"So why—"

"Sometimes, it's disrespectful to ask questions," Gambo curtly said. He paused and said, "I suspect the Desert Magician did more to you than change the marking on your face."

"How does it look, Ejii?" Dikéogu worriedly asked.

"It looks like now you can fight anything and win," Ejii said. It was true. Dikéogu's tattoo reminded her of war paint.

"Kola?" he said to the owl. "Well?"

The owl hooted and then flew from her perch in front of Ejii, softly landing on Dikéogu's shoulder. She leaned her feathery head against Dikéogu's cheek and Dikéogu puffed his chest with pride. Kola left his shoulder and launched into the air.

"Make sure you can find us!" Dikéogu called as the bird rose into the sky.

"I don't think you have to worry," Ejii said.

"She doesn't know this place," Dikéogu said.

"How do you know?" Ejii asked.

They passed several roads that branched off to small villages. Through the trees, Ejii could see the homes and buildings. She squinted. Was she seeing correctly? The houses were so oddly shaped. Some of them were actually round.

As they walked up a steep hill Jaa, Buji, and Gambo moved in front of Ejii and Dikéogu to talk. "Only to avoid trouble," Jaa was saying to Buji. Ejii and Dikéogu strained to hear. "Personally I feel—"

"We know how you feel, Wife," Gambo said.

"Gambo, let her finish," Buji said.

Jaa shrugged. "I've said how I feel."

"It's tradition," Buji said. "My mother still expects you to act like a wife."

"It's as much my house as both of yours," Jaa said.

"It's just courtesy," Buji said.

"Should I smile, too, as I bow to your father?" Jaa asked, annoyed.

"It will help," Buji said.

"I won't," she said.

"Just behave," Buji said.

"In my own house, I do what I want," Jaa snapped annoyed.

"Must we always have this conversation?" Buji said.

"After what happened before? Yes," Gambo said.

They reached the top of the hill and the view pushed away all Ejii's question about their conversation. She was reminded of an old photo she found on the Net during her infatuation with the United States. The photo of the pre–Great Change

New York City skyline before the two tall towers were destroyed by airplanes. She'd always marveled at how huge those two towers were, and she never thought she'd see anything close to that great city. But what she was looking at surpassed New York City by a thousand times! Her time with Allah had not shown her this part of Ginen.

"It's like . . . the Cross River rain forest mixed with the glowing buildings of Tokyo," Dikéogu said.

"Please, can we stop for a moment?" Ejii called to Buji, Gambo, and Jaa.

"Of course," Buji said. "One's first sight of Ile-Ife should always be given a moment."

"Is that what it's called?" Dikéogu said.

"Or you can call it the Great City, or just plain Ife," Buji said.

"But Ile-Ife is a city in Nigeria."

"No, that's the name of a *town* there," Jaa said. "*This* is a city. The real thing."

The skyline glowed as if the buildings themselves were made of a luminous material. The skyscrapers were amazingly high. People and cars moved about in the streets below. Trees and bushes and plants grew between the buildings. Thick green-brown vines linked every building like veins and arteries. There were wide screens on the sides of buildings that flashed undulating designs.

The people *did* look West African, though their styles of dress were wholly unfamiliar to her. She saw a woman wearing a heavy-looking dress made of tiny beads, a man with vine bracelets like Buji's, and a woman wearing a dress that flashed with blue fist-size mirrors. Lastly, she focused on the down-town area. She looked at the tallest tower and zoomed her eyes in as much as possible. When she saw the cellular makeup of the building, her suspicions were aroused. "They're all plants!" she said.

"The tallest one is the Ooni Palace," Buji said. "That's where the meeting will be. On the top floor. It's the government's center. It's over a thousand years old."

"Do they still . . . grow?" Dikéogu asked.

"Mm-hm," Buji said.

"I see the top," Ejii said. "Oh!" The very top of the Ooni Palace bloomed into a giant soft-looking flower with a blue center and long purple petals.

"The blossom is a digital transmitter for the whole kingdom," Buji said. He cocked his head. "Do you see anything else near the top?"

"White birds—owls but with thicker feathers," Ejii said.

"It's almost a mile into the sky," Buji said. "So it's very cold."

"Lower down I see . . . are those ants? They're white and really, really big!"

"Ogoni ants. They maintain the Ooni Palace," Buji said. "That tribe of ants has been living on and caring for it since it sprouted. Those ants can be deadly if anyone tries to hurt their sacred plant. They've killed more than a few people over the years."

"So there are people in there? In a giant plant?" Dikéogu said.

"Yes. They're sturdier than earth buildings. They may not be as clean but they smell better . . . unless some creature defecates in a corner," Buji said, with chuckle.

"We have to go *in* there?" Dikéogu whispered to Ejii.

"If they let us," Ejii said.

"I hope there's a balcony," he said.

"Are you sure you want to go outside when you're a mile in the sky?" Ejii asked.

"I'll wear a coat," he said.

✛

CHAPTER TWENTY

THE VILLAGE OF THE RED QUEEN AND HER KINGS

T HEY rode well into the Ooni Kingdom, very close to its heart. Jaa, Buji, and Gambo's village was in the downtown part of the city, just before the first plant tower. But Ejii was already overwhelmed before reaching their village. It started when they entered the city boundaries, the more rural part of the Ooni kingdom behind them.

When they'd entered Ginen, they came into what Buji called Northern Ooni. Here, Ejii got her first up-close look at Ginen's people. She was reminded of Agadez because people spoke loudly and laughed freely, restaurants were open for business, goats and hens walked about, and the air smelled of cooking oil and goat droppings.

Nevertheless, here there was no Islam, and that meant no mosques and no people on mats kneeling and praying. There was no Arabic writing on walls, the camels had longer necks and some had black hair, and there was no sand. There were people talking on netphones but the phones weren't made of plastic and wires; they looked like curvy green-and-orange gourds with screens. Ejii had seen a few of these in the Agadez market. The streetlights were large light-producing plants shaped like white trumpets. Ejii wondered if the light in the homes was also a plant by-product. Even a group of men sitting on a porch playing cards had a giant lily lighting their game.

Ejii laughed when she heard the music coming out of shops, restaurants, and from people's porches. Hip-hop. "Buji," she said. "Isn't this music from earth?"

"Earth and Ginen have always exchanged bits of culture. Even before the Great Change. Through secret openings."

"Like in America?"

Buji nodded. "One or two, but most are in the Sahara Desert."

The people of the North wore beautiful flowing dresses and pants and shirts that clicked with tiny mirrors. Some had round mirrors sewn into the hip of their pants, others had them embroidered into the hems of their skirts and cuffs of their shirts. One proud-looking woman had a whole dress made of mirrors.

Ejii tried to ignore the Ginen cars that zoomed around them on the street. Their speed terrified her. Buji said they weren't even made of metal; instead they were made from a tough fiber called hemp. "You crash in a Ginen car and you usually drive away," he said. "They're very safe. That's why a lot of drivers aren't very careful."

There were different types of plants everywhere, between

houses, on top of houses. She even saw a tree that grew through a house's roof. Ejii wondered how the place was kept so tidy. Then there were the people. Since they had entered Ginen, a crowd of people had followed them.

"What'll you do?" a man shouted. "The Golden Dawn is useless as golden urine!"

"They can do nothing," another man answered. "We're all doomed."

"Go back where you came from, and stay there!"

Ejii asked Buji, "How do they know about the meeting? I thought it was secret."

"Secret?" Buji said. "When the Great Change happened, there were demonstrations and protests and riots all over Ooni."

"That was when many found out that Earth existed," Jaa told Ejii, shaking a woman's hand. "It was a shock. Most people thought Earth was a myth."

"Since then, to avoid riots, the chief has kept the people informed," Buji said.

"Please, try your best, Red Queen," a woman said, coming up to Jaa.

"I will," Jaa said. A red flower fell from the sky into the woman's hands.

"We are counting on all of you!" the woman said.

As they moved along, Buji pointed out that the people of the North were distinctively different from his people of the Northeast.

"Ooni's divided along ancient lines of trade and art into five parts," Buji said. "Historically, the Northwesterners are great cooks. The Southwesterners love beads. The people of the Southeast work with metal. Northerners work with mirrors. My people, the Northeasterners are botanists. We cultivated most of this city."

"*Many* built this city, husband," Jaa said. She turned to Ejii and Dikéogu. "One of Ooni's biggest problems is tribalism, when one tribe thinks it's better than other tribes."

Buji rolled his eyes. "It's understood that Ooni is more than its tribal parts."

"Not always," Jaa said.

The people of the North were very proud and always looking at themselves in their mirrors as they followed, talked, walked, and chatted. Most of the time, their comments were aimed at Jaa, Gambo, and Buji. But a few looked at Ejii with suspicion. Someone even made the same sign that people back in Kwàmfà made to ward off the "evil eye," circling a hand over his head and snapping. Apparently shadow speakers also carried a stigma in Ginen. What was odder was the way they treated Dikéogu.

"Sunny day," many said to him. Jaa said this was the traditional greeting similar to saying "Good afternoon" or "Hello." Many children pointed and smiled at Dikéogu, a few girls blew kisses at him and said, "Rain is life." Dikéogu shyly nodded and smiled, not knowing what else to do. Ejii bristled, imagining scaring those girls with her eyes.

"Why do you think they like me so much?" Dikéogu asked.

She shrugged, annoyed. She didn't want kisses blown at her, but she didn't want to be treated like she had some contagious disease either. When they stopped to cross a street an old woman walked up to them. She handed Dikéogu a white flower with a red center. "For you," she said, grinning widely enough to show all her white teeth. "Rain is life."

"Thank you," Dikéogu said, taking it. Ejii rolled her eyes.

"Buji," Dikéogu said, once they were far from the old woman. "What's all this about?"

"Later," he only said. "Keep smiling and saying thank you."

It was obvious when they crossed the border into the Northeast. One moment there were proud, mirrored people; then, what seemed like a moment later, there were quiet, friendly people with plants growing around their wrists. All of them had dirt under their fingernails. These people had more encouraging words than insults. And they must have had things to do because few even followed. Here, the buildings were far more elaborate. There were sweet-smelling flowers growing in complex patterns, graceful multistoried homes, and large buildings that were really farms.

A spiky cactus fence surrounded Jaa and her husbands' village. Jaa said that all the homes within the village were part of the same giant blue plant. When they got to the cactus fence, Buji climbed off his camel, stepped up to the fence, and touched one of the cactuses. As soon as he touched the plant, its thorns retreated into the body, and the cactuses in front of him bent to the side and flattened themselves to the ground.

"They remind me of plants we had in my village," Dikéogu whispered to Ejii. "You touch them and they wither, then they go back to normal a few minutes later."

"I'll bet the cactuses only wither for people who live here," Ejii said.

"Welcome to Osizugbo, our village," Jaa said proudly.

The camels stepped over the flattened cactuses. Once they were over the gate, Jaa touched the cactuses and they came back up. Quickly after that, all the commotion began.

"Ah, ah! He's here, *o*! And he's brought his lovely, crazy wife!"

"Who are these two children? Has it been that long?!"

"Let me look at you three!"

"What were the wastelands like?"

"Did you bring us anything?"

"The girl is a mau girl. And so young!"

There was singing, dancing, hugging. All the people who lived in Jaa and her husband's village had some kind of twisted hair, be it long dreadlocks or short bumpy twists. Ejii and Dikéogu were squeezed by several people.

"Everybody, back off. Let us see our sons and daughter," a short woman with a rough voice said. She was Jaa's height. Behind her a man, also quite small, followed.

"Papa, Mama," Buji said, grinning.

His parents looked him over. "The wastelands have somehow kept you young," his mother said, patting his cheek.

"Not so young. Look at his forehead. Got lines like an ant's trail," his father said.

"I am so glad to see you," Buji said, giving them each a tight hug.

"Gambo!" his mother said, grabbing and hugging him.

"My second son." She planted a kiss on his forehead.

"You look beautiful, Mama Nyambe," Gambo said, kissing her hand.

"Papa Nyambe," Gambo said, giving him the handshake of respect by grasping his hand and snapping fingertips afterward. "It's good to see you."

Mama Nyambe turned to Jaa. "Oh, and here she is!"

Jaa and Buji's mother stood looking at each other for a moment. Then Jaa knelt down and bowed to both Buji's parents. They looked very pleased.

"She's learning," Buji's mother said. Papa Nyambe tapped Jaa on the forehead and Jaa got up.

"Who are these two?" Buji's mother asked.

"This is Ejii Ugabe from Kwàmfà village of Niger, and this is Dikéogu Obidimkpa from Arondizuogu village of Nigeria," Jaa said. "They're our students."

Mama Nyambe stepped up to Ejii, who stood a little taller than she did. Still she looked straight into Ejii's eyes. Mama Nyambe's face was a deep brown, wrinkly, with a small mole on her left cheek and brown eyes with long eyelashes. She smelled of honey. Ejii couldn't help but read her a little, though she was beginning to wonder if it was really "reading" anymore. *At first there was sweetness. Honey. Buji's mother loved honey. She was a honey seller. And her heart was as sweet as her honey.*

"It's g-great to meet you," Ejii said. She smiled broader than she wanted to as she tried to play off the slight dizziness in her mind.

"Sunny day. Welcome, mau girl," Mama Nyambe said,

holding Ejii's hand. She put an arm around Ejii, holding her up. She laughed and shook her head. "Nosy girl." Then she took Dikéogu's hand and said, "Welcome, rain boy."

"Yes, welcome. Now, come in, all of you," Buji's father said.

Ejii couldn't stop looking at the walls. They were light green and soft looking, like padding. Inside was larger than Ejii thought. There were three stories, reachable by an uneven staircase. There were red tapestries, red floor rugs, red wooden masks, and red statues. There were ferns with red flowers growing in every corner, their green leaves free of dusty spores. And there were all sorts of red flowers growing through the tables. The lights grew on long stems and tilted their glowing centers to shine pink light into the room. But it was the wall that Ejii was most interested in.

As Buji sighed with happiness, glad to be home, Jaa and Buji's mother discussed cooking dinner, Gambo and Buji's father talked about going to the late-night market, and Dikéogu looked at a bowl-like plant growing on the banister. Ejii walked over to touch the wall. She still couldn't believe that the house was a plant. Jaa said she'd personally planted it years ago.

"Right now, there should be a room about the size of a closet next to the master bedroom," Jaa had said. "In a few years it'll be another two rooms."

Aside from it being a plant, there were all sorts of wild-life inside it. Ejii saw large, bright blue spiders, transparent-skinned geckos, lizards with long metallic-looking nails, and all sorts of beetles; she even saw a tiny red-orange monkey clinging to the ceiling; it ran off the moment she stepped toward it. Mama Nyambe said that having creatures in the house was good. In an Ooni house, one was never more than a foot away from some creature.

"Nothing will bother you here if you don't bother it," she'd said. "But don't be surprised if something decides that you are interesting to watch, bathe with, or even spend the night with." She smiled. "And watch where you step. We sweep up every morning and evening but creatures must void themselves whenever they must."

Ejii looked more closely at the plant wall. It was so green. She could see the individual green bits inside each cell. Chloroplasts, she thought, remembering what she'd learned about plant cells in school. They contained chlorophyll. She pressed her finger against the wall. It was tough but not like wood or concrete. It felt alive.

"It closed when I touched it!" Dikéogu said from the stairs. "And did you see the size of that gecko that just ran up the wall? What the hell else lives here?"

"Ejii, you can stay in this room," Mama Nyambe said, when they went to the second floor. "I'll get you some towels so you can wash up."

Ejii looked into the room and grinned. It was plain with only a mirror, a large bed with a white blanket, and an empty closet. But it smelled like lilacs because there was a large lilac bush growing in the center of it, its leaves having spread across the ceiling. A green grasshopper with long antenna and short, thick legs rested on one of the flower bunches. There was another on the window.

"Don't worry about the grasshoppers. They won't bother you and they sing a nice tune at night when in the mood," Mama Nyambe said. She motioned Dikéogu to the room next to Ejii. "And you, rain boy, can sleep in here."

He shook his head. "I . . . I can't sleep indoors," he said. "I . . ."

"Oh, no problem," Mama Nyambe said. "Come on. Follow me." She led them back downstairs and outside to the back of the house. The garden took up the whole yard. And the yard fed into the yards of neighbors, who also had gardens, though not as well kept.

"An abode seed is cultivated to grow into a home," Mama Nyambe said. "That's nothing new. But that woman, Jaa, no one knows how she did it, she somehow made this abode seed sprout into multiple homes. Her plant has kept many families together."

Ejii thought of what had happened in the desert with the mango seeds and again, noted just how much she and Jaa were alike. She walked over to where the house narrowed into a very wide vine that plunged into the ground. Next to the house were five large, white boxes. Ejii could hear the bees softly buzzing inside.

"Honeybees," Mama Nyambe told Ejii. "Don't worry, they'd never hurt a fly unless provoked."

Sitting in the center of the village's yards was an enormous tree with a trunk wide as a house itself. It looked like a monkey-bread tree, its wide low branches fanning out as if it wanted to give all the houses a big hug. Buji's mother led them into the garden. Dikéogu flicked on his flashlight to see his way. He still tripped over a tree root.

"Dikéogu, you can sleep out here, or wherever you like," Mama Nyambe said. "We have all kinds of animals that live around here, but none will hurt you."

Dikéogu looked around the garden. "I'll probably sleep there," he said, pointing to a palm tree and cluster of pink flowers near the house.

"I'll get a mat and blanket then," Mama Nyambe said.

That night as Ejii closed the door to her room, took off her shoes, spread her cover on the floor, knelt down, and prayed, she felt wonderfully close to Allah. When she finished, she snuggled into bed, her hands behind her head. They would be in Osizugbo for one day and then go on to the Golden Dawn Meeting. Jaa had warned her that starting tomorrow, there would be protests and demonstrations; things would get heated. This was why they would be leaving so early in the morning the day after tomorrow.

Ejii pushed all this from her mind and concentrated on the fact that she was in a bed that grew from a giant plant that grew in the soil of Ginen; that she could now close her eyes and see the very cells that made up her eyelids; that she could fall into people; and that she had died and now she was alive, in Ginen. She dreamed of flowers, trees, wind, and angry, shouting people. In the morning, Jaa, Gambo, and Buji were gone.

"They had some contacts to meet with," Mama Nyambe said as she prepared their breakfast.

Ejii helped to peel, slice, and fry the plantains. The

plantains were different from the ones from Earth in only one way. They weren't green or yellow, they were red. But once peeled, the inside was the same—a large, tangy, starchy banana. As she worked, she thought of her mother. She quickly pushed the thought away.

Ejii lowered the plantains into the pot of boiling oil. How can plants produce electricity? she wondered. And how can those tiny, white mushrooms grow near the heat without frying? When a beetle fell into the boiling oil, Mama Nyambe simply flicked it out with a spoon, and to Ejii's shock, the thing flew on its way.

"Osizugbo's awake early today," Mama Nyambe said, speaking of the house like an old friend. "He usually takes a while to get moving in the morning."

"Mama Nyambe, why do they call me mau girl? Is it like shadow speaker?"

"I don't know the term 'shadow speaker,' but mau people have always been a part of Ooni society," Mama Nyambe said. "Ginen is older than your Earth; it knows more. 'Mau' means 'to see' in the old Ooni language. Many believe mau folk are witches, the wicked kind. They can see only the harm a mau person could do as opposed to the good. Dikéogu, he's a rain-maker, judging by his markings."

Ejii nodded. "I think he believes that now, too."

"That's why everyone here loves him so much," Mama Nyambe said. "Ginen is forest, jungle, meadow, and lightning cleans the air, so rainmakers are loved. Now, I have a question for you."

Ejii turned the frying plantains and cracked several large, soft-shelled eggs into a bowl. Lizard eggs. "Okay," she said.

"You witnessed Jaa kill your father, no?"

Ejii nodded.

"That woman is crazy, *o*. I know this more than anyone," Mama Nyambe said. She circled a hand over her head and snapped. "But I'm not surprised that my wild son married that type of woman and that he's one of two husbands." She sighed. "But you should not have witnessed your father's death."

"They never found his head," Ejii said, a lump in her throat.

"I didn't mean to upset you," Mama Nyambe said.

Ejii quickly turned the plantains around. They were burned black on one side and still a mushy yellow on the other.

"No . . . I'm okay. My father believed in a religion called Islam. But he wasn't a good Muslim." She used a fork to pick out the half-burned plantain slices and put them on a plate Mama Nyambe had lined with spongy leaves that Ejii soon found tasted like sweet-salty peppers.

✦

CHAPTER TWENTY-ONE

EARRINGS

"**E**VERYTHING seems better here," Ejii said to herself, as she leaned with her back against a tall tree and looked into the afternoon sky. The creatures that lived in the house liked to leave piles of stinky droppings, and Mama Nyambe said that because the houses were alive, they could also catch diseases and die, leaving people homeless; but even the best things had to have their not-so-great side. Jaa and her husbands had returned an hour ago, and inside Mama Nyambe and Jaa talked in the kitchen.

Ejii closed her eyes and concentrated on her body. She moved her head the slightest bit and her mind shifted like a radio antenna. Now she was picking up . . . *silence, watchfulness, the taste of soil and water, delicious* . . . the giant plant whose body was Jaa and her husbands' village? "Oh," Ejii said. She opened her eyes, pulling her mind back.

"Amazing," she whispered. She'd always thought that it would be the shadows she learned to speak to and manipulate to tell her whatever she wanted to know, be it the future or the color of someone's soul. Now the shadows were a part of her and she was part of them. She no longer heard them speak because she was their voice. To think, just a few weeks ago, I only wished to be a good wife, she thought. Ejii cursed her father and made a circle over her head and snapped her fingers.

"Who are you protecting yourself against?" Jaa asked, coming from the house.

"No one," Ejii said, looking at her feet.

Jaa put her hands on her hips and laughed to herself. "So, do you like my home?"

She nodded. "I like how it's the home of many . . . though I wish that the bird that lives near my room's window would coo more softly at night."

Jaa smiled. "How are you feeling now?"

"Strange," she said. She cocked her head and chose her next words carefully. "Jaa, this meeting, how do you plan to argue for peace?" Ejii didn't want to let on that she knew of Jaa's plan to kill the chief, but she also wanted to see if Jaa might have changed her mind. The glint in Jaa's eye was all Ejii needed to see to know Jaa's intent.

"You're here to observe," Jaa said, patting Ejii's arm and turning to leave. She looked over her shoulder. "Don't meddle in what you don't understand."

Ejii spent most of the day in her room. Dikéogu didn't come looking for her, so she figured that he too wanted some time alone to think. That evening, she found him in the giant monkey-bread tree. She paused at the base of the tree, noticing a pile of dead wingless flies and mosquito-type insects on the ground. When Jaa said this tree repelled certain insects, she wasn't kidding, Ejii thought. She slowly climbed up. A leaf touched her arm producing a spark. Dikéogu, who lay on a branch on his back, glanced at Ejii and laughed. When he kept laughing for some time, Ejii asked, "What?"

"Ah, nothing," he said.

"Okay," she said, sitting on a branch. "Weren't you supposed to water the garden?"

Kola clicked her beak in agreement. Ejii looked up. She hadn't noticed the owl.

"Kola says that she's seen some of the others," Dikéogu said.

"What others?"

"For the meeting, I guess," he said. "All this is starting to make me nervous."

"I know," Ejii said. She told him about her brief talk with Jaa.

"That woman's nuts," he said.

"Yeah, and her husbands are no different," Ejii said. But neither am I, she thought. At least part of me. "I think my mother and Jaa are opposites. My mother believes in creation. My teacher, Mazi Godwin, liked to say that 'the opposite of war is creation.'"

She climbed to the top of the tree and tilted her head back to look at the plant towers. She could see several Ogoni ants clipping dead leaves near the top of the Ooni palace and a sad-looking young woman gazing out one of the windows lower down. She looked as if she'd been crying. Ejii frowned. What's that all about?

"Tell me about your home," he said. "Who do you miss most?"

"My mother . . . and Arif and Sammy." she said. "I'm so far from them."

"Your mother is probably worried."

"And angry," Ejii said.

"You're lucky," he said with a sigh. "Who are Arif and Sammy?"

"My best friends," Ejii said.

"Oh."

"Arif gave me these earrings," Ejii said.

Dikéogu said something under his breath.

"Huh?" Ejii asked.

"Nothing," he said, looking irritated.

"Hey," someone said from below. It was Jaa. "I know it grows late and we have a long day tomorrow, but do you two want to see something amazing?"

"Yeah!" Ejii said, climbing down.

Dikéogu, however, stayed where he was. "What?" he asked.

Jaa sucked her teeth. "Come and find out, boy."

Ejii contemplated taking the egg stone from her pocket and leaving it in her room. Since she'd left home, she'd kept it with her, except when the Desert Magician took it. She decided to keep it in her pocket.

"It's late and I'm kind of tired," Dikéogu asked.

"You're young; how much sleep do you need?" Jaa asked.

Ejii jumped to the ground and looked up at Dikéogu. "Are you coming or what?"

He shook his head. "I don't want to see anything new for a few hours."

CHAPTER TWENTY-TWO

✛

THE BURNING BUSHES

"**T**HEY'RE called the burning bushes," Jaa said as they passed the cactus gate.

"You mean like the burning bush in the Bible?" Ejii asked.

Jaa laughed. "Possibly. Maybe it's more of that odd crossover between Earth culture and Ginen culture." She took Ejii's hand. "Get to the side of the road."

The moment Ejii did so, a car zoomed by. Jaa saw her jump and laughed. She's certainly in a good mood, Ejii thought. Knowing Jaa a bit better now, this didn't make Ejii feel comfortable. She moved as far off the road as she could, which put her in the soft grass that grew between the road and the homes and buildings they passed. She stepped on something hard and flat, it made a garbled sound and spit something on her dress. Ejii jumped back, disgusted.

"Disk beetle," Jaa said, wiping Ejii's dress with a leaf. "Harmless but foul tempered. Watch where you step."

Thankfully, they soon came to the start of a dirt-pounded sidewalk. As they walked, Jaa told her about the burning bushes. They were a field of green plants that were inconspicuous, except for one night every twenty-five years. Tonight was that night. Right after sunset, the bushes' long, round, green leaves began glowing a hot-red orange.

A week ago, singing wasps, wasps that also glowed red-orange and made an eerie sound with hollow funnels that grew on their behinds, had hatched from the centers of the burning bushes. They had taken the week to lay their eggs inside the burning bushes' centers and then explore the forests. Tonight, the wasps returned to their burning bushes to present themselves as food for the bushes.

"The bushes feeding on the wasps are an amazing sight," Jaa said. "People come from all over to see, some people even worship them. They believe the wasps' song is the voice of God." She sucked her teeth. "People are the same everywhere."

As they walked in the opposite direction of the Ooni Palace, though the sidewalk remained and the occasional car zoomed on the road, the homes and buildings were farther and farther apart, more vegetation growing between them. Ejii began to see glimpses of forest here and there. Ejii also sensed something else. She looked behind them but didn't see anything strange. Still, she had the odd feeling that they were being followed. A mile up the road she saw something.

"What is that?" she whispered to herself.

"That's where we're going," Jaa said.

"What is it?"

"Our transportation to the field of burning bushes," Jaa said.

The mutatu were like large birds except they had three long, thick legs, no wings, and what would have been feathers was soft, downy, black hair. Their big red beaks looked like they could crush large bones in one crunch.

"They're vegetarian," Jaa said as they stood before the mutatu's slow procession.

They had the spicy smell of fennel seeds, and leisurely followed each other in a line that went from south to north. Ejii and Jaa joined a group of women lined up before the passing creatures. They all gasped when they saw Jaa, several eagerly greeting her.

"The bushes will bring you luck for tomorrow's meeting," one woman said.

Ejii glanced at the clump of forest to their right and could have sworn she saw something lurking in there. The line moved up as each woman climbed onto a passing mutatu. Two women got in line behind them. Neither greeted Jaa.

"Every year the mutatu migrate from some distant land in the Greeny Forest, up north," she told Ejii. "They don't mind us riding them. Think of them as public transportation, Ginen-style. Public transportation for women, at least. They won't let boys or men ride them. No one knows why. We'd have had to take a car and then walk half the way if Dikéogu had come with us. Get on the one behind mine. Do it fast." Then as swiftly as she hopped on her large camel, Jaa grabbed a handful of a mutatu's long, thick, black hair and climbed onto its back.

"They have a groove in their backs, near their heads," Jaa said.

Ejii ran up to the next mutatu. She grabbed as much hair as she could, hoping that she didn't hurt the creature by doing so. The mutatu cocked its large black head to look at her but kept walking. Ejii grunted as she pulled herself upright and swung a leg over. She slid into the groove and found that she was quite comfortable. The creature's gait was soothing and, up close, its fur smelled even more strongly of fennel seed.

She rested her hands on the creature's fur, feeling the hard flesh underneath. It was easy for her to learn what she needed. *Seeds, tasty seeds. Preferably the orange, flat type because they produced a scent in his fur that he found lovely. He was excited to reach the migration spot, a group of trees that all looked alike and therefore hummed the same tune.* Ejii patted his head and he produced a sweet whistle from a hole in his head.

Hello, Ejii said to him, wondering if it would understand.

I don't enjoy talk, he told her. He blew air out of the hole in his head again but this time it sounded more like a loud, wet fart.

There was a roar behind her. One of the women was trying to get on the next mutatu but it didn't seem to like her. Jaa turned around and frowned. The woman was tall and plump and wore a long veil. It tangled around her legs as she scrambled back, and she fell. Jaa chuckled and turned back around. The mutatus soon left the road. Once in the forest, following a mutatu path, they picked up the pace. Ejii felt her belly flip. She was too aware of the power the beasts possessed and that she controlled none of it.

"Watch for low branches," Jaa called back. And indeed

there were quite a few, which Ejii had to flatten herself against her mutatu's back to avoid. An hour passed. Occasionally, they slowed down when they came across a village. During these times, some people hopped off or got on mutatus. The mutatus seemed to slow down whenever they came to places of human habitation.

"We're almost there," Jaa said, after a while. They must have traveled at least thirty miles, maybe more. Ejii could hear the chatter of people on mutatus ahead of and behind them. They were all probably going to the burning bushes. She yawned and looked at the sky. It was close to midnight.

"Get ready to jump off," Jaa called back.

"Okay." She could see the other women getting off a quarter of a mile ahead.

"Now," Jaa said, a minute later.

Ejii threw herself off and landed on her feet. She turned and watched her mutatu just keep on going without even a glance, as if she hadn't been there. She followed Jaa and the other women down a narrow path perpendicular to the path of the mutatus. They walked in silence, the woman in front holding up a glow lily, the sound of their feet on the ground mixing with the thousands of forest sounds around them.

The last in line, Ejii stuck close to Jaa. She turned around, thinking she heard something behind. Whatever it was, it leaped into the bushes before she could focus on it. There was movement in the trees above, and when she looked up she met the eyes of three red parrots. They squawked quietly but did not look away.

"Jaa," she whispered. "I think there's someone behind us."

"We're in the forest. There are probably a thousand things watching us. Relax."

The women started singing a wordless tune and soon, as the path opened to the grandest sight Ejii had ever seen, their voices joined the voices of hundreds of other people and thousands of wasps. Jaa took Ejii's hand and led her around the field, past men and women and a few children praying, singing to, and staring at the spectacle. There were large, ancient-looking black rocks strewn around the perimeter of the field where people sat, though some people preferred to sit on the ground or stand.

As Jaa pulled her along, Ejii stared at the fields of glowing orange-red bushes and orange-red wasps. As the wasps flew and sang their song, they were snapped up by the bushes' stems which opened to mouths of thorns. No one dared walk into the fields. At the center of the field was a large red flower that raised itself above the bushes on a thick green stem. It didn't glow and its thick waxy petals were opened wide.

"Here's a good spot," Jaa said, sitting on a large rock. But Ejii didn't want to sit.

"I know," Jaa said. "This place is . . ." After a moment she said, "Twenty-five years ago, a few years after the Great Change, I met Buji. I'd done so much . . . I was having a crisis of self. He brought me to Ginen so I would heal. He brought me here to see this. My mind must have snapped at the sight of all this because . . . I took off and ran into the field. It was suicide. I don't remember what happened next except that something spoke to me." She paused and Ejii knew she wasn't going to tell her what the voice said.

"Buji dragged me out," Jaa continued. "Minutes passed and I felt more like myself, strong, healed. 'Thank you,' I said to Buji. And that was when the first flower fell from the sky to accompany my words."

A red flower with glasslike petals landed at Ejii's feet. "So this place is sacred," Ejii said, picking up the flower.

"Maybe," Jaa said.

"The song the wasps sing, I've heard this song before. I hear a voice now," Ejii whispered. Tears fell from her eyes and she fell to her knees facing the field. She closed her eyes to better hear the insectile messengers of Allah. When she opened her eyes, she saw Jaa's sword flying in front of her face. *CLANG!* Whatever struck her sword ricocheted off it, hit a nearby tree, and blew into fluffy, white puffs. Another pinged off the amulet Ejii's mother had given her, knocking the wind from her chest. As she gasped for breath, Jaa grabbed her and pulled her between a tree and the rock.

"Stay down!" Jaa shouted, then rushed from their hiding place. Ejii coughed and sputtered, her eyes watering. She heard more clangs. There was so much noise from the wasps and the people singing to them and it was so dark that no one else seemed to register that something was happening. Jaa came back unharmed but looking very angry.

"They're shooting seed compacts," she said. She cursed.

"What's . . ." Ejii coughed.

"You were lucky. That seed should have torn your chest

open, and if that didn't finish the job, the poison from its touch would have two minutes later," she said. "They've been following us since we left. One of them tried to get on that mutatu right behind us. He was dressed as a woman. Stupid man, mutatus can always tell a man from a woman. I thought they were just watching us. I *knew* that bastard would try something. I just thought he'd do it at the meeting! What's the point of killing me out here?"

Ejii was horrified. She was in the middle of an assassination attempt. And I thought I had to stop Jaa from killing the chief! she thought. Everyone's gone mad!

"Let me peek," Ejii said, rubbing her chest.

Jaa looked at her and then nodded. "Stay low," she said.

Ejii slid on her belly, ignoring her chest's soreness, and looked around the tree. She could see several of them. They wore black pants and tops and carried what looked like metal rings. They ran from tree to tree, assuming that they had the cover of darkness.

"There are about ten," Ejii said. "What are those rings they carry?"

"Compact seed shooters," Jaa said. "And they've probably got pheromone disks. You'll see now. Earth people don't have a chance in hell against these weapons. They can make the very trees and ground attack you. If they declare war on Earth, we're done for."

"So what are we going to do?"

"Not we," Jaa said. "I'll fight, but you run. If they take me, you take my place."

"Run where?" Ejii asked. "You're alone!" She started to shudder with panic. Her eyes fell on the ground. She grabbed a stick. It was too small. She grabbed another.

The man was silent as he sprang from the bushes and ran at Jaa with some sort of weapon raised. He swung it at Jaa, who dodged it and swung her sword, slicing the man in the belly. Ejii stumbled back, nauseated. She blinked as the world went metallic.

"They're not after you, Ejii," Jaa said, kicking the man aside.

Something whizzed past Ejii's ear. She dropped to the ground as she saw another man come bursting from the trees on Jaa's right.

"Jaa!" she shouted, grabbing whatever she could. "He's coming."

She swung the branch. Heavy and thick, it smashed against the man's face, taking him by complete surprise. She felt pain as something snapped in her chest, and she fell with the man. When she came back to herself, her mind was filled with the song of the wasps, and she and Jaa were still behind the tree. She tasted blood in her mouth.

"Get up," Jaa was saying. Ejii's face burned as if she'd been slapped. "Whatever happens to you because you're a shadow speaker, you *have* to endure it and keep running. I can handle these men."

"I'm okay," Ejii said, getting to her feet. But even that was painful. She rubbed her chest. It felt as if someone had kicked her there with a shoe made of steel. She looked at the man she'd hit. He was either out cold or dead. Then she looked at the man Jaa had taken on. He was definitely dead, lying in a pool of blood. Some tiny green long-snouted animal was already sipping at it. She looked away, disgusted.

"What do you see?" Jaa asked.

Ejii scanned around them. The bush worshippers were still worshipping, the bushes were still eating the wasps, the wasps were still singing the song of Allah, and the flower in the center was still at peace. In the forest around, she spotted several dark-clothed assassins biding their time.

"That's the only way," Ejii whispered, pointing behind them. "Can you see?"

"I'll manage," Jaa said. "No matter what happens to me, you go. You have a duty." She paused. "Ejii, do you understand me?"

Ejii rubbed her chest but nodded.

"We run on your command," Jaa said, wiping her sword on her pant leg.

Ejii waited a moment for an assassin to hide behind a tree. They were almost surrounded, except for behind them. She was glad that Dikéogu had not come. At least one of us will be alive come daybreak, she thought. "Okay," Ejii whispered. "Go!"

They burst from the bushes, slapping branches aside, and jumping over fallen trees. More deadly seeds tore at leaves and tree trunks as they ran. Just a second before it happened, Ejii spotted two assassins in the trees above. Then there was a spraying sound and she heard Jaa curse. She chanced a look behind her and saw that Jaa had stopped running and was wiping at her clothes. Ejii stopped, too.

"No!" Jaa shouted at her. "What did I tell you? Keep going!"

A chittering sound came from nearby.

"Ejii, *go*!"

"It's coming from over there," Ejii shouted. "On your right!"

Jaa looked in that direction, her sword raised. Then Ejii saw the first creature come bounding from a bush, teeth bared, long, sharp claws ready. Jaa swiped her sword, slicing the large rabbit-like creature in half. Then a hundred more came at her and Ejii couldn't see anything but Jaa's sword and fur flying. Behind the battle, Ejii could see more assassins coming. "Go!" she heard Jaa scream at her.

Ejii turned and ran. Her face was wet with sweat and panicked tears. When she couldn't run any more, she walked. She had no idea where she was; she was exhausted and afraid to stop for fear of something biting, scratching, or eating her. All she'd come across were small rodents, insects, spiders, and birds, but who knew what was poisonous and what was not? The one constancy was the parrots. Red, blue, green, all colors. And as she progressed, she saw more and more of them.

"What are you looking at?" she asked two parrots who had the nerve to sit on a branch the level of her face and stare at her as she passed. They didn't answer. She cursed as her nose started bleeding and her head started pounding. I'm in real trouble, she thought. But her trouble wasn't as bad as Jaa's. "They killed her. The chief of the Ooni Kingdom had her killed," she bitterly said to herself out loud.

She let her guard down, Ejii thought. I infected her with stupid ideas that I don't even believe. She started sobbing as she trudged along. Then she stopped and picked up a large stick. She had a duty and if anything tried to stop her, she'd bludgeon it to death.

She didn't know how long she walked. Her stomach grumbled and she didn't care. She still had the egg stone in her pocket and she didn't care about that either. Jaa was dead and she had a duty. It was her job to represent Earth at the Golden Dawn Meeting. But she couldn't do that because she was lost in a Ginen forest, not a village in sight. Not even in *her* sight. She considered climbing a tree to see above the forest, but the trees around her were so tall and their lowest branches were too high, and she was afraid of what might live in them.

She came to a grassy field and sighed with relief. She was beginning to feel claustrophobic among the tightly packed trees. But she was still weary. Grassy fields might mean snakes. She threw some rocks in hopes of scaring any snakes off. Some sort of round, green-and-white, amphibious-type creature, about the size of her head, scrambled away. It made a clicking-croaking sound as it did so. It acted so flabbergasted and looked so terrified that Ejii couldn't help laughing tiredly.

She walked slowly into the field, slapping the area ahead of her with her stick. When she got to the field's center, she looked at the sky. Her mouth fell open. The night sky wasn't the deep blue of Earth on Ginen; it was purple-blue. She saw two moons in the sky, one was full and one crescent.

"Wha . . ." was all Ejii could say. The great merge, she

thought. And then she started to panic. Had she walked into another . . . another place? She felt movement in her pocket. She plucked out the egg stone and it was warm to the touch. Something was vibrating inside it.

Three parrots landed in a tree on the edge of the field. As Ejii watched, more of them arrived. And then more, and then more. Soon all the trees were full of parrots of many different colors. Suddenly, all the birds flew into the air. She grasped her stick more tightly, bending her legs, ready to strike when the time came. The birds intuitively flew in the same direction, squawking loudly, spiraling up into the sky and then arching back toward the trees.

"Go back to where you came from, beast!" it said. Its voice rattled in her brain. *"You are not welcome here. You will never be welcome here!"*

Ejii clasped the egg stone and raised her stick. "Yet I saw you where I came from. Wasn't that your kind I saw near the burning bushes?" She paused, noticing that she was speaking in her own language of Hausa, not the language of Ginen. "I go where I please."

"Go back to where you came from."

The birds cycled faster, their motion producing a rhythmic noise that affected her senses, then several flew at her. She slapped at them with her stick and they came faster, their feathers slapping at her skin. Their noise suddenly increased and she felt a painful popping in her ears, an ache in her forehead, and a wave of nausea. She crumbled to the ground. As her world went fuzzy, her hand still grasping her stick amidst the attack of birds, she thought she saw something in the sky. Something yellow.

She felt the egg stone, still vibrating, slip from her fingers. The queen bird, she thought. The first to taste me. I hope she chokes on my eyes. Then she knew nothing.

✝   ✝   ✝

Jaa?! she thought frantically. Are you . . . ? The wind. She turned her head and found her face buried in a mass of brown bird feathers that smelled of crushed flowers and oil. They were rough against her face. Her arms were around a head. She clasped more tightly when she saw that they were flying high above the trees. She raised her head and looked more closely at the bird's feathers, she could see individual strands. Hair. She read the bird for a moment. *Flight. Trees. Deserts. Oceans. A thousands lands* . . . She pulled away, dizzy.

"You awake?" When the head turned and she found herself looking into the dark-brown face of a man, she almost let go. He clasped her arms more tightly. "Good. You've been out for a few minutes." He paused. "Don't worry. You're safe."

She saw him for what he was. A windseeker. He wore yellow pants and a yellow top. Like most windseekers, he had seven long, thick dreadlocks. On windseekers, they were called dadalocks.

"You saved me?" she asked groggily. Her head ached thickly and she groaned.

"My name is Sunrise. I'm a friend of Buji's, but it was the

idiok baboons who learned of what would happen." He paused. "You listening? Don't go back to sleep."

"I'm here," she mumbled.

"The idiok can see bits of the future. You'll meet them. They told me you'd be where you were. I found you just in time." He sighed. "They'd have torn you apart."

Ejii closed her eyes and took a deep breath.

"Talk, Ejii. Until I can get you back," he said. "You've been through a lot. Oh, here." He pushed something warm in her hand. The egg stone. "What is that?" he asked.

"I . . . I have no idea," Ejii said, relieved.

"Whatever it is, it saved us. It was making so much noise that the parrots flew away from you just long enough for me to grab you."

She looked at the egg stone, now quiet in her hand. She yawned. "Why do those parrot people hate humans so much?"

"Not any humans," he said. "*Earth* humans. They can smell the difference. The Agonians have officially allied themselves with the Ooni chief."

"Why does the Ooni chief hate Earth people so much, then?"

"Because of their contamination, of course," Sunrise explained. "Pollution."

"I understand that, but nothing's really happened yet."

"Eh? Says who?" Sunrise asked. "Didn't Jaa tell you about the envoy she sent a few years ago?"

"No," she said, frustrated.

Sunrise laughed bitterly, maneuvering slightly in the air.

Ejii could see the Ooni palace in the distance. "Jaa is a proud woman. Her kind rarely talks about their failures."

Ejii snapped back to alertness. Jaa is dead, Ejii thought. Torn apart by those monsters. I have to take her place. "Tell me," she said.

"About two years ago, to improve relations with Ooni, Jaa sent a group of men to meet with the Ooni chief," Sunrise said. "These men were ignorant fools, especially the leader, Atachee. I don't know why Jaa hired him. Maybe she wasn't directly involved in the process. What I really can't understand is why the magician let them into Ginen."

"He's tricky," she said.

"Indeed," he said, nodding. "Well, they came driving their large trucks full of 'Earth's finest.' The moment those trucks crossed into Ginen, they began a path of destruction. The vehicles spewed smoke and fumes, poison to this land. If I were to take you over the area—it's not far from here—you'd see how all that land has turned to ash—the soil can't grow even a fungus! There's no place in all Ginen where a flower cannot grow! I have seen every inch of this planet and no such place exists! Until that envoy came."

"But I don't understand" Ejii said. "Even Earth can deal with pollution."

"*That's* the point," Sunrise said, annoyed. "Ginen is a *clean* place; it has no tolerance for that poison."

Ejii was reminded of something she'd read about the Native Americans in the United States. How they had no tolerance for alcohol, so when the Europeans brought it to them, it wreaked terrible havoc on their bodies. Whereas the Europeans could guzzle their whiskey like water and not be so pointedly affected. "I think I understand," she said.

"Good," Sunrise said. "Anyway, the chief was so angry that before the envoy could make it to the palace, he had his men slaughter every single one of those Earth people. And he had all that they brought burned to waste. I know that Jaa had specifically ordered Atachee to never bring such vehicles to Ginen. But Atachee wanted to impress the chief with something the chief had never seen before. He'd never been to Ginen, he didn't realize our technology put Earth technology to shame a thousand times over. Now, since the great merge, the chief has decided to act on the offensive.

"War has never solved anything and the Earth people will fight back. We have better weapons, but look what just one of their vehicles did to Ginen soil. Earth could use *that* as a weapon. Jaa must convince the chief of peace."

Ejii didn't know what to say or think. With Jaa dead, this was up to her.

"What did the . . . the idiok baboons say about Jaa?"

"Nothing," he said. "Why?"

"You don't know?"

"I was told only where to find you," Sunrise said. "What? What is it?"

"The reason I was there was because Jaa and I were attacked. Jaa said the assassins were sent by the chief. We were going to see the burning bushes. . . ."

"Eh! Attack? Is she . . ."

"I'm sure of it," Ejii said, a sob suddenly escaping her chest.

"*Chey*, this can't be! I have to get you back!" he said. "Close your eyes if you have to." And before Ejii could say anything more, Sunrise gripped her arms tightly around his neck, dropped many feet, and picked up incredible speed. Ejii didn't close her eyes, but she did scream.

✛

CHAPTER TWENTY-THREE

DAWN

"**E**JII!" Dikéogu screamed as Sunrise set her on the ground outside the house.

He came running and Ejii, despite her sadness and the pain in her chest, smiled. He hugged her until she coughed. "What happened?" he asked. Then he noticed Sunrise.

"Is anyone here?" Sunrise asked Dikéogu.

"Inside."

They hurried inside and Ejii stopped at the entrance. Lying on a mat in the middle of the room was Jaa. Her clothes were torn and she had scratches on her face, but she was very much alive. She grinned when she saw Ejii. Aside from Buji, his parents, and Gambo, there was a woman with skin lighter than the Arabs. If it weren't for her long green dress, many long brown braids, and three gold nose rings, Ejii would have thought that she was from the United States or Europe. The woman dabbed Jaa's bleeding arm.

Ejii was acutely aware of everyone watching her. "I thought you were . . ."

"I'm not," Jaa said. "Takes more than a few pheromone-enraged slashrabbits to take me down."

"I saw a lot more than a few," Ejii said, kneeling down beside her.

"Are you sure it was the chief who sent them after you?" Dikéogu asked. "I mean, maybe it was terrorists or . . ."

"It was the chief," Jaa said. "One of the assassins told me so. Of course, I had to squeeze him a bit first."

"Plus his solders have obvious traits," Buji said, bitterly.

Jaa took Ejii's hand. "I'm glad to see you." She paused. "Just as you had to leave me, I had to leave you. All I could hope was that you'd find your way back, as I did."

Ejii nodded. "I understand." And she did.

"Meet Jory," Jaa said. "She's a close friend of mine from Lif. She's also a gifted medicine woman, like your mother."

"Well met," Jory said, looking Ejii up and down.

"Same here," Ejii said nervously.

"Jaa, tell me what happened," Sunrise said stepping forward.

As Jaa, her husbands, Sunrise, and Jory discussed things, Ejii and Dikéogu slipped away to the garden where Dikéogu had spent the previous night. Ejii sat down hard on his mat and sighed a long exhausted sigh, rubbing the middle of her chest. Dikéogu sat beside her and she told him everything.

"Goddamn," was all Dikéogu could say.

"Yeah," Ejii said.

She showed him the large dent the compacted seed had made in her silver amulet and the welt the impact had left on the skin underneath.

"Goddamn," Dikéogu said again.

They lay down where they were and soon fell asleep. Two hours later, Mama Nyambe shook them both awake. "Time to bathe and get dressed for the big meeting."

"We're still going?" Ejii said groggily. "Even after what happened?"

"Of course. The chief even sent a messenger to make sure you're on time."

"So he tries to have Jaa killed and then turns around and expects her to show up for the meeting he planned, in his palace?" Dikéogu asked, wiping his face with his hand.

"He denies having anything to do with it," Mama Nyambe said. "He's a two-faced monster. But this meeting must succeed. So, you two, get up."

A half hour later, Ejii stood in a heavy dress made entirely of tiny red beads. Mama Nyambe had bought it yesterday and it fit perfectly. "It's from the Southwest, obviously," Mama Nyambe said. "I knew it was perfect for you the moment I saw it." Ejii was glad the dress weighed so much, it felt like a strong hand grasping her. Dikéogu wore a long, red caftan that reached his ankles, and matching pants. There were mirrors sewn into the pant cuffs. Mama Nyambe said his outfit was from the North.

Outside, Ejii could hear a crowd and it made her nervous, especially after last night. The cactus fence must have kept everyone out. She peeked from her room, where she had a good view. There were two large glow lilies set up to give them light. The crowd of two hundred people had been demonstrating for a half hour, at least that was when she'd started to hear them. She saw people wearing beaded clothes like hers, outfits with mirrors, people who had vines around their wrists, chubby people wearing white. All of them were lively, despite the early morning. Ejii could see journalists running about questioning and recording.

"Save us, *o*!" someone shouted.

"Why should we trust you or the rest of them? You aren't from here!"

"We won't accept Earth's witchcraft!"

"War to the wastelands!"

"Red Queen, I love you!"

"Don't let Chief Ette control you!"

"War! WAR!"

The shouting grew louder the moment they came into the view of the crowd. The flat, dark-purple car pulled up close to the cactus gate so that the crowd could only shout and watch on the other side. The chief had insisted on them being driven in the plush car to the palace, which irritated Ejii.

"I hope he hasn't rigged the car to blow up when we get inside," Dikéogu said.

Ejii couldn't have agreed with him more. Still, she had to admit that she understood the chief a little. With the actions of Jaa's envoy, any good leader would have reacted the way he had. A leader's primary concern was for his or her people.

The volatile crowd put Ejii on alert, but her attention shifted when she got inside the car. She'd never been inside one before. Gambo was the last to get in. He'd thrust his fist into the air, causing the crowd to burst into applause or curses depending on what they thought of him. Ejii noted that at least a third of the crowd cursed him.

"They worry me," Jaa said. The scratches on her face looked better, thanks to Jory's skills.

"Everything worries me right now," Gambo replied.

The long flat car was also dark purple on the inside and everything was very soft. "I always imagined the insides of cars to have more space," Ejii said.

"You've never been in one before?" Dikéogu asked. Ejii shook her head. "Then switch with me," he said, climbing over her so that she could sit near the narrow window. "The first time I was in a car when I was small, I threw up! The motion's going to feel funny to you."

"Close your eyes if you feel dizzy," Jaa said.

"Here's some gum," Buji said. Ejii popped it in her mouth. It was hot and minty.

"You'll be fine," Gambo said.

Ejii and Dikéogu were in the middle row, and Jaa, Gambo, and Buji were in the back. The ceiling was purple-tinted glass and the seats were so reclined that Ejii was almost lying flat. The minute she was settled in, a purple cloth belt wrapped itself around her waist and crossed itself over her chest. Tiny puffs of flowery-smelling mist came from near the windows and filled the car. Ejii immediately felt like sliding down her seat and, despite her serious mood, giggling. The driver looked in his rearview mirror.

"Welcome," he said. Then they were off.

"Whe-e-e-e!" Ejii couldn't help shouting. It was as exhilarating as flying with Sunrise except it felt more dangerous because they were zipping about on the ground. She didn't get sick or dizzy, but she did giggle a lot. Because of the car's speed, it was hard to take notice of the city that flew by. Minutes later, when they arrived at the Ooni Palace, they encountered more demonstrators.

"This is even bigger than before," Buji said, looking out the window.

"Well, look what's at stake," Jaa said.

The car slowly drove through an opening in the gate of vegetation surrounding the southern part of the palace. They were dropped off in front of two very high, purple doors. Ejii got out, still tickling from the car ride. She looked up. Now she felt dizzy. The Ooni Palace was so huge. She could see the Ogoni ants hard at work, disappearing and reappearing in the thin clouds that hovered at the very top of the palace.

"Allah is the true architect," she whispered, her legs shaky.

Dikéogu actually stumbled as he looked up. "Is it falling? It looks like it's falling!" he said, stepping back, shielding his eyes with his hand.

"No, no," Buji said. He was wearing white silky pants and a shirt with a vine belt. "It only looks that way because of its height. Relax. The palace has been standing for thousands of years."

Gambo looked intimidating dressed in his New Tuareg-style indigo turban-veil and flowing garb. Jaa wore a long red dress with a billowing indigo cape attached to her shoulders that matched Gambo's attire. She also wore vines around her wrists as Buji did.

"Buck up," Jaa said, looking sternly at Dikéogu. "From this moment on, you two are dignified adults. This is the crossroads of all our fates."

Ejii and Dikéogu nodded.

"You aren't to speak unless spoken to," she said. "You have met some of the masters, yes, but this is a formal meeting. Not all of them are human, and some are volatile."

The purple doors were guarded by four soldiers, each wearing striped red-and-purple skirts that ended just above the knee, showing brawny legs with gold bracelets around the ankles. They wore no sandals. Their outfits would have made Ejii laugh if she weren't so nervous and the soldiers weren't carrying large, greasy-looking black swords. Next to one of them stood a black furry creature with five sticklike brown legs and a long, equally sticklike brown snout. Standing about four feet high, it looked more weird than scary.

"Sunny Day," one of the soldiers said. The others just looked at them. The furry creature sneezed and shook itself out. Ejii glanced at Dikéogu, who looked disgusted by the creature.

"We are Jaa, Gambo, and Buji," Gambo said.

"And these two?" the soldier said, nodding a head toward Ejii and Dikéogu.

"Our apprentices, Ejii and Dikéogu," Gambo said. "They go where we go."

"Step forward, Dikéogu and Ejii," the soldier said. He clucked at the furry creature, which immediately scrambled forth, its long legs shuffling with an intricate, spiderlike swift-ness. "Don't run from the phoonsniffle," the soldier warned them. "Stand still and it won't harm you." Ejii and Dikéogu froze as the creature slapped them around with its thin, hard snout. It was sniffing as it slapped. With one last slap on the side of Dikéogu's face, it scrambled back to the soldiers and sneezed loudly.

"Swear to the one or ones that you worship that you come here for the Golden Dawn Meeting and to make the day sunnier," the head soldier asked all five of them.

"We swear," they all said.

"Welcome to the Ooni Palace. We hope that the meeting bears fruit, for the sake of all of us."

Once they stepped in the hallway, the large door shut behind them. Inside the Ooni palace the air was warm, humid, and woody smelling. Though the hallways were wide and long, no sound echoed.

As they walked, Ejii's eyes migrated to the carpeting. The patterns were infinite, symmetric swirling designs of every shade of purple. So much purple. Even the large glow lilies on the walls gave off a lavender light. A few times, Ejii saw purple scarab beetles and periwinkle geckos walking up the walls or hiding in corners. As they walked, they passed closed doors with soldiers standing in front of them.

Jaa looked straight ahead. "The chief of the Ooni Kingdom, Pilfenkwo Ette VIII, will soon meet us," Jaa said quietly. "Neither of you will like him and not only because of what he did last night. But be respectful. Do *not* bring up last night. Dikéogu, if you are Ejii's friend, keep *your mouth shut*. And however you see me behave here, know it is for politics only. A means to an end. Now, get behind us."

Dikéogu and Ejii worriedly looked at each other as they moved close behind.

"He sounds like a monster," Dikéogu whispered.

"He's just a man," Ejii said.

No sooner had she spoken then they heard a bellowing laugh come from down the hallway. Wall geckos scampered into shadows and scarab beetles flew to the safety of the ceiling. Then eight soldiers wearing short-skirted uniforms marched around the corner. These solders looked as if they were having a great time. Though they maintained their stiff march in unison, they had smiles on their faces, and several of them were laughing.

They lined up on both sides of the hall, their smiles still present. Behind them came ten women and girls, some Ejii's age, and some closer to her mother's age. They all wore long but tight-fitting purple dresses and sandals. Their nails were painted purple and they wore purple lip balm and eyelid shading, and had necklaces that glowed purple. The chief's wives. None of them were laughing. What miserable-looking women, Ejii thought.

They sat at the feet of the soldiers, still looking sad. Ejii recognized one of the wives as the woman she'd seen yesterday sitting at the palace window crying. Then she saw Chief Pilfenkwo Ette VIII. He was extremely fat. So fat that he apparently wasn't able to walk. He sat on a motorized purple throne with wheels. The throne was made of some sort of tree, the roots snaking and weaving into a knot above the vehicle's tires. It shed leaves as it came to a stop.

"Sunny Day," he said in a robust voice. "Welcome! I'm glad you could make it."

He was the kind of fat that only came from eating more than a camel ate in a day. Ejii's mother would have been disgusted. His body broadcasted excess and greed. He carried a large glass of what looked like palm wine.

But it wasn't just his obvious excess. There was something else that Ejii didn't like about this man. Something more sinister. His attire was complex, an outfit that was probably centuries old. Gold metal straps stretched from his ears over his portly cheeks to hold a large round disk of gold over his nose. It had tiny holes in it so he could breathe. His ample flesh was squeezed into a leather suit. Even his feet and hands were encased in leather. He must sweat gallons, Ejii thought.

The suit was embroidered from neck to toe with white cowrie shells and tiny mirrors that clicked with his every movement. The nails of his costume's feet and hands were smooth shells. Whoever made the suit loved detail. On his head was a crown of long black feathers. Though the costume was obviously made to accommodate his fat, he looked like a sausage, and he was breathing heavily. On his lap was an equally ornamented tusk of some great beast.

"Sunny Day, Chief Pilfenkwo Ette the VIII," Buji said, stepping forward and kneeling. Gambo and Jaa did the same. Then Buji and Gambo gave the chief an elaborate handshake.

Jaa stood back, wordlessly, still kneeling. Ejii didn't like that.

"It's good to see you," Chief Ette said. "How was your journey?"

"Mostly eventless," Buji said.

"Ah, one day I would like to see this Earth you all live on," the chief said.

"I'm sure it can be arranged," Buji said.

The chief glanced at the still-kneeling Jaa. "Seems you and Gambo have been nicely disciplining your wife." He chuckled. "The scratches on her face become her."

"We never lay an angry hand on her, Chief Ette," Gambo said. "Jaa met with a few unkind Ooni folk. But she handled them nicely."

"Ah, well, I must apologize for my people. They're so high-strung these days." He smirked. "Why is it that you have no children? This woman seems very . . . able."

"It's not the time, Chief Ette." Buji said.

The chief nodded, wiping sweat from his brow. "Yes, we are in strange times," Chief Ette said. He looked at Ejii and Dikéogu. Ejii felt her blood pressure rising. Oh, she did not like this man at all.

"These must be the apprentices," Chief Ette said. He motioned them to come closer. As they stepped forward, Jaa whispered to her. "Kneel." Ejii lightly elbowed Dikéogu. He nodded and they both knelt before the chief. Up close, he smelled strongly of sweat and leather and perfumed oils.

"A rain boy and mau girl," he said. "It seems this one's abilities are wasted, with her being a girl and all. Femininity is the destroyer of greatness." He laughed. Ejii looked at the ground, her eyes shut, holding back a rage much stronger than what had launched her at her cousin Fadio back home. She now knew what it was she disliked about this man. He reminded her of her father.

"But she does have a pretty face, even with the eyes," he said. "Up, boy."

Dikéogu stood.

"Ah yes, a true rainmaker, bold and loyal," he said. "What is it you think you'll gain from attending the Golden Dawn?"

Let Dikéogu talk and ignore me? Ejii thought angrily. The way her father did with her and Fadio. Maybe I can learn something of his plans for today, she thought. While she had the chance, she looked into the things the chief of Ooni carried.

Purple. Always purple. He was one of over thirty children. His father had many wives. Little Ette the VIII never liked this. He was the eighth son, but his father had especially liked his mother and thus gave Ette extra attention. Still he'd never liked this, either. He preferred to be alone so he could eat. He would hide in the pantry and eat sweetmeats and honey until his belly ached. His mother was only twelve years old when she gave birth to him, but she loved him dearly. She especially loved how he loved her when she gave him food. His father eventually was murdered in a coup d'etat when Ette was ten. And Ette witnessed it. Never had he felt so helpless and sad as when his father fell to the ground, his throat slashed. So much blood.

Ejii worked hard to hold herself from the abyss of the chief's sorrow. *Ette's oldest brother was the murderer. This same brother who often spat at Ette, one day saying that Ette was just an eighth son and did not deserve his father's attention. And when his brother became chief, he decided that Ette should be allowed only bread, water, and vegetables. Food for a peasant. A life fit for a peasant. So Ette chose revenge. When he was eighteen and strong and lean, he murdered his murderous brother. And became chief. He imagined that all of Ginen cheered his actions. That every plant bowed. Eighth son indeed, he thought. I am chief! And he started eating again. . . .*

Dikéogu suddenly started cursing at the chief, forcing her to pull back.

"I won't hold your stupidity against you, because you're young," Chief Ette said. "Normally, I'd have had your head and hands. Maybe that will come to pass when you're a few years older." He laughed. Dikéogu looked livid and Buji and Gambo were standing protectively beside him.

"Women, get up," Chief Ette. He swooped his hands dramatically in the air, his leather costume creaking. "We all have a meeting to attend!"

Ejii slowly stood up. Though Ette's childhood was sad and he was full of resentment and insecurity, she still despised him. He was the type of man who had to bring others down to lift himself up, and he was a lot to lift. He was the type of man who used truths, like the fact that Earth cars poisoned Ginen land, to mask his own cruel plans. Ejii understood why Jaa wanted to kill him. He was capable of doing harm that extended far beyond himself.

Ette and his wives and soldiers went one way down the hall, while two soldiers led Ejii and the others to an elevator in the opposite direction. It was nothing like the elevator at the

Yellow Lady. This one was part of the plant tower's flesh. All parts of it were made of a strong, smooth, waxy but clear material. It was flat on the bottom but domelike on the top, where a light-green plant with spirally leaves grew. A chameleon clung to one of the leaves, looking down at them. Jaa pulled Ejii and Dikéogu close.

"This plant is thousands of years old. It won't drop us," she said.

Slowly, Ejii reached for Dikéogu's hands and his fingers locked around hers. The stocky soldier with very muscular arms tilted his head back. He opened his mouth wide and loudly breathed, "Ha-a-a-a-a-a." The plant began lifting immediately but smoothly. Very, very fast. Ejii's stomach went to her feet and she grasped Dikéogu's hand more tightly. The ground shot away from them, and suddenly they were in the predawn sky, the city of Ile-Ife growing smaller and smaller. Then she could see beyond the city, to the outer parts of the Ooni Kingdom where all was forest and jungle.

"Allah is many," Ejii whispered.

They seemed to rise forever. After a while Ejii's body grew a little accustomed to the sensation. Then the elevator stopped and the clear doors opened. They were at the top floor. For a moment, Ejii was light-headed. The air was a little different here. She took a deep breath and felt as if she couldn't quite fill her lungs. She took another deep breath and her head cleared.

"Easy," Jaa said. "The plant regulates the air but it's still a little thin up here."

The soldiers walked slowly to accommodate Ejii and

Dikéogu's slow pace. The hallways were small gardens. Bushes and trees grew through the floor and the ceiling was carpeted with a dense rug of tiny, dark-green buds. Butterflies, red flies, and bees flew about, some snapped up by wall geckos, chameleons, and tree frogs. There were two blue scarab beetles on the branch of what looked like a stunted iroko tree. One of them multiplied into three and they all walked in different directions.

The soldiers led them into a large elaborate room. There was a mirror embedded into the wall. Palm trees reached the high ceiling in all five corners of the room. At the room's center, plants with large bell-shaped white flowers grew next to the chairs and large round table. And vines with star-shaped leaves crept around the large windows on the far side of the room.

"The meeting will be in the conference room in twenty minutes," the stocky soldier said. When the soldiers left and closed the doors, Ejii relaxed.

Dikéogu sat hard in one of the chairs, his arms wrapped around his chest. "Inflated, evil, camelshitting, fat-assed bastard. How can *he* be the chief of this place?"

"Chiefs don't always represent the places they rule," Buji said.

Ejii wondered how much of a say his wives had in their plight. Probably very little. She thought of how her father was going to marry her off to his cook's lazy son.

"He could have killed you," Gambo said, sternly, striding up to Dikéogu.

"What happened?" Ejii asked.

"I wasn't afraid of the man who beat me in that slave camp, and I'm not afraid of that walking food machine!" Dikéogu snapped. Outside Ejii heard the rumble of thunder and then saw a flash of lightning. The sky had been clear when they arrived. A more-than-mild breeze sprung up in the room, blowing dried leaves about and rustling fresh ones. Dikéogu stood up, acknowledging Gambo's challenge. Ejii blinked. Dikéogu didn't seem afraid of Gambo at all. He must have forgotten what Gambo *was* and what he had done to those crazy, confused Americans in the desert. Or maybe he didn't care.

"We asked you to be careful, Dikéogu! Are you deaf?" Gambo said.

"But what happened?" Ejii asked again.

"Didn't you see? Are you blind, Ejii?" Jaa said. "Or maybe your attention was elsewhere?" She smirked.

"I won't accept slavery," Dikéogu said. "People should live as they choose."

"You now know one of the greatest problems that will arise from the great merge," Gambo said.

"Whatever," Dikéogu said, looking away.

After that, things quieted. While Jaa, Gambo, and Buji sat at the table and quietly talked, Ejii and Dikéogu sat looking out of the large window.

"That was another one," Ejii said, pointing as a shape zoomed by. "It had blue eyes, too."

"I wish they'd fly by slower," he said.

The window gave them a spectacular view of Ooni and

beyond. A flash of lightning lit up the sky from far away. Ejii looked sideways at Dikéogu. She looked away when she saw that he was looking at her.

"You did that, didn't you?" she asked.

He nodded. "The Desert Magician, I think he . . . rewired me or something. I can feel the control now, like the sky is part of me."

"I can imagine."

There was a rumble of thunder outside.

"Dikéogu, try not to get so angry," she said. "The chief is a sad man. His fat is different from most people's. His is like a coat of sadness, and he gets fatter every year and it gets heavier and harder for him to carry it around."

"You looked into him?"

"How could I not?" She said. She gasped and pointed. "Dikéogu, look!"

Kola landed on the outer edge of the window. Dikéogu pressed his face to the glass and put his hand on it. Her wings were encrusted with frost. "Kola!" Dikéogu shouted, smiling. "I didn't know you could fly so high!"

The owl opened her beak and must have hooted; Ejii couldn't hear through the glass. Kola clicked a talon on the window where Dikéogu's hand was. The sight of Dikéogu and Kola, hand to talon, made Ejii's heart flutter. Then Kola launched herself into the sky and flew in a broad circle. As Ejii watched Kola fly off, she spotted something else in the sky.

"That's Sunrise!" Ejii said.

They watched as Kola and two huge white owls flew with

him in a large circle, like a delicate dance in the sky. Then Sunrise descended, all three owls following him.

The soldiers came. It was time for the meeting. They were led down the hall to two large, purple metal doors. Ejii reached into her pocket and held the warm egg stone tightly in her fist. I hope I know what to do with this when the time comes, she thought. A scarab beetle flew past her head and landed on her shoulder.

"Get off me," Ejii grumbled. It was so close to her ear that she could hear the beetle folding its wings.

"Better those than the red flies. I think they bite," Dikéogu said, scratching his arm. "I'll get it." He plucked it up and it made a noise that sounded oddly like a soft giggle as it wiggled its antennae. Another appeared on Ejii's shoulder. It spread its wings and flew away.

The doors opened and as they entered the room, Ejii and Dikéogu moved close to each other and tried to hide behind Jaa, Buji, and Gambo. All the way around the room were windows, giving Ejii a 360-degree view of Ooni. The ceiling was high and domed, covered with green hanging vines. Among the vines, to Ejii's horror, was a noisy flock of frolicking red parrots. Below the parrots was a wide round table around which many different types of people sat. The chief sat on the farthest side, flanked by two soldiers.

"Sunny Day," Jaa said, her high-pitched voice echoing around the room.

There was a man who looked as if he was made completely of metal. His skin shone like mercury. He wore a long silver caftan. Every time he moved, Ejii heard the tinkle of bells. Three small, brown, fluffy-looking baboons with large golden eyes sat next to him. Two more sat on the conference table, and Ejii thought she could see the tops of the heads of another two sitting on the floor. All of the ones she could see carried small pads of paper. These must have been the future-seeing baboons who'd saved her life by telling Sunrise where to find her. Next to them was a large gray-furred gorilla wearing a green-jeweled necklace.

Next to the gorilla was a man with skin as dark as Ejii's, but his long hair grew in large, shiny curls. He was bare-chested and Ejii wondered if he wore any clothes from the waist down. Next to this man was . . . Ejii didn't know what it was. It looked like a cross between a rabbit and kangaroo. It had white fur and large black eyes with gold pupils.

Jory sat next to this creature. She wore a green dress and yellow bangles all the way up her arms. She raised her chin at Jaa, who did the same. Next to her sat Sunrise. Next to him was a group of four-inch-high people sitting on the table. They each had various shades of oily, green skin, wore all black, and had large bulbous noses. And close to them, farther down the table, a wisp of smoke hovered above a chair.

Jaa's greeting was met with words, grunts, jingles, silence, and squawks. The parrots had all squawked in unison and Ejii had to work hard to not tear out of the room screaming. Gambo turned and motioned for Ejii and Dikéogu to step forward.

"These two are our apprentices," Jaa said. "Dikéogu and Ejimofor."

"The shadow speaker is the one on what she called 'walka-bout?'" Jory asked.

"Yes," Jaa said.

"I think they were both on walkabout," said the man Ejii thought was naked.

"Enough," the chief said. "Jaa, Gambo, Buji, sit down." He motioned to the three empty seats at the table. Ejii and Dikéogu remained standing.

"Masters, make these two less ignorant," the chief said, sighing with boredom.

Ejii wanted to shield her eyes as the naked man with the long, beautiful hair stood up. She sighed with relief when she saw that he was wearing a blue loincloth. He said his name was Djang and he was a shaman from Australia. Ejii almost laughed. No wonder he knew about walkabout! The furry baboons all gestured wildly as they each stood up. The gray-furred gorilla stood up, slow and shaky, clutching his chair for balance.

"I am Obax," he said in a gruff voice. "A chief from the Greeny Jungle of Ginen. These are the idiok and they do not call each other by name. Just call them friend."

The silver man, who called himself the Shining Wizard, jingled as he spoke. His motions were smooth and fluid. When he spoke, his voice was accompanied by the sound of clanging bells. He was from a world called Ngiza. When he finished introducing himself, a few of the parrots flew around Ejii's head. Thankfully she found the courage to stand tall. Then they quieted. "We waste time on these children," they squawked in unison. "We have important things to discuss. I want to return to Agonia." The sound of their voices was unnerving.

"Relax, Aku," Chief Ette said. "We have a few minutes."

"Tanah, I am," the giant kangaroo-like creature said in a soft voice. She sounded annoyed but her face remained blank. "Also, I from Agonia. I am in agree with Aku. No time for learners."

"I am Jory of Lif," Jory said. "I'm glad to see children here."

"I represent Ginen," Sunrise said. "But Arroyo, my mother, is from Earth. It's good that you're here."

"We're the Kad'an from Lif," said a voice that echoed around the room. The little people stood before a plant bulb that grew in the center of the table. The bulb served as a microphone. "I am the spokesperson, Tsirita," one of them said.

It was the puff of smoke's turn. When it spoke, Dikéogu jerked and had that look of fright on his face. Ejii grabbed his arm, though she, too, was horrified. The voice vibrated inside her head. "I am Smoke from Ngiza," the voice said. "I have seven minds, two in the future, one in the past. We should treat these children with respect. Welcome."

"Thank you," Ejii and Dikéogu said.

"Now, both of you get out of the way and let us talk," the chief said.

There were two mats on the floor behind Jaa, Gambo, and Buji, for Ejii and Dikéogu. They quickly took their seats and let out sighs of relief.

"Thank goodness that's over," Dikéogu whispered.

"I know," Ejii said. Her heart was still beating fast. She looked at her egg stone and looked around the room. No sign of what to do with it.

"Masters," Chief Ette said loudly. He turned to the window. "The sun rises. We're right on schedule."

Sunrise laughed loudly as the room began to light up with sunshine.

"This has nothing to do with you," Chief Ette said, irritably.

"If you say so," Sunrise said, still smiling.

"Representatives of the five worlds, the Golden Dawn is officially in session," Chief Ette said, squinting in the sunshine. "You have been called for this meeting because of your connections, your vision, and your power. Something has happened and things will never be the same."

"What's happened has happened," Jaa said. A red flower with a spiky stem bounced off of Chief Ette's head. He grunted with annoyance, catching it and throwing it aside. "Now how will we prevent war?" Jaa looked at Chief Ette as she said this.

"War isn't a problem yet," said the Shining Wizard.

"It will be," Jaa said. "There are no longer any borders between the worlds. Ginen, for one, can't rely on the guardian to maintain order. The Desert Magician loves trouble, as all gods do."

"Sunrise," said Djang the Australian. "Tell us what you've seen."

Sunrise stood up. It was obvious that he liked to hear himself speak. He walked with his hands behind his back as he looked out the window. "Ngiza, Agonia, Earth, Ginen, and Lif all hold a place in my heart," he said. "Even the guardians allow me to move freely. So you can imagine how I feel now that all five of these places are suddenly one, open and known to each other.

"What have I seen? Cultures spilling into other cultures, plants fighting with plants, people fighting with people, people fighting with plants, disease. There are no wars on a grand scale, like what happened on Earth. But there will be if nothing's done. All of us here have influence. We can spread the word. Many people don't understand what has happened and so everything new is perceived as an attack."

"*Earth* humans are the problem," squawked Aku. Several of the birds flapped their wings. "Many have already migrated to Agonia from an Earth place they call China. They think that the birds there have no spirit energies and they slaughter us for food! They shoot us down! Next they will bring their poison machines. We Agonia people are against killing, but what else can we do? Soon, we will fight back."

"And what of the Agonia bird tribes that flew into China?" Sunrise asked. "There is nothing left of the food the people planted there. Do you expect Earth humans to rely on spontaneous forests for substance? And I saw human bodies, too. Slaughtered also, flesh gnashed by strong beaks. At least the Earth people do what they do because they seek food. Those humans were killed for sport. I've seen it."

Aku was quiet.

"Even here, Earth people wreak havoc," the chief said.

"Since when?" Jaa demanded.

"Since you sent that envoy of idiots!" Chief Ette screamed. "And every day there are more reports to me of human foreigners. It's only a matter of time before one of them brings another of their poison machines! Our world is a place of . . ."

"Earth people don't want to do any of what you've said," Jaa said. "You can't base everything on ten stupid men who acted against orders."

"Says who?" the chief retorted.

Jaa ignored his comment. "Ginen technology is far superior. Go to the markets on Earth and the best products are from Ginen! How do you think those things got there? Obviously Ginen people are migrating to earth, too!"

"Small, small woman," the chief said, looking at her with disgust. He was breathing heavily. "I won't let Ooni be turned into the wasteland Earth has become!"

Ejii found herself growing angry as she listened.

"Such human behavior," Obax the gorilla said, shaking his head. "It's a cycle." The idiok were vigorously scribbling and showing each other what they had written and scribbling more.

"Look at what they've done to themselves," Ette continued. "They're the reason for all this in the first place! I don't want their kind here!"

Gambo put a hand on Jaa's shoulder and told her to be quiet. "So what do you suggest, Chief Ette?" Gambo said, through clenched teeth.

"I'm prepared to do what I have to do!" Ette shouted. The

fat under his chin jiggled. "Nip the problem in the bud before it blooms!"

"Chief Ette has my full support," squawked Aku.

Tanah kicked her strong kangaroo-like legs under the conference table, making that side of the table bounce up several inches. "We join you if we must," she said. "This what I wanted learn today. About these toxic Earth humans."

"*These* people are supposed to decide what's to be done?" Ejii whispered loudly.

"Ejii," Dikéogu said. "Quiet down!"

"We agree," Tsirita said into the voice amplifier. "We cannot live in a world like the Earth. We breathe through our skin. We'll become extinct!"

"This is ridiculous," Djang said. "I'm from Earth and I live with my tribe off the land. We belong to the land. I didn't come here to . . ."

"Neither did I!" Jory said. "Chief Ette, your warmongering sickens . . ."

"Earth is the problem!" Ette bellowed, shaking his fat fists. He calmed himself. "Gambo, Djang, you have my respect as Earth men." He flashed a look at Jaa. "But Earth is corrupted. Look at how nothing makes sense there—spontaneous forests, indeed! I strongly suggest you move to Ginen, for my allies and I plan to have Earth subdued."

Ejii gnashed her teeth. Jaa looked daggers at Ette, the sides of her eyes twitching.

"That's enough," Buji shouted. "This is outrageous, you can't . . ."

"We will!" the parrots all squawked.

The Shining Wizard's bell jingled.

"This is pathetic," Sunrise said.

"Was this meeting even meant to be a meeting?" Jory nervously said.

"Who will join hands with me?" Chief Ette asked ceremoniously. "Who will . . ."

"No!" Ejii yelled, standing up before she knew what she was doing.

Chief Ette sucked his teeth loudly. "Jaa, shut this girl . . ."

"Enough!" Smoke's voice didn't have to be loud to be heard. Everyone yelped and quieted. Even Chief Ette. His soldiers, who up to now had barely even blinked, clapped their hands over their ears. "Let the girl speak."

All eyes turned to Ejii.

"Huh?" she said.

"Speak, Ejii," Smoke said. "Clearly. Now!"

The tension in the room seemed to squeeze at her face. "Um . . . you . . ." Ejii stammered, afraid to speak, afraid of saying the wrong thing. Most of the masters seated before her had blood on their hands just as Chief Ette, Jaa, Buji, and Gambo did. She could practically hear what her father would have said had he been here: "Sit down and close your mouth. How dare you speak before such great men!"

"Speak, Ejii," Smoke said. "Speak before your moment passes."

She took a deep breath and when she spoke, her voice was steadier. "You . . . you all call yourselves 'masters'? Masters of what? I can't believe the . . . the . . . the *stupidity* of what I'm hearing." She paused. Her words tasted good. "Chief Ette, you're Ooni's leader and that's a feat in itself. Even if you *did* murder your own brother years ago and try to assassinate Jaa last night, I respect your work as a leader. You're a great man, but have you ever *been* to Earth?"

Ette only glared at Ejii.

"Then *who* are *you* to judge it? Aku, why are you so angry? Your people have done the same thing as Earth humans. And Tanah, Tsirita, you are not here to react in anger. Dikéogu and I are children of . . . of change. I've spent most of my life under my father's thumb. He made me think that my abilities were a deformity, a waste. *You* remind me of him, Chief Ette. He couldn't accept change. When Jaa killed him, even *I* was glad, his own daughter!

"Dikéogu's parents let him get sold into slavery because they couldn't accept their own son's ability. We've suffered because of your type of backward thinking. There is no Ginen, Earth, Ngiza, Agonia, or Lif! Things have *changed*! You talk of war . . . what you're defending now belongs to all of us. Together. We'd just be fighting ourselves. So . . . stop it! This is the kind of thinking that caused the Great Change in the first place!"

The room was silent as they all just stared at her.

"Then what we do?" said a voice from her left. It was Tanah.

"We should listen," Ejii said. "Listen to each other. Talk. Understand. We're all from different places but we have a lot to share. Chief Ette, didn't you hear Sunrise and Djang? They said Earth humans *respect* Ginen's technology. That envoy was a terrible mistake and Jaa is sorry for it. Send Ginen people to Earth to teach people about Ginen's machinery. *Peacefully* cause the Earth vehicles to go extinct."

Ejii took a step back, nervous. She'd just insulted Chief Ette, several times, along with several of the others. One of the idiok climbed onto the table and walked up to Ejii. It motioned for her to step forward. He touched her forehead with a small warm hand.

"That means, 'Well spoken,'" Obax the gorilla said.

"Sit down," Chief Ette spat with a disgusted look. "Better yet, guards, remove these children. Take them down, like a stone." The guards roughly grabbed Ejii and Dikéogu. Ejii tried to snatch her arm away but the guard was too strong. Dikéogu managed to run halfway across the room before the guard caught him. They were dragged out of the conference room.

"If you hurt them," Ejii heard Jaa say. "I will kill you."

"No!" Ejii shouted as the guard dragged her out. "Jaa, no!"

"Now as I was saying," Ette continued. "Who is with me?"

"Vile man. I didn't come here to talk, anyway," Jaa said jumping up and pulling out her sword. Ejii saw Gambo leap up and a wind gusted around the room, slamming the conference room doors shut.

Ejii screamed, pulling at her arm. Dikéogu was wordless as he tried with all he had to get away. But the soldiers were too strong. They easily dragged the two of them down the hall. "This isn't your battle," one of the soldiers said.

306

CHAPTER TWENTY-FOUR

✦

ORDERS

HE soldier tilted his head back and breathed, "Hh-h-o-o-ok" and Ejii and Dikéogu dropped so fast that Ejii's tears ran up her face. Thankfully it was only about five floors. They screamed the entire way. The soldier holding Ejii laughed when the elevator finally stopped. Ejii and Dikéogu slumped against the wall.

"Sorry," the soldier said grinning. Ejii was so angry that she wanted to kick his muscular legs and punch him in his privates.

The other soldier shrugged with mock sadness. "Chief Ette's orders."

"I didn't hear him say anything," Ejii snapped. She put the egg stone, which her hand had absentmindedly been trying to crush for the last fifteen minutes, into her pocket.

"That's because he told us this morning," the soldier said with a smirk.

So the chief planned this, too, Ejii thought. Dikéogu took a deep breath and Ejii immediately slapped a hand over his mouth before he could shout his string of obscenities about Chief Ette. "Th . . . thank you for the ride," Ejii said, as Dikéogu struggled to remove her hand.

"Follow us," the soldier said. "If you run, we'll have reason to hurt you. *Also* Chief Ette's orders."

"Will you calm down?" Ejii whispered to Dikéogu as they followed the soldiers. It was like they were back in the Aejej again.

"Damn it," he hissed. "I hate that son of a . . ."

"Dikéogu! Not now, okay?"

In front of them the soldiers laughed. "All we need is a reason," one of them said.

Dikéogu pressed his lips together, his nostrils swelling. Now his hatred of Chief Ette is sealed, Ejii thought. They were shoved into a small room with no windows and only a dim withering glow lily to light it. The floor was carpeted with short, yellow, sickly-looking grass. The guards slammed the door behind them. "If you try to escape, we'll be right here to grab, beat, and throw you back in," one of the soldiers said.

"What have we done?" Ejii shouted. "We're *guests* here!"

"Not anymore," the soldier said.

Ejii slapped her hand against her thigh, stepping away from the locked door.

"I hate him," Dikéogu hissed as he sat on the floor. Ejii worried more about Dikéogu's hatred of being indoors in a room so small.

"You haven't known him long enough to hate him," Ejii said quietly.

"Yes, I have," he said. "Evil man. He said slavery was good for me because it toughened me up . . . and look what he said about *you*!"

She'd been too busy reading the chief to hear what the chief had said about her.

"And look what he's done!" he shouted. "This was all his plan! Probably his plan B, after he failed last night!"

"Fine, hate him," she said. "But we can't think about that now."

"Ooni's problems are probably all *his* fault," he said. "Now . . . those problems will become ours, too." Outside they heard the rumble of thunder.

"Oh, Allah, what's happening up there," Ejii said. "We have to go back!"

"How?" he said. "This place is crawling with Ette's stupid yes-men and his sad, beaten, damned wives and his messed-up children. What can we . . ."

"But remember those ones that brought us to the room before the meeting?" Ejii said. "They seemed kind enough. They can't all be like the ones guarding the door."

"If you're not part of the solution, you're part of the problem," he said.

Ejii sat down next to him and leaned against the wall. "Oh, Allah, what will become of us all?"

Suddenly Dikéogu jumped up and ran for the door yelling, "LET US *OUT*! DAMN IT! OPEN THIS DOOR!" Before Ejii could get up to stop him from slamming himself against the door, something grabbed her from behind. At least it felt that way. Whatever it was grasped her roughly and pulled her deep. And then she saw through a purple haze:

Aku, a flurry of parrots with one consciousness, was attacking Jaa. Like the slashrabbits, the parrots were no match for her and her sword. Within moments, she'd chopped many of them in half. The Shining Wizard shouted something, the sound of bells complimenting his voice. He rushed at Jaa. Before he got to her, a gust of wind blew him toward the large window. The blast of wind was powered by Gambo. CRASH! Out Gambo flew in a burst of glass, taking the Shining Wizard, Smoke, and Sunrise with him. Over a mile above the ground.

Ejii could feel the pain from the huge broken window.

The kangaroo-rabbit, Tanah, gave Buji a rib-breaking kick in the chest. One of the idiok whipped a pen at her, giving Buji the chance to get up. Some of the Kad'an, the little people, tried to stick poison spears in Buji's foot as he swung at Tanah with a dagger. Jory ran for the door. She was about to pull it open when she suddenly collapsed instead. Buji accidentally stepped on a few of the little people as he swung at, and eventually stabbed, Tanah. Djang the Australian, snatched up the remaining Kad'an, ran to the door, and threw them into the hallway. Now Jaa was slowly walking toward the chief who still sat in his chair. . . .

When the vision let go, Ejii slumped over. Dikéogu was still shouting and kicking at the door. Ejii was too weak to call his name. Terrible things had happened in the conference room. She wasn't sure if everyone up there was dead. But as she lay there sideways, her shoulder to the floor, her back against the wall, watching her friend succumb to panic, a plan came together in her mind. This time, instead of the plant grabbing her, she reached out to it.

The plant was ancient and she knew to read such a creature was dangerous, but she didn't know what else to do. *Purple. She was falling into something so vast that she could feel her mind shuddering, about to break.* Oh Allah, she thought, what have I done? I'm going mad! Then something grabbed her. If it hadn't, she'd have remained there on the floor, saliva dribbling from the corner of her mouth, her eyes blank . . . forever.

Control yourself, the voice said. *Or you'll have no self.*

Ejii was like a chameleon who had shot its tongue at an insect and realized at the last moment that it was pure poison. In her physical body, she felt the pain of her strain.

Good. Ejii, I am Oily Jada, the voice said.

Hello, Oily Jada, she said. *Have you been hurt?*

You have to return to my top room. They're fighting.

Soldiers guard our door, Ejii said.

I will take care of some of them. Get up. Now. The one named Gambo has gone to bring the others who wait close by. I feel the Ooni soldiers gathering from all parts in me and outside me, swarming. The glass breaking . . . they were given orders in case something happened. War is at hand. Get up. Ejii felt herself pushed forward and she rolled onto her belly. With all she had, she pushed herself up.

"Dikéogu," she said as loud as she could. It came out more like a grunt and he didn't hear her. She rested for a moment, noticing the red dots on her arms. Burst blood vessels from the stress of her encounter with Oily Jada.

When the door swung open, she almost laughed with delirium. Dikéogu jumped back, his fists up. When no one came at him, he ran out. Slowly, Ejii stood up and on weak legs made for the door. When she was almost out, Dikéogu came running back in, a stunned look on his face. They looked at each other for a moment. He took her hand.

"I'm weak," she said as they stepped into the hallway.

Dikéogu grunted, looking around.

"What do you think you're doing!" a voice shouted. They looked up to see one of the soldiers held tightly in a tangle of vines.

"Please, help us down!" the other pleaded.

"Eat camelshit," Dikéogu said, pulling Ejii along.

"I . . . I spoke to it," Ejii said.

"Huh?" he asked, turning to her. He stopped and touched her chin. "Are those dots blood? What happened to . . . ?"

"Stress," she said. She smiled, still out of breath. "Anyway, the palace, this palace. Her name's Oily Jada." She took a few breaths. "We have to get back up. The elevator! She'll help us. I think I remember the way."

"Me too," he said.

Ejii explained as they moved. "She said Gambo went to bring people to fight or something. I think they're coming now. I think this is how the war will start."

"Stop!" the soldier shouted. He stood with two others in front of the elevator and next to them was a phoonsniffle, the furry beast that had sniffed them for weapons. All three of the soldiers leveled some sort of disk-shaped weapons at them and

312

opened fire. Dikéogu instantly dropped to the floor, but Ejii stood tall, almost welcoming the shots.

In the back of her mind, she could hear the song that Allah had sung to her and she felt at peace. There was nowhere to escape and she'd tried to do what was asked of her. Pink sticky globs smacked into her chest, then her leg, then her arms, then her face. She stumbled back, involuntarily tasting the pink ooze. Whatever it was was . . . sweet?

"Ugh!" she heard Dikéogu groan. "What the hell is that?"

Ejii wiped the gunk from her face and slapped it onto the floor.

"The phoonsniffle will lock these cuffs on you," one of the soldiers said. "Make one move and you will have trouble."

Dikéogu stood up and grabbed Ejii's hand as the furry creature scrabbled toward them on its four long legs, the fifth leg held up as it carried what looked like vines.

"Move with me," Dikéogu said.

"What?" Ejii hissed.

"Come on. Both of us can take that thing down easy!"

They started moving away from the approaching creature. Without a word, the soldier pressed something on the side of his weapon. It instantly began vibrating, making a strange buzzing sound. The phoonsniffle stopped, waiting. Then a louder buzzing sound came from behind Ejii and Dikéogu. They turned and saw a black swarm of what looked like fat, fuzzy bees coming at them.

"Oh, Allah!" Ejii said. "I think this sticky stuff makes me a target."

"Put your arms around my waist," he said. "Do it now, so you won't get hurt."

She threw her hands around him, looking with horror at the approaching swarm. A thousand insect stings, she thought. What a horrible way to die! Before she could think anything else, a mass of electric-blue electricity burst from Dikéogu. It flew through Ejii, standing every hair on her body on end, and then filled the hallway.

Immediately, the insects fell to the floor writhing, their wings burned away. The phoonsniffle was left standing, every hair on its body singed off. It sneezed loudly, now a sticklike body on sticklike legs. The soldiers all fell to the floor, the muscles on their arms and legs jerking uncontrollably. Their clothes were practically burned to ashes, and the remains fell away as their muscles cramped and kicked.

"Learned I could do that yesterday," Dikéogu said. "Remember those dead bugs under the tree? Wasn't sure if it would kill those men, though."

Ejii nodded, staring at the furless phoonsniffle. Dikéogu grabbed her hand. "Come on!"

The phoonsniffle tried to scramble away from them as they passed. Instead it fell over, its legs also jerking about.

When the elevator opened for them, there were three more soldiers pulled tightly against the walls by strong vines; vines were also wrapped around their heads and across their mouths. Ejii and Dikéogu stepped in, ignoring their muffled pleas for help. As the elevator took them back to the top, Ejii wiped more of the pink gunk from her face and clothes, and tried to look outside for any sign of approaching armies. However, the elevator's speed forced her head down. When it stopped, she looked outside.

"Oh no!" she said. She pointed. "There. I can see them coming!"

"Many?" he asked.

"Too many. In Ginen cars and on foot. They wear red uniforms. We have to hurry," she said turning from the window. They ran to the conference room and when the doors opened for them, what they saw washed over them with despair. It was terribly cold in the room because the windows were all shattered. Dead parrots parts lay strewn about; the ones that still lived cowered among the vines hanging from the ceiling. On the floor, in the middle of wet, green splotches were several crushed little people. Jory's body lay close to the door. What looked like two large green quills were sticking out of her left cheek, the poison spears of the Kad'an.

In the far corner, Buji was slumped over and coughing, his hands pressed to his chest. Not far from him lay Tanah's body in a pool of a clear, sticky liquid, her large feet limp. Djang sat on the table sadly looking at Ejii. "You're late," he said. To the right, Ejii saw a tuft of fur pop up, then she met the golden eyes of one of the idiok baboons.

"Stay back, both of you!" Jaa said. She was breathing heavily as she crouched on the table. Her left eye was swollen shut and her nose was bleeding. Before her, in his chair, sat the chief, shaking like a freshly born goat. His motorized throne was toppled over on the far side of the room. He whimpered, pleading to Ejii with his eyes. His tight elaborate suit had split down the middle and his immense dark-brown belly hung out. The strange golden-metal nose screen he'd been wearing on his face was gone, but he still wore his crown of black feathers. Jaa was holding her green sword at his neck.

"What have you all done?" Ejii asked quietly.

Dikéogu ran to the open window and looked outside.

"It's not finished," Jaa said, grinning wildly as she looked into the chief's eyes.

"W . . . where is Gambo?" Ejii asked.

"Gone," Djang said. "He will bring the others who wait only a few miles away."

"It was always war! For both of you!" Ejii said. "What kind of leaders are you?"

Before Ejii could say more, she saw the chief's hand whip lightning fast across Jaa's face, as his other hand swiped her sword from his neck. Jaa tumbled off the table but managed to regain her footing. Ette groaned as he pushed himself to his feet. He grinned once he had his balance. "Come on, you undergrown witch," he snarled, spittle flying from his lips. "I'll stop your breath with my own hands. You go see pepper now!"

"Shut your mouth and come on then," Jaa said. She raised her sword and sprung at Ette, and Ette lumbered forward to meet her, holding out his large arms and hands, fingers spread. It would have been a sword fight if they'd both had swords. In many ways, it still was because Ette wielded his hands like two thick swords, slapping away Jaa's advances with rapid accuracy.

Ejii realized that it had been those fast hands that made Jaa's eye and the entire side of her face swollen. With one eye swollen shut, Jaa was at a definite disadvantage now. Her small size and limited reach were also weaknesses in close combat.

The chief was a man trained to fight using his natural and unnatural advantages, his speed and his weight. Jaa's sword bit at, but did not slice, the leather sleeves of what remained of his traditional outfit. Ejii could only guess at the type of animal the leather came from. He fought Jaa to the wall.

Jaa dodged Ette and leaped to the side, knocking over a potted plant that landed on Tanah's dead body. Djang helped the ailing Buji move out of the way. Ejii could only stand there, mouth agape, unsure how to stop them without getting decapitated or slapped unconscious. Ette snarled and went after Jaa again, this time, trying to corner her between him and the conference table. His leather bound feet crunched on dead parrots.

He landed a hard smack that connected with the swollen side of Jaa's face. Then he grabbed her by the neck and began to squeeze. Jaa tried to bring her sword up but Ette's arms were too massive. Ejii ran up and kicked Ette in the side, but it was like kicking a thick slab of fatty meat; it did nothing. Jaa was choking. Ejii wanted to kick Ette some more, maybe bite his arms or hit him with something hard, but instead she found herself stumbling backward. Something had pushed her away. In her ear, loud and clear, it said *Get out of the way*.

Her skin grew warm and her head felt light. "What's hap . . ."

Not this way, it said.

The entire room went many shades darker.

They burst from within and outside of Ejii, fluid, swirling darkness that was warm and humming. The shadows. They went for Ette, wrapping around his wide girth, snaking up to his eyes. Then over Jaa's arms. Over her face and body. For a moment, the two were completely enveloped in darkness. The shadows pressed and shifted, moving Ette's hand from Jaa's neck, separating the two. Then as quickly as they came, they left, some of them flying back into Ejii's chest, others melting into the shadowed places around the room.

Ette and Jaa stood staring at each other, Jaa pixie-like and Ette like a giant. Jaa raised her sword and Ette readied his hands. Ejii wanted to cry. It wasn't over. Jaa slashed at him with her sword. He slapped it away. She slashed. He slapped and moved forward. His hands were fearless. However, though his hands were quick, his body wasn't. Whichever way he went was the way he had to go until he could steer his enormous girth in another direction. When he was sure he'd cornered Jaa between himself and the conference table, he moved in for the crush. He didn't count on Jaa slipping to the left at the very last minute.

He ran belly first into the conference table, knocking the air from his lungs. Jaa took advantage, grabbing his arm from behind and pulling him back into one of the chairs, trapping him like a turtle flipped on its back. She jumped onto the table and pointed her green sword at his soft exposed belly. "Death by disemboweling is slow and painful, *sabi?*" she said, squinting at him with her good eye. A tiny line of blood ran down from where the tip pressed his flesh.

"Ejii," Jaa said calmly, though she was breathing heavily. "If you didn't understand then, understand *now*. Imagine that this is your father. Imagine that, instead of a small town, he had control of *five worlds*. This giant pig would take vengeance on Earth, starting with the Sahara, your home. That was his plan. You were there last night and you see how it went today. *That's* why I brought you, to see! This one would have killed me, killed my husbands, and taken the rest of you prisoner while he gathered the others to 'subdue' Earth."

"Remove your sword!" Ejii shouted. Behind her, she heard the crash of thunder and a breeze flew through the room, sending more red feathers, papers, leaves, and debris into the air. "Look at him!"

"No, *you* look at him," Jaa said, her voice as steady as ever. "Bloated with fear and malice. So . . . hungry, for power, food, women! He wants to consume all things. You see how he can move, his fat is unnatural, immoral. I've been through *too* much to watch Earth suffer a second death."

"Look at *yourself*, Jaa," Ejii said, lowering her voice. "What I *see* is that even those with the best intentions can be corrupted by power."

From outside, water splashed in and a crash of thunder made them all jump, except Jaa. Her sword was as steady as ever. "It's going to start whether you like it or not," she said. "I'm from Earth, but even here I have many people and they are coming. We squash it *now*, here in this tower, before others from the other places can decide and gather. This way fewer people die." She turned to the chief. "*You* die today."

"Then what are you waiting for?" Ejii spat. "Why isn't his throat open already?" She stepped forward. "I know you, Jaa. Your mind works fast . . . when things are clear."

Jaa looked at the chief but said nothing. A whip of wind slapped the room.

"Call it off," Ejii said.

"No," Jaa said. She grasped her sword tighter and straightened up.

"Argh, argh!" the chief babbled. "I'll do whatever you say. Please! P . . . please." He lowered his voice. "Whatever you say . . . queen, m-m-my queen."

"*Your* queen?" she said. "You already have sixty of those, no?" Her face hardened. "Many about Ejii's age? You think I want such a title from you?"

The chief's face suddenly changed and he bared his teeth like a wild animal. "You're nothing short of goat's piss!" he sneered. "I could crush you with half my weight! Grind you to dust between my fingers! Filthy, low, common beast of a woman. Kill me! You are only going to kill a man!"

Jaa laughed an ugly laugh. "You quote the revolutionary Che Guevara now? How ironic. I thought you hated Earth people."

"There will be others after me who will finish my job," Ette said. "Earth lives on borrowed time. The wilderness is *not* ready for me. I'll return tomorrow in my oldest son! None of you will leave this palace in the bodies you came in!" He smiled evilly. "And when I reincarnate in my son, the first one I will take as my concubine slave will be that little animal there." He pointed at Ejii.

As his finger centered on her, Ejii felt more than saw the rage whisk through Jaa.

"No!" Ejii screamed, running forward. Words weren't going to stop Jaa; communication was never her way. Jaa's will was focused to a hot precise point. Her muscular arms flexed as she pushed the sword with all her might. The blood dribbling down the chief's belly doubled . . . but that was all. Jaa pushed her sword again, but it wouldn't penetrate the chief's belly.

"It would be wrong!" The plume of smoke appeared and hung over the chief.

"Why?" Jaa asked, her voice even icier. "Smoke, you know this is the only way."

"The girl is correct," Smoke said.

Ejii felt wetness on her upper lip. Her nose was bleeding again. The chief was now shaking even more vigorously, spittle running down the corner of his mouth. Smoke continued shielding him. "Do any of you wonder why the Ooni ants who guard this plant tower have not run in here and torn you all apart for breaking that window?" Smoke asked. "If you kill the chief, I will tell the ants to come."

"Do it then! Let us all die, as long as this man doesn't live," Jaa hissed, pushing at her sword with all her strength. At first nothing happened, then slowly, her sword began to press at Ette's belly. A nauseating feeling washed over Ejii, and the world around her turned that strange metallic color, as if all things around her had sharp edges.

"No! Stop it! You make me sick!" Ejii screamed.

"Be sick then," Jaa said through gritted teeth, pushing harder.

Swimming in queasiness, Ejii pushed herself up and wrapped her hands around Jaa's blade. She felt it slice into her flesh, and no matter how hard she pushed, Jaa was still stronger and the sword only moved deeper into the chief's flesh. Still grasping it, Ejii looked at the sword. Looked into it.

Clear green metal from Ginen. Homegrown. It had a taste for blood and it had fed well. Now, like a planted mango seed, it was ready to do what it was made to do. She could see its molecules and understand its thoughts. The sword had fed on the blood of her father and so many others; it had even tasted her own blood back at the Yellow Lady Hotel when Jaa had attacked her. *All you need is some help remembering,* she told the sword. *You weren't put in the world to only feed. You also are to grow. Ah, there you go. Start right from there.*

Ejii wasn't sure if the ripping sound came from within her or outside of her. Then the green sprout pushed out from the tip of Jaa's sword. Soft, shiny, and round, not pointed. Creative and fruitful. Another popped out from the sharp edge of the sword and snaked up toward Jaa's face, touching her cheek like a kiss. Jaa gave the sword one last push, but instead of piercing the chief's chest, the bud at the tip was crushed and the sword began to bend. She cursed and threw her sword on the conference table, where it proceeded to further germinate, burrowing yellow-green roots into the surface.

Ejii slumped to the floor, holding her bleeding hands. "This bastard will live."

Smoke hovered between Jaa and Chief Ette. Jaa glared at Smoke and, through Smoke, at the chief. She got off the table and moved away from them and eyed her sword, which was now a fast-growing plant with a remotely sword-shaped center, spreading itself over the middle of the conference table.

"Now what?" Djang asked.

The boom of thunder was so loud that they all jumped, even Jaa this time. Ejii turned and was surprised to see Dikéogu standing before the window, still as a statue. She walked over to him, but did not touch him. She looked out at the storm he'd called up. What he'd done was genius. It was possibly the greatest storm Ooni had ever seen. It churned around the palace in a mile radius. Ejii wondered what the people of Ooni thought as the red-clothed armies had marched through their streets toward their palace and then had to take cover when a wild and sudden storm rushed in.

One of the idiok jumped onto the right side of the conference table, avoiding the lively plant at the center. Obax the gorilla stood beside the table. "We've all behaved badly," he said. "Human beings bring out the worst in all people." Another idiok baboon jumped onto the table and began motioning wildly to Obax. The gorilla signed back to the baboon. Then to Djang, Obax said, "Not all of you."

Obax signed with the idiok again and then turned to Jaa and the chief. "They have an idea," Obax said. He signed with the idiok again. "They say there is still time."

Yet another idiok baboon hopped onto the table. In its small black hands, it carried a pad of yellow paper and a pen.

"An Nsibidi pact," Obax said. "You both will take it and it cannot be broken."

Jaa shook her head. "I'll not participate in any juju unless I'm given a detailed . . ."

"It is good," Obax said.

"You know Obax doesn't lie," Djang said. "And lies cannot be spoken in the language of Nsibidi, regardless. Not for it to work. It's a good idea."

They watched the one idiok scribble strange elaborate symbols on the paper, while the other idiok occasionally gave their input. The process took several minutes. Then the idiok who'd done most of the writing signed to Obax.

"Your sword," Obax said to Jaa, motioning toward the plant. "A part of its edge is still sharp. Use it to draw blood from your hand. Then dip your finger in the blood and make a fingerprint on the paper . . . in the top left corner." After Jaa did so, Obax turned to the chief. "Dip your finger in the blood on your chest and do the same atop Jaa's."

But the chief only grunted and looked away. None of them said anything. Even Ejii understood that for this juju to work, it had to be done by choice. Finally, the chief touched his bloody chest and pressed his fat finger to Jaa's fingerprint. Ejii had expected a green perfumed wave or something similarly dramatic to happen, but all that happened was that the paper crinkled a little at the edges. The idiok raised their fists in triumph.

"It is done," Obax said. "For the next three years, peace between the leaders of Earth and Ginen will get a chance. If either of you declares war against the other, no one will listen, no one will feel the passion for blood and ruin."

"Three years is not that long," the chief grumbled. "I can wait, but it wasn't only Jaa and Ejii's passion."

"Only a fool waits to die," Jaa said. She and the chief glowered at each other, but neither of them could kill the other, so that was okay with Ejii.

"Now there is hope," Smoke said, as he settled his essence on one of the chairs.

Ejii had started to stare off into space, her mind clouding from excess adrenaline and the pain from her bleeding hands, when there was suddenly a horrible racket. It seemed to be coming from everywhere. Those with hands closed their ears. The noise stopped and even through her numbed senses, Ejii felt the vibration at her hip, from her pocket. "Oh," she said, bringing out the egg stone. It grew hot to the touch and she dropped it. It bounced and rolled to a stop on the conference table. They all watched as the egg stone's hard shell shivered and became like tough cloth.

They were quiet enough to hear the tearing sound. A black, spiky leg pushed through, then another. Then a shiny black head with two large raspberry-like compound eyes. When the two-inch long insect lifted the rest of itself out of the egg stone, Ejii shivered. I've been carrying this icky thing with me all this time? she thought.

"What is that?" Ette asked, irritably.

"I don't know," Ejii said.

"Well, get it out of here, I don't want it multiplying in the palace," he snapped. He motioned to the plant that used to be Jaa's sword. "We've already got *that* growing in here; we don't need any more foreign beasts."

One of the idiok moved toward the insect and it immediately began to make the terrible noise again. It slowly lifted itself in the air. Ejii frowned. It had no wings that she could see. Wasplike, it flew to the edge of the table and then underneath it.

"Ejii, maybe you should try and get it," Jaa said. "It might recognize you."

Ejii sighed tiredly and crawled under the table. It had landed on the underside and was looking at her, at least she thought it was. It made no noise. It flew to the center of the table's underside, hovered for a moment, and then right before her eyes it disappeared. She looked more closely and realized that the insect hadn't disappeared after all. There was a patch of what looked like a shadow suspended in midair in the middle of the table.

She stared for a moment. A long moment. Then she wanted to laugh really hard. She shimmied all the way underneath the table for a closer look. One of the idiok baboons was looking at her from the side of the table and she put her finger to her lips. The baboon only looked back at her. When she was eye to eye with the patch of shadow, she looked through it.

It was like the aerial view she'd had when she was flying with Sunrise, except instead of forest, below she saw the lopsided and collapsed tall buildings of a ruined city. But even in its destroyed state, she recognized this place. It was New York

City. All this time the chief had fought so hard to keep Earth and her ugly ways out of Ginen, and here Earth was, right in the palace. Ejii could almost hear the Desert Magician's crazed laughter.

"I crushed it," Ejii said, when she came out from beneath the table. She'd decided to keep the knowledge of the tiny hole to herself. For the sake of peace.

The chief grunted and said, "At least you're good for something."

CHAPTER TWENTY-FIVE

✛

CLEAR SKIES

E JII put a thick blanket around Dikéogu's shoulders and sat next to him on the wet floor in front of the window. She pulled at her blanket. She could still taste the sugary stuff the soldiers had shot at her on her lips. Buji said it was a pheromone that enraged winged battle ants to sting, and anyone covered with it was doomed. Of course, the insects didn't know that standing next to their target was a rain-maker who had finally understood what he was capable of.

Outside, the midday sky was clear. Normally she would have been terrified of sitting so close to the edge, so high up in the sky. But she'd changed. So had Dikéogu.

"Not bad," she said.

"One day, I'll make a storm strong enough to blow away that damn chief."

"Maybe," Ejii said.

"I fought with Gambo," he said.

"Oh?" Ejii said.

"Yeah. He knew what I was doing, even from far away. He

was the one bringing the others to fight the Ooni soldiers. He was crazed, like Jaa."

"A taste for war eventually becomes an appetite," Ejii said.

Dikéogu nodded. "He was stronger, but by the time he blew my storm away . . ."

"I'd stopped Jaa and the idiok had gotten her and the chief to sign the Nsibidi pact," Ejii said, finishing his sentence.

"I hate when you read my mind."

"I didn't."

"How can I be sure?" he asked with a laugh.

"You'll just have to trust me," she said.

"Maybe one of these days," he said. "Give me some time."

✛

E-LEGBA ENTRY 783

To: Myself
Subject: Details and Life
Date: The Tenth Orie Market Day, Rainy Season,
      40yrs Post-Wahala

We're traveling, so not much time to type this in, but I want to get these details down. My eyes and skin are dotted with burst blood vessels. I'll heal. Also, probably because of what I did to Jaa's sword, my finger and toenails grew two inches in a matter of hours, as did the hair on my head. I cut my nails, but left my hair.

You know when Jaa, Buji, and Gambo left during our one day in their village? The day just after we arrived in Ginen. They were going to see to their armed forces of Ginen folk who had agreed to their cause. Yes, Jaa had more support in Ginen than I thought.

And, oh, Dikéogu's storm. It stopped everything on the ground. It uprooted trees, spawned two tornadoes. It was

Ginen's worst storm in centuries, according to many. But maybe that has more to do with when Gambo blew Dikéogu's storm away with his own. No one died in the storm, thankfully. Ginen houses are not easily uprooted, even by strong winds. And Ginen cars are so low to the ground that high winds pass right over them. Most important, Jaa's army was so busy running for cover that they couldn't make it to the palace in time. Once the pact was signed, all the fight left their hearts.

Oh, and I had to get ten stitches in both of my hands.

No one knows what happened to the Shining Wizard after he was blown out the palace window with Sunrise and Smoke. Unlike Smoke, he couldn't just float back in; and unlike Sunrise, he couldn't fly. Jaa said that beings like him won't die from such a fall. He must have returned to his lands, angry. That worries me. I feel the same way about the Kad'an little people and the half dead Aku. Uneasy.

Jory is still recovering from the Kad'an poisoned spears. She's conscious, able to pick out the medicines she needs, but she still can't speak. The chief's healers say she will recover in a few days, but she may always be slow when speaking.

I got a glimpse of Sunrise the windseeker as he flew by on his way to goodness knows where. The idiok are in possession of the Nsibidi pact, and they have since disappeared into the northern forests that go beyond the Ooni Kingdom. That pleases me. The document will be safe with them, I think. Three years isn't a long time, but it's not short either. Especially for five worlds that have become one. That will be three years of it inhaling and exhaling and, well, growing. A lot can happen.

I could fall into Jaa and try and see what lies ahead. I think I can do that now, see the future. Oily Jada said that, for now, it's best to dwell in the present. She's been in the same place for thousands of years, so I think she knows much better than I do.

Sincerely,
The Mau Girl

CHAPTER TWENTY-SEVEN

✦

HOME

EJII knew when they left Ginen. The air made her cough. It made them all cough. But that was all the journey back to Earth did to Ejii. Traveling was no longer a problem for her. The desert soon spread before them and they camped under the cover of a small spontaneous forest of palm trees. Ejii slept deeper that night than she had since she'd left home, and she felt her body and mind settling like a freshly sown field. When she woke that morning, she stared at her tent ceiling listening to Dikéogu's soft unbothered snore. He was just outside her tent.

It was only Jaa and Ejii who traveled south to Kwàmfà. Dikéogu and Kola went with Buji and Gambo to meet up with Ali Mamami, head of Timidria, the section of the Nigérien Bureau of Investigation that specialized in the eradication of slavery. They were going to make a trip to Assamakka and a few other places where child slavery was practiced. As Dikéogu said, they planned to "kick asses and clean house."

"I'll come to Kwàmfà before going anywhere else afterward," he'd told Ejii.

"If you want to go home first, I'll under . . ."

He held up a hand. "I'll come see you first. After that, I'm more likely to go with Buji to Ginen for a while. Buji says that they have super old rainmakers there who could teach me stuff." He'd given Ejii a long hug and whispered in her ear, "Thanks for saving me." She'd given him a kiss on the lips and he'd touched her cheek, looking into her eyes. Then he climbed onto Gambo's camel. The markings on his face had remained red and white after they'd left Ginen, no longer the markings of a slave. Kola landed on Ejii's shoulder, holding her talons away from Ejii's flesh as always. She pulled a feather from her wing and held it out to Ejii with her beak.

"Thank you," Ejii said. Kola hooted and took to the sky. Ejii put the feather in her pocket as she watched Buji, Gambo, and Dikéogu's camels walk into the night.

"Come," Jaa said, after a while. "It's time to go home."

They traveled swiftly, mainly in silence through the night, Ejii sitting behind Jaa on the camel. Jaa used the stars to navigate. They saw a flock of hummingbirds pass overhead, a caravan of men traveling in the opposite direction, and something silver and shimmering lingered with them for three hours before going elsewhere.

"People and creatures know who to leave alone," Jaa said, after the shimmering creature had gone. Ejii hadn't realized that Jaa could see it in the dark.

They camped for a few hours, during the hottest part of the day. Ejii was still wary of Jaa. She always would be, but she had learned that she herself was something to be wary of too. Ejii slept deeply right next to Jaa in Jaa's tent.

When they arrived in Kwàmfà, it was the middle of the night. Ejii felt as if she'd been gone for years. She paused when she got to the front door of her house. Slowly she touched the deep gashes that splintered the heavy wood. These hadn't been there when she left. As she ran her fingers over the wood, she could hear them. *Shouts and screams.* These gashes had been made with machetes.

"Mama," she whispered as regret washed over her, cold, wet and heavy. She swayed on her feet, thinking about the young, ambitious wives of her father. She looked back at Jaa, who motioned for her to go forward.

Quickly she knocked on the door. It didn't take long for her to hear her mother's footsteps. The door opened. The first thing Ejii noticed was the healing wound on her mother's forehead and some sort of large blue jewel hanging from a pale gold chain around her neck. She was wearing the long, pink cotton nightgown she always wore to bed and the blue wool robe she usually wore when it was cold.

Most important there was a triumphant smile on her mother's face. Protectively standing behind her mother, were Arif and Sammy, wide-eyed, daggers in hand. Her mother pressed her arms to her chest. What has happened here? Ejii thought. But before she could ask or read anyone, her mother snatched Ejii into her arms.

"Things have changed since you've been gone," her mother said into Ejii's ear.

And then there were only cries of joy and amazing stories to tell.

ACKNOWLEDGMENTS

❖

I would like to thank Jaïra Placide for believing in this book and helping me realize just how wild it could be when I put my mind to it; my agent, Janell Walden Agyeman for her faith in me and her sense of wonder; my parents for everything; my fellow creative forces, Ifeoma, Ngozi, and Emezie; Tom Wagner for putting it into my head just how cool a novel about futuristic Africa would be; professor Cris Mazza and my novel-writing workshop for their help back when Ejii was in her infancy; the Eagle-Eyed Anyaugo and the Mighty Onyedika; Pat Rothfuss, Nalo Hopkinson, Jamal Jeffries, Tayannah Lee McQuillar, and Neil Gaiman for lending me their eyes; the Jump at the Sun team for jumping at this novel; Kelli Martin and my editor, Jennifer Besser, for putting it all together; my family back in Nigeria and around the world for being the inspirations for so many of my characters; and Nigeria and the greater Africa for being my muse.

NNEDI OKORAFOR-MBACHU
is the author of *Zahrah the Windseeker*, as well
as several award—winning short stories. She
earned her PhD in English at the University of
Illinois, and currently lives in Chicago, where she
is a journalist.